Daragh Smyth

A GUIDE TO IRISH MYTHOLOGY

DARAGH SMYTH

A GUIDE TO
IRISH MYTHOLOGY

IRISH ACADEMIC PRESS

This book was typeset by
Gilbert Gough Typesetting Services, Dublin, for
IRISH ACADEMIC PRESS
Kill Lane, Blackrock, Co. Dublin
and in North America for
IRISH ACADEMIC PRESS
c/o ISBS 5804 N.E. Hassalo Street, Portland, OR
97213, USA.

A catalogue record for this book
is available from the British Library.

ISBN 0-7165-2612-3

First edition 1988
Second edition 1996

Printed in Ireland by
ColourBooks Ltd, Dublin.

To my parents

Contents

Preface

I wish to express my gratitude to all those involved in the first edition of this book.

This second edition has new entries including the rites of sovereignty and the *tarb fes* or bull feast.

It has an expanded entry on the Fir Bolg or Belgae, and a new entry on the Dál nAraide.

Some dates have been changed and some AM dates have been left unaltered even though they are questionable, precise dates being unavailable.

Much of early Irish history has been regarded as mythology; why this should be is unclear. There is abundant evidence of an early historical period. Irish recorded history starts at AD 431. Why this should be so remains unclear to me. However, this is a book about mythology and not about history; yet they do overlap; as Robert Graves put it, 'Irish mythology is history'.

A historical rather than a romantic bias is suggested as an approach to reading this book.

Introduction

If this book had a Gaelic title, it would be *Foclóir na Síde*, which means 'dictionary of the mounds'. The *síde* were popularly known as fairy-hills. In these hills, from Mesolithic or Middle Stone Age times (6000 BC), the bodies of the ancients were buried, and within these walls, these hills or tumuli, the spirits of the ancients are said to reside.

Notable among the *síde* is the Síd an Bróga, the legendary home in the Boyne Valley of Aengus, the harper to the gods. At Síd ar Cealtrai at Downpatrick, Co. Down, there is one of two burial sites associated with Oisín, son of Finn mac Cumaill. Unfortunately this mound was ransacked.

Countless are the stories associated with these mounds, for they contain the myths of Irish folklore in a pure form; these myths are but guides to a symbolic understanding of our ancient culture, masks behind which truths may be discovered.

The last popular surviving remnant of the *síd* cult is the belief that all the mounds open up at the Samain (Hallowe'en) and that the gods and goddesses connected with them roam the land. The Síd ar Cruachain — the fairy cave at Cruachain — near Tulsk, Co. Roscommon is especially associated with the Samain. During this time of year popular belief had it that hosts of spirits leave this cave, led by the Mórrígan or 'Great Queen'.

Scholars have further interpreted the word *síd* as a 'star', pointing to stellar worship. Others see the word emanating from the Greek word meaning 'a seat of the gods'. The veneration of the *síd* included a communion with all natural phenomena — rivers, mountains, wells etc. This affinity would appear to be a valuable possession, as important to us as the three possessions of the Dagda, the Irish Zeus, were to him. The Dagda is said to have had a club, a harp and a cauldron. These three items might act as symbols of the three areas with which this book concerns itself. The club may stand for the warrior aspect; the harp for music and poetry; and the cauldron for the Celtic spirit which, although on the edge of Europe, still retains its power and vitality.

The ancient stories or sagas of Ireland are divided into four cycles of tales — the Mythological Cycle, the Ulster Cycle, the Fenian Cycle or the Ossianic Cycle and the Historical Cycle or Cycle of Kings.

The chief source of knowledge of pagan Ireland is the Mythological Cycle, concerning itself with heroes who inhabited the country before the coming of the Gaels. This cycle's central theme is that of a race of people who withdrew into fairy-mounds, 'where they still dwell, and from whence they sometimes emerge to interfere in the affairs of men'. This cycle includes the pantheon of the gods belonging to the great mystical race, the Tuatha Dé Danann (translated as People of Dana, associated with Danu, Anu and Donn).

Thus if one wished to build up a picture of the **Mythological Cycle** one should earmark the following entries: Aengus, Aed, Áine, Badb, Balor, Banba, Bel, Boand, Bodb, Brigit, Dagda, Ériu, Fódla, Goibniu, Gráinne, Grian, Lug, Lugnasa, Macha, Mag Tuired, Manannán mac Lir, Midir, Mongán, Mór, Mórrígan, Nuadu, Ogam, Otherworld, Samain and Tuatha Dé Danann.

The **Ulster Cycle** is concerned with the Craeb Ruad or Red Branch Knights based at Emain Macha, present-day Navan Fort, two miles west of Armagh city. This cycle largely revolves around the hero Cúchulainn and it is set in the first century of the Christian era in the reign of Conchobar mac Nessa, king of Ulster, and Medb, queen of Connacht. Associated with this cycle are the following entries: Bricriu, Conchobar mac Nessa, Cruachain, Cúchulainn, Emain Macha, Fer Diad, Fergus mac Roich, Gaé Bolga, Loegaire Buadach, Medb, Scáthach, Sualdam mac Roich and the Táin.

The **Fenian or Ossianic Cycle** is set in the reign of Cormac mac Airt, who is said to have reigned at Tara in the third century of the Christian era. These tales revolve around Finn mac Cumaill and the Fianna with their ancient capital at Almu on the Hill of Allen in Co. Kildare. These stories are included under the following entries: Caoilte mac Ronáin, Cormac mac Airt, Finn mac Cumaill, Gabhra, Goll mac Morna, Gráinne, Imbas forosnai, Oisín and Tara.

The final cycle, the **Historical Cycle or Cycle of Kings** includes entries under: Conn Cét Chathach, Cormac mac Airt, Niall Noígiallach and Togáil Bruidne Da Derga, which includes the king Conáire Már.

Rather than construct themes through a list of characters one can associate stories related to the various cycles. The Wooing of Étáin (see under Midir), the Battle of Moytura (see under Mag Tuired) and the Children of Lir (see under Oidhead Cloinne Lir) are three major tales of the Mythological Cycle.

The Táin Bó Cualgne, Bricriu's Feast, the Love Story of Deirdre and Naoise and Scél Mucce Meicc Da Thó are four tales from the Ulster Cycle. These stories can be checked under the following entries: Táin, Bricriu, Longes mac nUsnig and Mesroida mac Da Thó.

Stories from the Fenian Cycle are generally included under Finn mac Cumaill; the great romantic story of the Pursuit of Diarmuid and Gráinne is under Gráinne.

The Plunder of Dinn Rig (see under Labraid Loingsech) and the Destruction of Da Derga's Hostel (under Togáil Bruidne Da Derga) may be two variations of the same story, reputedly occuring in the third century BC These tales can be included within the Historical Cycle or Cycle of Kings. This cycle has been termed 'a mixture of genuine history with symbolic fiction'.

Whether it is possible or not to separate fact from fiction in any mythology, the question does inevitably arise as to the historicity of the main characters, events and races mentioned in the book. Broadly speaking, events before AD 200 could be seen as fiction, and happenings after that date might be taken as fact. However we shall see that certain events even as late as the seventh century AD can be classified as fictional whilst some very ancient battles (such as the destruction of Dinn Rig) would be considered historical.

Eminent nineteenth century scholars felt that great personages such as Cúchulainn, Conchobar mac Nessa and Queen Medb really did exist. Standish O'Grady states that 'Cúchulainn, and his friends are historical characters, they are not literary phantoms but actual existences'. The German scholar Ernst Windisch held that 'it is possible, even probable, that there was once a King Conchobar of Ulster, and a Queen Mahb of Connacht, that Ulster and Connacht waged war with each other over similar causes as were described in the sagas'. However, it has become increasingly common to regard the tales as being based on myth rather than on history.

Myth or history, fact or fiction or, as more likely, a blending of both, what do we know of the chronology of these stories? During what age did man first appear in Ireland? Archaeology tells us that it was before 6000 BC, between the Paleolithic and Early Mesolithic Ages, sometime around the late Stone Age and the beginning of the middle Stone Age. The *Annals of the Four Masters* place the arrival of the first colony in Ireland in the year 2678 BC. Archaeology confirms that it was during this period, a time of warm dry weather that the first megaliths appeared.

Much of the method of recording Irish history was established by Christian monks in the sixth and seventh centuries. These monks referred to chronological systems established by early Christian scholars, such as that of the third century Eusebius of Palestine and the sixth century Isidore of Seville. Eusebius dated events from Anno Mundi ('the beginning of the world') abbreviated AM. Thus early historians recorded the first colony as having arrived in the year 2520 AM. As with dates, the monks placed happenings and characters of Irish history into the Christian context. They had their own world chronicles and synchronized major events with the Flood, the Bible and the reign of Assyrian kings. Thus the progenitor of the Irish becomes Adam rather than Donn.

Later historians applied their own personal belief and the culture of their time to the task of interpreting Irish mythology. T. F. O'Rahilly regards our historians as being euhemerists — that is, treating the divine in our tales as humans from a distant age. Thus Manannán mac Lir becomes a navigator who lives in the Isle of Man rather than a sea god. The scholar Alfred Nutt has said that 'the mythology of the Celts has suffered more than that of any other race from the euhemerizing methods of investigation applied to it'.

Academic interpretations vary from century to century; the nineteenth century was more romantic than scientific in its approach, the twentieth century more scientific than romantic. However, apart from these theoretical considerations, it is from the physical world of the *síde*, these scattered hillocks and underground caverns, that the underlying theme of this book emanates.

NOTES

Where sources mention AM times these are included alongside their equivalent BC times in the text. The year AD 1 is equivalent to the year 5198 in the Anno Mundi system, and so it is possible for the reader to convert one to the other by subtracting BC times from 5198 AM. Thus 2520 AM is the same as 2678 BC.

Throughout the text some well-known names are given in their modern Irish or English form. Otherwise forms are given in old Irish orthography taken from T.F. O'Rahilly, *Early Irish History and Mythology*, and other sources.

Cross references: Names and other words which have their own entry are indicated by an asterisk (*). Words which are explained in the Special Notes are identified in the main text by the symbol °. The superior figures in the main text refer to the numbered sources given in the list of Source Material.

Aed   Lord of the Otherworld, ancestor or creator of mankind, Aed (his name in Irish means 'fire') is a sun god and god of thunder and lightning. He occupies a similar position in the Celtic pantheon to Jupiter and Zeus within the Graeco-Roman system, appearing under various names.

Aed Álainn is king of the western Otherworld and possessor of the venomous spear which Jupiter and Zeus wield in the form of a thunderbolt. Aed Álainn is another name for the Dagda,* king of the Irish gods. Elsewhere, Aed Álainn is Bodb Derg,* son of the Dagda. This apparent contradiction can be explained by the tendency for local dieties to be related to the king of the gods in different ways.

Aed mac Ainninne, the sun god, came to the various lakes of Ireland and cast a spell under each so that they dried up.[1]

Aed mac Fidga was slain by Finn mac Cumhaill,* being killed by his spear as he was leaving one *síd°* (mound) to enter another. Finn mac Cumhaill's traditional enemy Goll mac Morna* was also another manifestation of Aed.

T.F. O'Rahilly mentions that the overcoming of the gods by the Hero, as in Finn's slaying of Aed, is recorded 'partly because of the myth-tellers bias in favour of the Hero, and partly because the myths have been recorded at a time when paganism was a thing of the past'.

Aed Ruad was drowned in the waterfall at Ballyshannon in Donegal; this waterall, now called Assaroe (Ess Ruad), and the adjacent *síde* are both called after Aed Ruad. We thus have the god Aed, presiding over the *síde*, being identified with the Aed Ruad who was drowned in the neighbouring waterfall, i.e., according to pagan belief, lived beneath it.

Aengus   The Otherworld* god of the Tuatha Dé Danann,* the race of Danu.° Sometimes referred to as Aengus Mac Ind Óg or Mac in Dá Óc, 'the son of the two young ones', his father was the Dagda* and his mother Boand,* from whom the Boyne river is named. Harper to the gods and a friend to poets, Aengus was probably conceived at the fertility rites during Samain* at Bruig na Bóinne.°

In the famous *Aisling Aengusa* or Dream of Aengus, he falls in love with a girl whom he has seen only in a dream. Ill with longing, he eventually discovers that she can be found at Loch Bél Dracon in Co. Tipperary. He learns that there, during Samain, the girl, called Caer Ibormeith (yew berry), along with one hundred and fifty others, will change into swans. On his arrival he sees all these swans, Caer among them, and he himself changes into a swan and flies with her back to

Bruig na Báinne where they act as protectors to lovers. We see an instance of this when Aengus, as god of love, appears in the adventures of Diarmuid and Gráinne* as protector to that couple, putting a mantle of invisibility over Gráinne so that she can escape from the Fiana or Fenians (*see:* Finn*).

Later, in the medieval romances, Aengus was seen as a wily character by Christian scribes who may well have felt it important to belittle this greatest and wisest of magicians of the Tuatha Dé Danann. Later still we find him in folklore as a frightener of cattle: '. . . the plough teams of the world and every sort of cattle that is used by men would make a way in terror before him.'[3] This role of Aengus may be less puzzling when one notes that his mother, Boand, is the white cow goddess.

The death of Aengus is said, according to some stories, to have occurred during a battle near the Boyne. A woman named Caitleann killed him with a stone thrown at his head. He died in the river and is buried in Síd an Bróga° in Bruig na Bóinne.

Aengus Ollmugaid Aengus the Great Destroyer became monarch of Ireland in the year AM 3773 (1425 BC) after his victory at the battle of Cliú (near Knockainey, Co. Limerick) the previous year. Among his most famous battles were Cuirce; Sliab Cailge against the Martini in the province of Corca Baiscinn;° and the battle of Ros Fraechain in Muirisc,° Co. Mayo. Two lakes burst forth during his reign — Loch Aenbeithe (lake of the birch tree) and the present Bellahoe Lough, on the borders of Cos. Meath and Monaghan, south of Carrickmacross. The sea also erupted between Eabha (now Magherow) and Ros Cette, an ancient name for a point of land, now called the Rosses, lying between the river of Sligo and Drumcliffe, in Co. Sligo. It was Aengus Ollmugaid who cleared the plain of Mag Muccrama (the counting of pigs), which lies immediately to the west of Athenry, Co. Galway. Aengus also cleared Mag Luachra Deadaid, a level tract of land on Sliab Luachra, near Castleisland, Co. Kerry. He was killed at the battle of Carmann (now Wexford) by Enna Airgtheach.°

Aengus Tuirmech Temrach Monarch of Ireland for sixty years (AM 4816-4875 or 382-323 BC). His cognomen, Tuirmech, is explained by Keating as *náireach* (ignominious act). This act is supposed to have been incestuous and he had two sons by this relationship — Fiacha Fermara[4] and Enna Aighneach. Other scribes, namely the Four Mas-

A drawing, one twelfth actual size,
of a stone found at Knockmany, Co. Tyrone

ters[5] and O'Flaherty,[20] derive the name differently, from *tuirmeach* (prolific), because he is the common ancestor of the great families of Leath Chuinn,° Alba,° Dál Riada° and Dál Fiatach.° The *Annals of Clonmacnoise* make no allusion to Fiacha Fermara as the offspring of an incestuous relationship. They speak of 'Enos Twyrmeach' (Aengus Tuirmech) as follows: 'Enos succeeded and was a very good king. He left issue two goodly and noble sons, Enna Ayneach and Fiagha Ferwara. The kings of Ireland descended from Enna Aighneach and the kings of Scotland from Fiacha'.

Aengus Tuirmech became king when he slew Fergus Fortamail at the battle of Tara* in AM 4815 (383 BC). Tara at this time was the scene of constant struggles for sovereignty. The reward for successful struggle was the kingship, if only temporarily. Fergus Fortamail himself seized the crown by killing his predecessor, Eochaid Ailtleathan. After sixty years as sovereign, Aengus Tuirmech 'died quietly at Tara, in his bed'. His son, who reigned for twenty years, was himself slain by Crimthann Cosrach, a man who four years later met the same violent end.

Áine   The wife or daughter of Manannán,* who is the Irish Neptune and travels by horse. Elsewhere described as the wife of Echdae, the horse of the heavens, indicating her connection with a sun deity moving through the heavens, Áine comes from the days of sun worship and represents that older pantheon of gods who, as travellers of the heavens, hark back to gods and goddesses moving across the skies like the Egyptian Amon Ra (god of the heavens). Áine's name is associated with meanings such as 'brightness', 'heat', and 'speed', and particularly with the midsummer ritual at Knockainey, Co. Limerick. Here, at the *síd* (mound) of Cnoc Áine,° men used go in procession round Áine's hill carrying poles with flaming bunches of hay and straw tied to them.

Áine has another mound and well in the parish of Lissan, Co. Derry — Cnoc Áine and Tobar Áine.° In this district she is regarded as a lady who was taken away from her husband's side at night by the wee folk and never returned. Áine has links with the family of O Corra (Corr), who are believed to be her descendants. It is said that when an O Corra is about to die, Áine is heard wailing in a plaintive tone in the wild glen of Alt na Síon,° adjacent to the fort of Lios Áine° (Lissan). Knockmany Hill, near Augher, Co. Tyrone, is associated in local legend with a fairy or witch named Áine.

Áine is represented, in the genealogy of the descendants of Éber,*

18

as a daughter of Fer Í, the son of Eógabal. This man was a brother of Eóghan who gave his name to the Eóganacht,* as the southern Gaels* called themselves. The connection between Fer Í (man of yew) and the names Eógabal and Eóghan is the Irish word *eo* (yew). According to some traditions Áine of Cnoc Áine was wife of Ailill Olum, father of Eóghan. Áine was also the name of a god named Ailill Áine whose son Labraid Loingsech* was the ancestor deity of the Érainn, a tribe from Munster.

Amergin   One of the sons of Míl* who came to Ireland from Spain (Galicia) *c.*300 BC. During this year he fought against the Tuatha Dé Danann* at Tailtiu (Telltown, Co. Meath), his two brothers, Éremon* and Éber, assumed the joint sovereignty of Ireland, and he built the causeway at Avoca, Co. Wicklow. One of the earliest poems in Ireland is attributed to Amergin, who is said to have uttered it from the deck on one of his invading ships. The metre of the original is called *rosc*.° Poems in this metre depend for their effect upon rapidity of utterance and upon a tendency towards alliteration; the repetition of images in the following poem, 'Amergin's Invocation', creates an internal rhyme.

Amergin's Invocation

I invoke the land of Ireland:
much coursed be the fertile sea,
fertile be the fruit strewn mountain,
fruit strewn be the showery wood,
showery be the river of waterfalls,
of waterfalls be the lake of deep pools,
deep pooled be the hill-top well,
a well of tribes be the assembly,
an assembly of kings be Temair [Tara].
Temair be the hill of the tribes,
the tribes of the sons of Mil,
of Mil of the ships, the barks!

Let the lofty bark be Ireland,
lofty Ireland, darkly sung,
an incantation of great cunning:
the great cunning of the wives of Bres,

19

the wives of Bres of Buaigne:
the great lady, Ireland,
Eremon hath conquered her,
I, Eber have invoked for her
I invoke the land of Ireland.[19]

Badb   Sometimes known as Badb Catha (battle raven). She was one
of a trio of war goddesses who appear in Irish legend. Sometimes she
appears as a crow, sometimes as an old hag or *cailleach*,* and sometimes as a beautiful young woman. Together with Macha* and the
Mórrígan* she made up the Mórrígna, a triple goddess of the battle-
field. Badb, like the other two, was both sinister and sexual; she
prophesied the end of the world and chaos:

> Son will enter his father's bed,
> father will enter his son's bed,
> everyone his brother's brother-in-law.[51]

Badb exhorted Cúchulainn* to fight his last battle and personifies
the *femme fatale* who both befriends the hero and leads him to his death.

Balor   Béimean (Balor of the
mighty blows), champion and
army general of the Fomorians,*
was engaged in the two great battles of Mag Tuired* (the plain of
reckoning, or lamenting), the
modern Moytura in Co. Sligo. In
the first of these (1821 BC) he slew
Nuadu* Argat Lám (Nuadu of the
silver hand). In the second, when
the Fomorians were defeated by
the Tuatha Dé Danann,* Balor
was slain by Lug.* It is related that
the weapons used by Lug in win-

Beltany stone head
(see under Bel)

ning this battle were forged by the Trí Dé Dánann,° the three gods of
artistic skill.[2] One of these was Goibniu* the smith, who forged the
lightning weapon which Lug sent through Balor's eye, and the others
were Luchta the wright, and Credne the bronze-worker.
    A story of Balor was recorded by O'Donovan[5] from Shane O'Dugan

of Tory Island in 1835. The story goes that a famous warrior called Balor had one eye in the middle of his forehead and the other in the back of his skull, the latter, with its 'beams and dyes of venom' able to strike people dead. He kept this eye constantly covered except when he wished to get the better of enemies by petrifying them with looks. (This is the reason the evil eye is referred to as Súil Bhalair° — Balor's Eye — in Irish.) Balor had been told by a druid that his only daughter would bear a grandson named Ó or Lug, who would kill him. In order to avoid this happening, Balor imprisoned his daughter in a fortress at the summit of Tor Mór (lofty rock) at the eastern extremity of Tory Island, off the coast of Donegal. The story relates that there was a chief called Mac Kineely who owned a generous cow known as the Glas Gaibleann.* It was Balor's ambition to get possession of this animal, and this he did, whereupon Mac Kineely sought the advice of a *leanán síde*° (familiar sprite). The sprite dressed Mac Kineely as a woman, who then crossed over to Port na Glaise (harbour of the green cow) on Tory. Mac Kineely went to Balor's daughter, left her pregnant, and returned to the mainland, where he was captured by Balor and be-headed at a place later called after Kineely — Cloch Chinn Fhaolaidh (Bloody Foreland), Co. Donegal. Mac Kineely's son avenged his father by thrusting a glowing rod from the smith's furnace through the eye in the back of Balor's head. This epic battle between Lug and Balor took place at Dunlewey. It is also recorded that he killed Balor with a sling stone.

These stories about the killing of Balor have similarities. The smith in both stories provided the weapon that killed him. Balor is the maternal grandfather of both Lug and Ó, and he was responsible for the deaths of both their fathers.

Another similar story which this author recorded in 1990 from 92-year-old Donal Duggan, concerns a medieval Balor who was a notorious pirate and a pagan. This man had taken on the mantle of Balor, and was also from Tory Island.

Balor is associated with worship of the sun, as represented by the single eye. As a sun god he threatened to burn Ireland; as a giant he may be compared to the Welsh god Ysbaddaden. T.F. O'Rahilly[2] states that Balor the sun god and Goibniu the smith god, though they were differentiated in later times, were ultimately one and the same, and secondly that in the primitive form of the myth, the Hero (as we may call Lug, Cúchulainn and Finn)* 'slays' the god (represented by Balor, the dog of Culann, and Aed)* with the latter's own weapon, the 'thunderbolt'.

Banba   Queen of the Tuatha Dé Danann,* Banba was slain by Caicher, one of the sons of Míl,* at the battle of Tailtiu,* a village and district in Meath, in AM 3500 (1698 BC). At this battle her sisters Éire* and Fódla,* were slain, as were her three brothers, Mac Cuill, Mac Cécht and Mac Gréne.

Banba symbolises Ireland in the warrior aspect; Fódla is Ireland in the intellectual or spiritual sense; and Éire is it in its earthy or geographical aspect.

Bel   An idol, found in Belteine, the month of May, which means in Irish 'the fire of Bel'. Whitley Stokes[6] says of Bel that 'a fire was kindled in his name at the beginning of summer always, and cattle were driven between two fires'. These fires were made by druids* with great incantations, and cattle were driven between them as a safeguard against disease. This feast of Bel is called Beltane in English and was celebrated on the first of May.

Offering table to Belenus or Bel

In northern Italy and Gaul he was called Belenus, and Belinus in Roman Britain. Places were named after him, e.g. Billingsgate (Belino's gate), London. He is also said to have been a pastoral deity. The largest celebration of Belteine was at Uisneach* in Co. Westmeath. This festival occurred at the same time as the convention of Uisneach, where a great annual fair was held.

Belgae (see Fir Bolg).

Boand   The white cow goddess, after whom the river Boyne is named. The Irish word *bóinn* means cattle; Buvinda is the name Ptolemy gave her, and her original name may have been Bou-vinda, meaning cow-white goddess. The wife of both Nechtan and Nuadu,* Boand also lived with the Dagda,* bearing him a son Aengus.* The Dagda won the love of Boand after he had ousted Nuadu from Bruig na Bóinne.°

As a cow goddess, Boand represents cattle, the different colours of

22

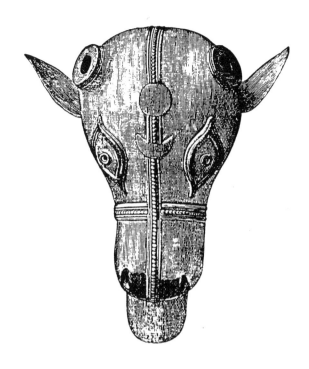

A bronze bovine mask probably of oriental origin; there are solar and lunar emblems on the harness of the mask.

the cattle symbolising various phases of the moon. Thus we get the white cow (*bó finn*); the *bó ruad* (red cow), the *bó donn* (brown) and the *bó orann* (dark).

In the end she followed the river Boyne back to its source and was submerged in it, thus becoming the divinized river. This fits in with the belief that supernatural beings have their dwelling below lakes and rivers. Boand is celebrated as an eponym of this, the great river of Irish mythology. Bruig na Bóinne,° the Boyne Valley region of hill forts, is called after her, and this area is noted for the ancient pagan fertility rituals that occurred there during Samain.*

Bodb   The son of Dagda,* commonly referred to as Bodb Derg, he is associated with Síd ar Femen, the modern Slievenamon in Co. Tipperary.

Bodb's pigs were reputedly supernatural and consistently reappeared after being eaten. There is a reference to the pigs of Bodb of Síd ar Femen in the famous story of Togáil Bruidne Da Derga.* Some stories mention that he had seven sons; others name his three sons as Artrach, Aed and Aengus. Falling out with their father, these three went to Conn's Cét Chathach's grandson, Cormac mac Airt* and were offered land in Tír Conaill (Donegal), where they stayed for thirty years.

Bodb, also lord of Bruig na Bóinne,° is mentioned[7] as having a great household of ten men, ten score and ten hundred, all of which were chiefs and territorial lords of the Tuatha Dé Danann.* It is as lord of Bruig na Bóinne that Bodb can be linked with Aed Álainn* and the Dagda.

Brehon laws   These take their name from *breitheamh* (lawgiver, judge). The brehons were a professional caste of judges and lawyers and part of a body of professional poets that came out of the druidic system. P.W. Joyce states[53] that 'the proper name for brehon law was *fénechas*° or law of the *féne*, or free land-tillers'. It was a law developed by judges rather than by government or kings. The brehon interpreted the laws and applied them to individual cases and, as Joyce states, had to be careful in this application, 'for he was himself liable for damages, besides forfeiting his fee, if he delivered a false or an unjust judgment'.

The basic territorial unit in Ireland was the *túath*, translated as tribe or petty kingdom. It has been suggested on the evidence of genealogies that there were probably at least 150 kings or *rí túaithe* in Ireland between the 5th and 12th centuries.[98] These kings ruled over an island population of less than half a million people.

Brehon law formed a great body of civil, criminal and military law. It outlined the five main classes of people and set down their rights, duties and privileges. The relations of landlord and tenant, the fees of professional men, such as doctors, judges, teachers, and builders, and the duties of father and son, of foster-parents and foster-children, of master and servant, were all carefully regulated. There is a large quantity of brehon law tracts in manuscript form. Eugene O'Curry[65] transcribed many of these and, with John O'Donovan, made preliminary translations.

The brehon law included laws of marriage, fencing of land, watermills, distraint, bee-keeping and timpanists. In the brehon law tract of the *Book of Ballymote* a list of the pay and rank of various professions is given. Social status was also determined: for example, among musicians, the harper (*cruit*)° was the only one recognised as being of the rank of the *bó airech°* class. This meant that he was entitled to four cows as his honour price. Other musicians, such as horn-player or piper, were not entitled to legal recognition in this way.

The sixteenth-century Clane scholar Domhnall O'Davoren[34] mentions that bells (*clothra*) were required by law to be attached to any dog inclined to spring upon people: a little bell has to be put on its neck, or something else which is heard ringing when it is going to commit a trespass.

Cows of the first quality, according to the laws, had bells round their necks, and penalties for stealing these were greater than those for the theft of ordinary cows.

Artists who made crescents of gold were paid in silver the equivalent weight of the crescent. Under the laws of fosterage and tutorage, according to O'Curry,[65] the sons of kings and chiefs had to be taught riding, swimming and the board game *fidchell,°* together with the use of sword and spear.

The emphasis in the brehon laws was not on punishment but rather on compensation. If a person caused another physical injury, then that person was responsible for having his victim nursed back to health at his (the culprit's) expense.[94] Capital punishment did exist, anyone having the right to kill an outlaw for a serious offence. Kings, however, had the power to ransom such outlaws, and were also able to proclaim emergency laws in certain cases, for example, after a defeat in battle or during a plague.

During the reign of Cormac mac Airt,* a hero by name of Aengus mac Airt, corb of the Déise of Meath, held the office of Aire Échta.° The holder of this office, according to the brehon laws, righted the wrongs of his tribe, as well as protecting the weak and the poor.

In marriage, the husband and wife were free to divorce.[38] Thus, the society reflected in the brehon laws was not strictly monogamous; for example, if a man's wife fell ill, her husband was obliged to maintain her but could take another wife as well. This was known as *cét muintir for muin araile* (the chief wife in place of another). The principal wife (*cét muintir*) had a higher standing than the other wives, but the latter were recognized. The bride price given to the secondary wife became the property of the principal wife. The chief wife was free from liability for anything she might do during the first three nights when the secondary wife was living in the home, short of killing the secondary wife. Bloodshed could be inflicted with impunity through rightful jealousy if the secondary wife took her place.[94]

According to manuscripts written between the 14th and 17th centuries the leading brehon families in Ireland were the mac Berkery (mac

25

Biothagra — short pleading), the mac Gilsenans and the O'Breslins of Ulster. The mac Aodhagáin or mac Egans were the most popular legal clan in Connacht and Munster; other brehons were the O'Davorens and the mac Clancys; the Leinster brehons were the O'Dorans.

Perhaps the ancestors of some of these families have been present when the king of Tara was being inaugurated at *leic na ríogh*, the inaugural stone, situated on the hill of Tara. The mac Berkery and the O'Breslin brehons were present at Tullahogue near Dungannon when O'Neill of Ulster was being inaugurated. The O'Clancys were the brehons to the O'Briens of Clare and acted as officials at the inaugural site at Quin, where Moyare Park (*magh adhar*) is situated. At Lisbanagher, Co. Kerry the mac Egans were the brehons to the king. The brehon's seat near Ballaghmore Castle (near Borris-in-Ossory, Co. Laois) was the seat where the mac Aodhaghána held court. Finally at Cnoc an Bogha at Ferns, Co. Wexford, the O'Dorans were judges to the mac Murroughs. The 7th century Andacht Morainn (the testament of Morann) is an example of a text relating to kingship, as is Tecosca Cormaic, 'the teachings of Cormac' (which also deals with the proper behaviour of kings, and contains important passages on court procedure); it may be suggested that these early legal or wisdom texts were the basis for the later legal texts.

Bres   The son of Elatha and Ériu.* Elatha was a Fomorian* king and ériu belonged to the Tuatha Dé Danann.*

After Nuadu* had his arm severed in the battle of Mag Tuired* the kingdom was offered to Bres. In AM 3304 (1894 BC) he took up the kingship of Ireland. Under him tribute was forced from the Tuatha Dé Danann. Their chief god, the Dagda,* built a fort for Bres, and the Tuatha Dé Danann, including Ogma,* had to supply him with firewood. That the Tuatha Dé Danann — leaders and gods — had to labour thus for Bres is indicative of their suppression under Fomorian rule. Bres' marriage to Brigit,* a daughter of the Dagda, is further example of inter-marriage continuing between the Tuatha Dé Danann and the Fomorians.

The difficult times which came about under Bres' rule led to co-operation between the three gods of the Tuatha Dé Danann, the Dagda, Ogma, and Lug.* By his demanding excessive tributes of milk and crops, it was felt that Bres had forfeited the kingship, for a king had a duty to be generous if he were to retain sovereignty.

Bres was challenged by the Tuatha Dé Danann poet Cairbre, who made him the object of satire, 'until boils appeared upon his face'. It is related that magic was used against him by Lug when Bres was required to drink milk from pails dipped in bog water so that he wasted away. Another version tells how he was required 'to drink milk which was not real milk from cows which were not real cows'.[8]

Bres resigned his kingship of Ireland after seven years, his resignation leading to the second battle of Mag Tuired between the Tuatha Dé Danann and the Fomorians.

Bricriu Known as Bricriu Nemthenga or Bricriu of the evil tongue. He is compared by Henderson[9] to the Greek satirist Thersites, to Conan of the Ossianic Cycle, and to Sir Kaye of the Arthurian Romances. Characterised by the motto 'Clearer to me is a whisper than to anyone else a cry', Bricriu is associated with Lough Brickland, Co. Down, near which was his palace of Dún Rudraige (Dun Rory). Bricriu has also been compared with the Scandinavian Loki, a demon from the Germanic pantheon of gods, who was involved in mischief making.

Fled Bricrend or the Feast of Bricriu is an early Gaelic story attached to the Cúchulainn* cycle and transcribed from older manuscripts into the *Lebor na h-Uidre* (Book of the Dun Cow) by Moelmuiri mac Ceileachair, a culdee° of Clonmacnoise in AD 1100. (The date AD 875 is given by Henderson as that of the older manuscripts.)

The story relates how Bricriu built at Dún Rudraige a palace similar to that of the Red Branch Knights at Emain Macha* (Navan Fort) and then held a great feast for Conchobar mac Nessa* and the Ulaid (the Ulster warriors), with the intention of stirring up trouble among them; by offering the champion's portion to the bravest warrior, he succeeded in creating rivalry (the champion or hero had the right to the first cut of the pig). This giving of the champion's portion to the most eminent warrior at a feast was an event of great importance to the Ulaid; on this occasion the portion included a cauldron full of generous wine, a seven-year-old boar, a seven-year-old cow and one hundred cakes of wheat cooked in honey.

The Ulaid present were Loegaire Buadach* (the triumphant), Conall Cernach* (the victorious), and Cúchulainn. Bricriu said to them, 'If the champion's portion of my house be thine, the championship of Emain (Ulster) is thine forever'. He then incited the wives of the warriors, offering them the queenship over all the ladies of Ulster if they were first into the banqueting hall. Each lady had fifty attendants, and the subsequent rush to enter the hall sounded like 'the noise of fifty chariots approaching. The whole palace shook and the warriors sprang to their arms'.[9]

The Feast of Bricriu story tells of the 'Champion's Covenant', the wager with the Bachlach° (giant or churl). This Bachlach was in search of Honour and his method of achieving it was by way of a wager; his search had brought him through 'Alba, Europe, Africa, Asia including Greece, Scythia, the isles of Gades, the Pillars of Hercules and Brigantium. On this quest he found no men to give him fair play'.[9] The Bachlach was asked by Sencha mac Ailill (an instructor and wise man in the court of Conchobar mac Nessa) to make his quest known, 'for it beseemeth not a great clannish folk to break a mutual covenant over any unknown individual', that is, the Ulaid would honour any agreement made with anyone. The Bachlach's reply was, 'Come whomsoever of you that may venture, that I may cut off his head tonight, he mine tomorrow night'.

Later, however, it was agreed that the Bachlach was to have his head severed first and that the covenant would be honoured by the warrior returning the following night. With that, Muinremur* (fatneck) of the Ulaid dealt a blow across the Bachlach's neck with an axe, 'till it stuck in the block underneath, cutting off the head, till it lay by the base of the fork-beam'.[9] Then the Bachlach groped for his head, and finding it set it on his neck again, saying that he would be back the following night in order to obtain honour. The next night Muinremur failed to appear and eventually, as Loegaire and Conall did not appear either, it was left to Cúchulainn to maintain the honour of the Ulaid. This he did by placing his neck on the block. The giant, however, hit him with the blunt side of the axe, and then announced that Cúchulainn had the champion's portion undisputed. Then the Bachlach vanished.

Bricriu was ill at Cruachain* during the battle of the Táin* Bó Cualnge. He got up after the battle and was made umpire between the contesting bulls, the brown bull of Cualgne, and Finnbennach, the white-horned. Bricriu's death came about as a result of being trampled by the bulls during their fight. Another version has it that Bricriu, having offended a warrior named Fergus during a board game, was struck in the head. The five pieces of the board game in Fergus' hand went into the head of Bricriu, 'and it was a lasting hurt to him'.

Brigit   A goddess of fertility, a mother goddess. Her symbol is fire, 'the fiery dart of Brigit', and she is associated with movement, represented by the sun symbol, Brigit's cross. A goddess of healing, Brigit is connected with the Brigantes, that large tribe which inhabited Yorkshire in Roman times and which has been traced to the south-east of Ireland. Her name is associated with the river Barrow in Leinster,

28

whilst Camden, the Yorkshire historian, connects her to Breconshire and Birgus. Other references mention Brechin in Scotland, Bargy in Wexford, Bregia (the plain of Meath) and the English river Brent. Brigit was culted by the river Brent near Glastonbury in Somerset. In Ireland Brigit was associated with the Úi Brigte, the name of a sept among the Dési° (the present-day Deasy families). And in Switzerland there was the tribe of the Brigantii with their capital Brigantion (now Bregenz) on Lake Constanz. An association has been suggested with the Sanskrit Brhaspati and the old Norse Bragi. Brigit is a goddess associated with the gods of artistic skill — Goibniu* the smith, Luchta the wright, and Credne Cerd the metal worker. These three with Brigit are referred to as *na Trí Dee Danann.*°

Brigit is referred as a poetess and daughter of the Dagda* and some accounts say that she married the Fomorian* king Bres.* A female sage, a woman of wisdom, Brigit is the goddess of poets.

Brigit's day is the first of February, the same day being the feast of Imbolc,° the old pagan festival of spring. This day was celebrated until recently in Donegal, with people going round their houses carrying Brigit's cross.

Brigit has strong associations with Drumeague, Co. Cavan. This location has been referred to as the 'highland of the Gods' and also as Sliab na dTrí nDé (mountain of the three gods). Here Brigit's head in stone was worshipped as a triple deity. It was hidden on the arrival of the Christian era in a stone age dolmen tomb. Later salvaged, it was eventually erected on a local church and popularly canonised as St Bride of Knockbridge. Thomas J. Barron[10] mentions that 'in 1847 the parish priest took Brigit with him in his gig to his church in West Knockbridge, and she has not been seen since'. According to Mr Barron her head may well have been thrown into a local bog.

Brigit's fire was kept alight from pre-Christian times in Co. Kildare until extinguished by the Normans in the twelfth century. This fire, which may originally have been looked after by vestal virgins, was protected by nuns after the Christian Brigid became abbess of Kildare in AD 525. It is recorded[11] that these nuns took precedence over the bishops until the papal envoy directed otherwise in AD 1151. The actual head or skull of St Brigid herself was reportedly taken away by the Normans to Portugal, and in modern times its veneration is said to include a ceremony in spring when cattle are driven by its presence.

Thomas H. Mason, writing on St Brigid's crosses[12] states that 'the crosses vary in pattern from simple to elaborate types. From the facts that I have gathered I am certain that the custom is of pre-Christian origin and is another adaptation of a custom which was so deeply rooted that it could not be eradicated by the early Christian missionaries and was taken over by them and given a Christian significance.' The St Brigid's cross, like the swastika, is well authenticated as a sun symbol and as such is found throughout the world. It has been noted that it reached the British Isles between 200 BC and AD 200.[13] The related three arm symbol, the triskele,sometimes found in a circle, as at Mullaghmast Stone in Co. Kildare, was used for the protection of beasts and found above the door of cattle sheds. This further demonstrates the association of the Great Mother Brigit with the protection of cattle. As a mother-goddess, she watches over childbirth, and folklore makes Brigit the midwife of the Blessed Virgin.

Bruiden   *Bruidne (pl.)* were hostels, located on hilltops and generally surrounded by three rings of ramparts. Feasting was associated with the *bruidne* and they had a secondary use as beacons or look-out points. Regarded as Otherworld* centres, they have been described as festival halls where the Otherworld feasts were held. Each *bruiden* had a cauldron full with enough food for everyone, and in this regard the Dagda's* cauldron can be mentioned, 'from which no one went away unsatisfied'. The *bruidne* contained inexhaustible supplies of pork, it being said that the pigs, killed and eaten today, were alive and ready for slaughter again tomorrow.

T.F. O'Rahilly mentions[2] four particular *bruidne*: one, Bruiden Da Derga, is connected with Bohernabreena, adjoining the Dodder river, a mile or two south of Tallaght, Co. Dublin. Henry Morris' attempt to place Bruiden Da Derga north of Lough Bray and south-west of the present Glencree Reconciliation Centre in Wicklow is described by O'Rahilly as 'of no value', because, he says, it is an Otherworld place and has no material existence. But Morris claimed that there is a connection between the name Moreen Brook (at Lough Bray) and mBruiden.[14]

The second name mentioned by O'Rahilly is Bruiden Forgaill Manaig about a mile north west of Lusk, Co. Dublin and known as Rathmooney. A third name is Bruiden Meic Da Thó. These two were again according to Morris, possibly sited at the hill above Lusk, from where there is a view of south Dublin and Kildare. (Bruiden Forgaill Manaig was attacked by Cúchulainn* in the saga of the Wooing of Emer.) The fourth name is Bruiden Da Choca, which has been identified by O'Rahilly as Breenmore Hill, situated eight miles east of Athlone. The hill, nearly five hundred feet high, has views over the Shannon valley and the midland plain. The traditional site of the bruiden on top of this hill is an oval fort standing ten feet above the surrounding ground.

A similar word, *bruíon*, a fairy dwelling, pronounced 'breen', may have an association with the Otherworld aspect of the *bruiden*.

Cailleach   Often translated as 'an old hag'; however, an aspect of the *cailleach* is that she can change from that state to being a young woman.

The Caillech Béri is associated with the Beare peninsula in south-west Cork, an area where she is also recorded as being a mother goddess to the Corca Duibhne,° and also with Carnberí, Co. Louth. A local story on Beare Island tells about a row between two cailleachs, one on the mainland, the other on the island. They threw hurling sticks or rods at each other, and the large standing stones in the middle of Beare Island west of Castletownbeare is where one landed; the other is close to Castletownbere.

The Cailleach Gearagáin° is traditionally regarded as being represented by the stone head in Clannaphillip Church in Co. Cavan. The lips of this head are shaped as if to represent the *cailleach* blowing with her breath; a feature which may be compared to the god Boreas, the north wind. This is the *cailleach* who is said to have been destroyed by St Patrick at Mag Bolc° (Moybologue) Co. Cavan.

Sliab na gCailligh (the witches' hills) or Lough Crew in Co. Meath were formed, according to legend, when a *cailleach* let the stones fall from her apron as she was flying overhead.

A story involving Niall Noígiallach* (of the Nine Hostages) and his brothers tells of a *cailleach* that they must kiss. However, she was so objectionable that all but Niall and his brother Fergus were intent on killing her. Fergus placed a quick kiss on her cheek and was rewarded. Niall not only kissed her but embraced her as well and his reward was the kingdom of Ireland, the *cailleach* changing into a beautiful woman. This story is an example of the sovereignty myth,* a pervasive myth that shows the supreme power of the *cailleach* in bestowing the kingdom of Ireland.

Cairbre Cinn Cait (Cairbre Cat-head)   An ancestor deity of the Érainn, a branch of the Fir Bolg* or Belgae. He was called CinnCait because his ears were like those of a cat:

> Thus was Cairbre the hardy
> who ruled Ireland south and north:

31

Two cat's ears on his fair head,
Cat's fur upon his ears.

A further description is included in a poem by Egan O'Rahilly: 'srub chait dono lasin Carpre' (moreover the nose or snout of a cat was worn by Cairbre).

The cat cult came to Ireland from south Wales; it was strong in a tribe called the Silures. This powerful and warlike tribe fought the Romans in AD 48, but a fortress (Isca Silurum, Caerleon) was established in their territory and by AD 78 they were overcome. Their town, Venta Silurum (Caerwent), became romanized.

In Caerleon, referred to above, many cat-eared heads have been found in stone. It has been suggested that these represent a feline deity of the Silures. They appear in Welsh literature as *cath paluc* or Palug's Cat. Thus a close association has been suggested between the stone heads of Caerleon and the mythological Irish figure known as Cairbre CinnCait. The cat god appears as an aggressive deity that was, legend says, originally in human form. Cairbre's son had a collar round his neck which referred to Cairbre as the cat-headed king of Ireland. Every son that had a snout like Cairbre was put to death. Cloghan CinnCait in Brandon, Co. Kerry, is also known as the stepping stones of Cairbre. This place is also associated with the Érainnn of whom Cairbre was the ancestor god.

Cairbre Músc An ancestor of the Múscraige, a branch of the Érainn° (who were connected with Co. Cork). A descendant of Oengus Músc and Mug Láma, Cairbre Músc went to Munster in the time of the sons of Oilioll Olum. A poet, he was rewarded for his poetry by the granting of land, receiving from Fiachaid Muillethan, extensive territory which stretched from Belach Mór Osraige to Cnoc Áine.

Cairbre had two brothers, Cairbre Baschain and Cairbre Riada. Their mother was Sáraid, daughter of Conn Cét Chathach,* and their father is variously identified as either Conaire Mór or Conaire mac Moga Láma. The Dál Cairbre spring from Cairbre Músc, and the Dál Riada from Cairbre Riada. The townland of Carbery in Cork has the names of these brothers as its origin.

Cairenn The daughter of Saxall Balb (stutterer), king of the Saxons. She was called Cairenn Chasdub° (Cairenn of the curly black hair). She was a mistress of Eochaid Mugmedón,* a local king from Co. Cavan.

He is said to have carried her off in a raid on Roman Britain.

Cairenn is said to have lived at Tara,* working with the slaves in drawing and carrying water, though it is also said that she lived near Sliab Guaire in Co. Cavan. She became pregnant by Eochaid Mugmedón and, as legend has it, Eochaid's wife Mongfhind, jealous of this, had her work up to the end of her pregnancy in the hope that the child would be lost. She bore a son on Tara's green and, for fear of Mongfhind, she dared not pick him up, leaving him exposed. Torna the Poet took the boy and nurtured him. This boy was to grow up to be Niall Noígiallach* (Niall of the Nine Hostages). Until he was fully grown neither he nor Torna returned to Tara and, when he did, he found Cairenn still drawing water. Niall told her to stop working, and Cairenn replied, 'I dare not for the queen'. To this Niall replied, 'My mother shall not slave and I a king's son'.[7] He then took her to Tara and dressed her with 'purple raiment'.

Caoilte mac Ronáin A member of the *fian*° of Finn mac Cumaill.* Regarded as one of the most courteous members of the *fian*, he is described as 'a soldier, a guide at need, and a brave man who entertained all'. In one of the stories of the Lays of Finn, it was Caoilte who had to pay a ransom in order to free Finn from Tara.* This ransom consisted in catching various types of animals, including 'a wild man'. 'The wild man left me, I was at the end of my strength, but I captured him in Crumlin'.[36]

It was Caoilte who explained to Oisín* about the famous Crane Bag. This was a bag which had once belonged to Manannán* and had eventually come to Conaire Mór, a mythical king of Ireland. It contained many treasures, including the king of Scotland's shears, the king of Norway's helmet, and an urn which Caoilte himself possessed.

Caoilte was one of the *fian* who survived the massacre at Gabhra* in AD 284. Legend has him fighting with Ilbreach against the latter's father, Manannón mac Lir. Caoilte killed Manannán and took over his *síd* at Síd Fionnachaid° (Slieve Fuad) near Newtownhamilton, Co. Armagh.

Cathaer Mór An ancestor of the Lagin, the tribe from which Leinster gets its name. King of Ireland for three years, Cathaer was slain by the *fian* of the Luaigne of Tara* in AD 122 and was succeeded in the kingship by Conn Cét Chathach.* The *Annals of Clonmacnoise* state that 'King Cahiers armie was overthrown and himself slain, and buried near the river of Boyne'. In an Ossianic poem, Goll mac Morna* of the *fian* boasts that he slew Cathaer Mór in battle.

The Lagin and the Luaigne are both traced back to the 'pseudo-historical' personages of Cathaer Mór and Conn Cét Chathach. Dermot McMurrough and Rory O'Connor, kings of Connacht and Leinster, were descendants of these earlier high kings.

Cathbad   A druid at the court of Conchobar mac Nessa* and, according to earliest accounts, the father of Conchobar himself. Conchobar's mother was Ness, queen of Emain Macha,* and a story about her and Cathbad goes as follows: Cathbad passed Ness one day and was asked, 'What is the day good for?' 'It is good', said Cathbad, 'for begetting a king upon a queen.' The child that resulted from this union was born beside the river Conchobar in Ulster from which he got his name.

Cathbad foretold the birth of Deirdre and the sorrows that she would bring to Ulster (*see*: Longes mac nUsnig*). Cathbad also prophesied the coming of Cúchulainn.* It is related that when Cúchulainn killed his own son Conlaí in battle, his grief was so great that the Ulstermen feared for their lives. Cathbad cast a spell on Cúchulainn so that, thinking the waves were warriors, Cúchulainn's anger was deflected and he fought them until he collapsed from fatigue.

Cathbad had a druidic school with eight students under him, the school including his own son Geanann, also a druid.

Ceasair   The daughter of Noah, came to Ireland forty days before the deluge in AM 2242 (2956 BC); all her tribe are said to have perished during the Flood. Bringing with her fifty girls and three men (Bith, Ladra and Fintan), Ceasair's arrival and her retinue are frequently mentioned in manuscripts.[5] In the *Chronicum Scotorum* it is stated that she was the daughter of a Greek.

Ceasair, the first woman to enter Ireland, is said also to have been the first to bring sheep to the country. Keating,[4] however, says that Banba* was 'the name of the first maiden who occupied Ireland before the deluge and that Banba gave her name to the land'. He mentions Ceasair ('daughter of Bioth, son of Noe') as having arrived *before* the flood, quoting a verse about her arrival.

> Ceasair, daughter of lasting Bioth,
> foster-child of Sabhall, son of Nionuall;
> the first valiant woman who came
> to the isle of Banba before the deluge.[5]

34

This source also states that Noah refused Bith and Ceasair permission to enter the ark, after which they forsook Noah's God and took an idol. The idol advised them to make a ship and, after being at sea for seven and a quarter years, they put into port at Dún na mBarc° on the fifteenth day of the moon. This location is probably the modern Dunnamark near Bantry, Co. Cork. They went from there to an area known as Cumar na dtrí-n- uisce° at the confluence of the rivers Barrow, Nore and Suir. Here the women were divided among the three men, and Ceasair herself went to Connacht where she died and is buried at a place called Cúl Ceasrach (Carn Ceasra).°

Some people say that this is Knockma Hill in Co. Galway on the summit of which is a very ancient cairn, locally known as Finnbheara. O'Donovan[5] states however that Carn Ceasra is on the banks of the River Boyle in Co. Roscommon and that this is where she died and is buried.

Cess Noínden Ulad   The sleeping sickness or the debility of the Ulaid. This weakness fell on the Ulaid at certain times of their history, most especially during the Táin Bó Cualgne* or Cattle Raid of Cooley when the Ulster warriors lay 'with the pains'. During this cattle-raid King Conchobar lay with the 'birth pangs' and was unable to defend Ulster against the Connacht men. Macha* herself whilst giving birth put this curse on Ulster — that in times of crisis they would be powerless.

According to Eleanor Hull[17] 'this curious idea has been supposed to have had its origins in some custom similar to the "couvade" which has been practised among many savage nations, and retains its hold even today among the Indians of Central and South America, the natives of Martinique and the islands near Panama, in parts of China and in the Congo in Africa.' She says that Diodorus and Strabo mention its existence in Corsica and other places in Europe. At the turn of this century it was to be found among the Basque inhabitants of northern Spain. Francisque-Michel says: 'In Biscay, in the valley, the whole population remembers, through its customs, the infancy of that society; the women get up immediately after the birth of a child and see to the needs of the household, while the husband takes to his bed, takes the tender creature in with him and thus receives the compliments of the neighbours.'

Cethlenn   The wife of the Dagda,* born in AM 3450 (1748 BC),[5] is

35

also referred to as the wife of Balor* Béimenn and grandmother of Lug,* who slew Balor in the second battle of Mag Tuired.* It is stated in the *Annals of Clonmacnoise* that Enniskillen (Inis Ceithlenn) is called after her.

Clíodna Together with Aibhell and Áine, Clíodna constitutes a triad of Munster goddesses. Her *síd* is said to be close to a large rock near Mallow, Co. Cork, known as Carraig Clíodna. As an Otherworld* goddess, she possessed three magical birds which ate apples from the otherworld tree. She is also recorded as a banshee (woman of the *síd*; the keening of the banshee predicted death) that rules as queen of the fairies over south Munster.

Her mortal lover was called Ciabhan, and he is said to have brought her to Ireland. As a *femme fatale*, Clíodna enticed men to the sea-shore and then drowned them, which reminds one of the superstition that it was unfortunate to see a woman just before you went to sea. Eventually a young man learnt her spells and plotted to kill her, but she changed into a wren and escaped. Some say that hunting the wren finds its origin in this 'event'.

Clíodna's birds had a healing power which lulled the sick to sleep and healed them.

Clíodna is said to have drowned in the harbour of Glandore, near Clonakilty, Co. Cork. The deep roar of the sea as it enters the caverns of the cliffs there was said to foretell the death of the king of Munster. This surge has been 'from time immemorial called Tonn Clíodna, Clíodna's wave'. Because of the way she was treated, Clíodna threatened to cause a very large wave which would completely cover Munster.

Conchobar mac Nessa King of Ulster in the first century BC. He gives his name to the Cycle of Conchobar mac Nessa and the Craeb Ruad° (Red Branch Knights) — the Ulster Cycle — one of the main headings under which a large proportion of early Irish tales falls. (The other headings are the Cycle of Finn mac Cumaill* and the Fiana; the Mythological Cycle; and the Cycle of Kings.) His palace at Emain Macha* also known as Emania, is now known as Navan Fort, located west of Armagh city. Here the Red Branch warriors were trained to defend the king and Ulster.

Conchobar's mother was Ness, and legend has it that his father was the druid Cathbad.* Ness lived with Fergus mac Róich,* king of Emain

Macha, on condition that Conchobar be king for a year. She then contrived successfully to make Conchobar king of Ulster.

Constantly protected by the Red Branch Knights, he was seen as a popular and wise king. At Bricriu's Feast Conchobar was present and a royal couch was erected for him high above those of the royal house. As high king, he had the ancient right to spend the first night with the wife of any of his warriors, and the story of Deirdre has its roots in this ancient custom. In this instance he had the woman guarded and kept solely for himself when she came of age. The story tells how by his lack of honour in deceiving the Sons of Uisneach to return home to their deaths, and in putting his foster-father Fergus mac Róich out of the way Conchobar was able to dispose of Naoise his rival for the affection of Deirdre. Legend has it that Conchobar was husband of Eochaid Feidlech's four daughters, Mumain, Eithne, Clothra and queen Medb.[97]

During friendlier times Conchobar and Fergus mac Róich crossed from Emain Macha to Cruachain Connacht* to be feted by Ailill and Medb;* king and queen of Connacht. During the Cattle Raid of Cooley (the Táin),* Conchobar was lying weak 'with the pains', this being an illness which affected the Ulaid (the Ulster warriors) during times of crisis. These 'pains' are known as the Cess Noínden Ulad.*

Conchobar's death resulted from a conflict with the perenial enemy, cattle raiders. Conchobar went into battle but was distracted by women who wanted him to stand aside so that they 'could see his shape'.

The cattle raider Cet put 'the brain of Mes Gegra'° in his sling and hit the crown of Conchobar's head, so that two thirds of the brain entered Conchobar's head'. The fallen Conchobar was brought by his attendant Cenn Berraide to Ardachad° of the Fews (the modern High-field, near Newtown Hamilton, Co. Armagh). Fingen, Conchobar's physician, stitched his head and told him that 'he must always remain relaxed, he should never become angry, never have connection with a woman, he should not over-eat and should not run'.[1] He thus lived on for seven years.

Some stories say that he died immediately, others that he fell at the ford of Daire Dá Baeth,° and a story with a Christian emphasis has him dying in a fit of rage on hearing of the death of Christ. The year 27 BC is the date given for his death in the *Book of Ballymote*.

Conn Cét Chathach Conn of the hundred battles (AD 177-212) was a famous high king of Ireland. The date of his birth coincides with the completion of the five roads to Tara.* Conn apparently came to power as a result of slaying Cathaer Mór* at the battle of Mag Ága°. At this time Ireland was divided between Conn and Eógan Mór of Munster. A boundary line called the Eiscir Riada° was drawn west from present day High Street in Dublin to 'Ath-Cleyth Mearie', in Connacht. North of this was controlled by Conn, south by Eógan Mór. (Eiscir Riada can be translated as 'gravel hills of the kings'; there are a series of hills travelling across Ireland in a rough east-west direction.)

At a later date Conn defeated Eógan Mór at the battle of Mag Lána, Co. Offaly and thus became high king of Ireland, holding sway until the usual internecine struggles for power resulted in his brothers plotting his death. Whilst preparing for the feast of Tara he was slain by Tibraithe Tíreach, grandson of the king of Ulster. Conn reigned for thirty five years and was almost a hundred at the time of his death.

Conn Cét Chathach is synonymous with Conn, the Otherworld* deity. It is said of Conn the king that once, when a magic mist had come upon him near Tara, he found himself in the Otherworld. Here he met Lug,* who foretold the kings who were to succeed him. T.F. O'Rahilly[2] says that Conn was one of the numerous names applied to the gods of the Otherworld and that the Celts believed themselves to be 'descendants of Conn'. He further states that the genealogists, following their custom, turned Conn the god into an Irish king, making him son of Fedlimid Nechtaid, son of Tuathal Techtmar.* The word *conn*[41] means 'head', 'reason' and 'chief', 'head' symbolizing the sun as well as wisdom and thus appropriate for a Celtic Otherworld deity.

A stone head of Conn, as a god of enlightenment, was discovered in a passage grave in Co. Cavan. This was one of the many stone heads of the Celtic pantheon of gods found at Sliab na dTrí nDé, Corleck Hill, Co. Cavan; now known as the triple-headed god from Corleck, it is to be seen in Dublin's National Museum. The word for Conn in France is Condus and Senocondus, and on both Gaelic and Gaullish monuments he is represented as a triple-faced head or as a triple head.

Cormac mac Airt   Called Cormac ua Cuinn or Cormac of the Gaels* in earlier Irish texts. The earliest known version of the name is Cormac Conn Loinges (Cormac of the exiles) and in this instance he is king of the Érainn.° During the year AD 226, at the battle of Crinna on the Boyne, Cormac defeated Fergus Dubdétach, king of Ulster. He was assisted in this victory over the Ulaid by the Cianacht,° whom he settled on the conquered territory.

In the four years from AD 227 Cormac fought twenty-three battles, among them the battle of Granard against the Ulstermen. Twice then among them the battle of Granard against the Ulstermen. Twice then he was driven by the Ulstermen into Munster and Connacht. According to O'Donovan[5] it was as a result of all these battles that he was forced to flee in AD 241. He went to Scotland, obtaining sovereignty there, but it would appear that he returned the following year, battles being recorded against Munster. These include the battle of Grian, in Co. Limerick and the battle of Samhain near Bruree, also in Co. Limerick.

Cormac's reign is often described as a golden age of plenty. However, being constantly ousted from his kingdom, it would seem that he ruled over an age less stable than the storytellers would like to admit.

Like many characters described in this book, the historical personage of Cormac is interwoven with legend. Thus we learn that Manannán mac Lir* gave Cormac a silver branch containing golden apples which produced music that calmed all. Cormac is associated with wolves, legend having it that he was suckled by them. His taboos (*see*: geis*) included a prohibition against pursuing the birds of Mag da Chó° or from swimming with the birds of Loch Ló.°

Cormac mac Airt died at Clettech in the Boyne valley after a reign of forty years. His death, caused by the lodging of a salmon bone in his throat, resulted from a spell which the druid Maelgenn placed on him after Cormac had turned against the druids 'on account of his adoration of God in preference to them'.[5]

Cormac is credited with composing Tecosc-na-Ríg (princely institutions) or Tecosca Cormaic, to preserve manners, morals and government in the kingdom. Tecosca Cormaic or the Instructions of Cormac was written down in the 9th century and is contained in a number of manuscripts. It was first translated in its entirety by Kuno Meyer in 1909. An extract from this early text is as follows:

> 'O grandson of Conn, O Cormac,' said Caibre, 'what is the best for the good of a tribe?' 'Not hard to tell,' said Cormac.

> 'A meeting of nobles,
> Frequent assemblies
> An enquiring mind,
> Questioning the wise,
> Quelling every evil,
> Fulfilling every good,
> An assembly according to rules,
> Following ancient lore,
> A lawful synod,
> A lawful lord,

Righteous chieftains,
Not to crush wretches,
Keeping treaties,
Mercifulness with good custom,
Consolidating kingship,
Weaving together synchronisms,
Fulfilling the law,
Legality of ancient alliances.'

He also called the chroniclers of Ireland to Tara,* ordering them to write the history of the country in one book. Named the Psalter of Tara, no fragment of this book has been identified as extant.

Crom Cruach According to the *Dindshenchas*,° the principal idol of all the colonies established in Ireland from earliest times to the sweep of Christianity. Crom Cruach is probably synonymous with Crom Dub whose festival, known as Domhnach Chroim Duibh, celebrating Crom's overthrow by St Patrick, is held in many places throughout Ireland on the last Sunday in July or the first Sunday in August.[47] His stone idol was situated near Ballymagauran in Co. Cavan on the plain of Mag Slecht.* Crom was a corn god to whom animal and human sacrifices were offered. 'Milk and corn they would ask from him speedily in return for one-third of their healthy issue: great was the horror and the scare of him.'[67] There were gatherings at Mag Slecht on the eve of Samain* and sacrifices of first-born animals and humans were made.

On this plain there were twelve stone idols all embossed in silver except Crom who was embossed in gold. When St Patrick overthrew Crom a large hole was dug and Crom was buried in it. However, part of the stone idol stuck out from the ground and there is a story that a farmer blew it up around 1900. The exhibit in Dublin's National Museum known as the Killycluggin Stone is said to be Crom.

Cruachain Originally known as Cruachain Connacht, the ancient kingdom of Connacht and seat of the kings and queens of the province. It is situated over an area of about ten square miles near Tulsk, Co. Roscommon. This royal site is among the major ones of pagan times. It consists of a series of ring forts, various graves which have been excavated and extensive lengths of ditches marking out old enclosures. There is the pillar stone of Daithi, an ancient pagan king, and also

Rathcruachan, the largest of these ring forts, being some fifteen feet high and one hundred yards in diameter. This fort, as Cruachain Connacht itself, has strong associations with Queen Medb.* The site of the pillar stone and excavated graves mentioned above is known as Reilig na Rí° (the burial place of kings). The view from Rath° Cruachan is excellent and on a clear day one can see far to the east over the plains.

Perhaps the most interesting aspect of Cruachain is that it contains the entrance to the Otherworld,* through the many caves in the area. According to local tradition these caves go back as far as Sligo. In accordance with the general Christianization of pagan tradition, one particular cave, the Síd ar Cruachain, is known as the Hell's Gate of Ireland. One may also cite the legend that has Ailill's warrior, Nera, destined to live there with his wife until the Day of Judgment.

Cruachain has many associations with mythical personages. The Ellén Trechenn* or triple-headed deity emerged from here and laid waste to Ireland until he was killed by Amergin, father of Conall Cernach.* From here too came a flock of white birds that throughout Ireland 'withered up whatsoever their breaths impinged on' until the Red Branch Knights killed them with their slings.

'Certain pigs of paganism emerged from the cave of Cruachain',[7] the pigs giving the name to Mag Muccrama (the plain of the counting of pigs), near Athenry, Co. Galway. There are references to Ailill and Medb counting pigs on the plain of Muccrama.

It was from Cruachain that the Mórrígan* came in a chariot 'pulled by a one-legged chestnut horse towards Cuailgne' (the Táin*).

Cúchulainn   The son of Sualdam mac Roich* (king of Cuailgne, Co. Louth) and Dechtire, who was sister of Conchobar mac Nessa,* high king of Ireland, and druidess daughter of the druid Cathbad.*

Cúchulainn's given name was Sétanta, and as a youth he went to Emain Macha* to train with the Craeb Ruad,° the Red Branch Knights. Around this time he killed the hound of Culann, who was smith to the king: the smiths closed in on their guests, the knights, with fire tongs, irons and a massive anvil, and it is recorded that this was the only time the knights ever feared for their lives. Bloodshed was avoided by Sétanta offering himself in place of the hound he had slain; thus he got the name of the hound of Culann mac an Gabhann, or Cúchulainn.

Cúchulainn and Emer

Cúchulainn went to woo Emer at Bruiden Forgaill Manaig, now called

Rathmooney, near Lusk, Co. Dublin. After describing themselves to each other Cúchulainn said, 'Good indeed are these virtues, why then should it not be fitting for us to become one?' Emer's reply was to ask, 'Yet one question, hast thou a wife already?' Cúchulainn told her that he had not, and they continued their courtship conversation with riddles, so that Emer's handmaidens would not know what was going on. 'I am the nephew of a man that disappears in another wood of Badb',* said Cúchulainn, referring to Conchobar his uncle; and, when asked his own name, he said, 'I am the hero of the plague that befalls dogs'.

However, Emer's father Forgall Manach (Forgall the Wily) found out about Cúchulainn and Emer meeting in Lusk and he said, 'The madman from Emain Macha has been here to converse with Emer and the girl has fallen in love with him. . . . I shall hinder them'. Forgall then went to Emain Macha and suggested that Cúchulainn go to Scotland for training as a warrior. This he did, but later he resumed his pursuit of Emer. After leaping over the three ramparts at Bruiden Forgaill Manaig, he defeated Forgall and his men and carried off Emer. Cúchulainn killed Emer's sister Scennmend when she rushed against him, the place where he killed her being ever since called the Ford of Scennmend. After much fighting Cúchulainn reached Emain Macha with Emer.

Cúchulainn in Scotland

It was the custom for warriors to train with Scáthach* (the shadowy one) on the Isle of Skye and this was Cúchulainn's destination. He first met the daughter of Donall Dornalla (big fist), who fell in love with him; being refused by Cúchulainn, she swore to be avenged, but Cúchulainn went on to meet Uathach, Scáthach's daughter. Travelling by the Bridge of Cliff, which 'no man can cross until he achieves valour' Cúchulainn was advised by Uathach to perform one of his warrior feats (that of the hero's salmon leap) in order to reach Scáthach. On reaching her, he was to 'set his sword between her breasts' until she yielded him his three wishes — to teach him, to allow him to wed Uathach, and to foretell his future. This Cúchulainn did; he then trained under Scáthach and later, fighting for her against Áife, a warrior princess, he 'seized her (Áife) under her two breasts, took her on his back like a shoulder load, and bore her away'. Áife had a son by Cúchulainn called Conlaí, who, back in Ulster later, was slain in ignorance by his father. His death was caused by his obedience to a command not to reveal his name.

Before Cúchulainn left Scotland, Scáthach foretold his future:

> Welcome, oh victorious warlike. . . .
> at the lifting of the kine of Bray (Bregia),
> thou wilt be a chariot chief in a single combat.
> Great peril awaits thee. . . .
> alone against a vast herd. . . .
> The warriors of Cruachan, thou wilt scatter them.
> Thy name shall reach the men of Alba (Scotland).
> Thirty years I reckon the strength of thy valour.
> Further than this I do not add.[17]

The Feats of Cúchulainn

Many stories tell of Cúchulainn, of his exploits and adventures, and of his extraordinary bravery and skill in battle. His particular abilities and techniques are described as his 'feats'. Included here is the Gaé Bolga* (spear of Bulga). Bulga, the god of lightning, was said to have been the inventor of the missile-spear and, by acquiring this, Cúchulainn was greatly strengthened in battle. It was with the Gaé Bolga that he slew his own son Conlaí.

Another feat Cúchulainn is noted for is that known as the 'apple feat', in which his abilities are described[18] thus: 'nine swords in his hand, and nine silver shields and nine apples of gold. He shoots each of them on high, and nothing of them falls on the ground . . .'

The 'dart feat' is the most celebrated of all, when, during a single combat in a ford, a friend floated a dart mid-water to Cúchulainn. He, receiving it between his toes, stuck it into the belly of his opponent. Said to have been a barbed dart, it entered the body, threw out a number of blades and inflicted a deadly wound.

The 'champion's scream' has been described by the nineteenth-century historian O'Beirne Crowe thus: 'he shook his shield and he bent his spears, and he brandished his sword, and he gave his champion's scream from his throat.'[18]

Cúchulainn in the Táin

The Táin Bó Cualgne* (Cattle Raid of Cooley) credits Cúchulainn with the killing of a hundred of Medb's* men. And, according to Ailill, king of Connacht, 'that is not the first abomination he has wrought us'. Medb, learning that the Cess Noínden Ulad* (a sleeping illness affecting all the Ulster warriors except Cúchulainn), was wearing off, sent three witches and three wizards to assail him. Cúchulainn killed them.

A number of notable single combats are recorded. One of these is that between Cúchulann and Fergus mac Roich,* in which Cúchulainn eventually mounted his chariot and fled. However, the fight between Cúchulainn and Calatín Dána and his twenty-seven sons was a different matter. Each of them was endowed with a poisonous quality, which also applied to their weapons, causing death to their opponents as soon as they drew blood. Cúchulainn, helped by one of Medb's scouts, Fiacha mac Firaba, defeated the sons of Calatín Djna.

Cúchulainn and Fer Diad

This most notable battle shows[17] 'a high ideal of chivalrous honour exceeding anything that the Arthurian Saga can show, and perhaps cannot be surpassed in any literature.'

It had been Medb's custom, in previous duels with Cúchulainn, to offer warriors bribes to fight on her behalf. These bribes included land, bondswomen, her daughter Findabair* in marriage, plus, if desired, Medb's own 'gentle thighs'. Many young warriors found either these rewards too enticing, or the opportunity to fight Cúchulainn as one not to be missed. Thus three Connacht warriors. Étarcomal, Nath Crantail and Forgamen died.

Fer Diad had been Cúchulainn's fellow-pupil under Scáthach.* Medb, using the promise of Findabair as a wife and, perhaps more effectively, the dread of satire, persuaded Fer Diad to offer combat. Cúchulainn was warned by Fergus mac Roich* that Fer Diad was going to come, but Cúchulainn, conscious of the opinion of his peers, nonetheless arose late, lest it be said that he had got up early through fear or dread of the forthcoming battle. When he did rise, and travelled to the ford where the battle would take place, Cúchulainn was surrounded by bocánachs° (demons of the air). Fer Diad asked why they were fighting since, when they had been at Scáthach's, Cúchulainn had been his attendant. Cúchulainn replied, speaking of that time,

> We were heart companions
> we were comrades in assemblies
> we were fellows of the same bed
> where we used to sleep the deep sleep. . . .'[17]

The fight began, lasting for three days. They fought on foot and by chariot with swords and spears. 'Their eight sharp ivory-handled spears fly backwards and forwards between them like bees on the wing of a sunny day.'[17] At the end of each day's fighting they exchanged medicines, their horses shared the same enclosure and their charioteers slept at the same fire.

On the morning of the third day Cúchulainn told Fer Diad that he was looking unwell, 'Thine hair has grown darker and thine eyes drowsy'.

Cúchulainn: O Fer Diad,
                        if it be thou,
                        thine honour is fallen low,
                        to have come at a woman's bidding,
                        to fight with thy fellow pupil.

Fer Diad: O Cúchulainn, inflictor of wounds,
                        O valiant man, O true champion!
                        A man is constrained to come
                        to the sod where his final grave shall be. . . .[17]

Then ensued the final encounter, for which Fer Diad wore an iron apron as protection against the Gaé Bolga.* Fighting in the ford of a river, at Ardee, Fer Diad threw a sword and buried it in Cúchulainn's body 'so that his blood fell into his girdle, and the ford was reddened with his gore'. Unable to endure this Cúchulainn asked his charioteer, Laeg mac Riangabra, for the Gaé Bolga. Using this weapon, Cúchulainn pierced the heart of Fer Diad. He retrieved it again, and hit Fer Diad a second time so that it protruded through his body.

Fer Diad: It did not behove thee that I should fall by your hand.

Cúchulainn: O Fer Diad, treachery hath defeated thee.
                        Unhappy was thy fate —
                        thou to die, I to remain —
                        grievous forever is our lasting separation.[17]

The Death of Cúchulainn

Cúchulainn's death occurred in the battle of Muirthemne (12 BC) in the modern Co. Louth. This battle was inpired by revenge for the deaths of Calatin, Curoí mac Dáire* (king of Munster) and Cairbre (king of Meath). After the fighting, exhausted and dying, Cúchulainn 'drank his drink and washed himself and came forth to die, calling on his foes to come and meet him'.[17] Wishing to die standing up 'feet on the ground, eyes facing the foe', Cúchulainn went to a pillar stone and tied himself to it. (This stone can still be seen at Knockbridge, near Dundalk in Co. Louth.) At first his enemies were afraid to approach. But then, seeing a bird settle on his shoulder and pecking at his eyes, they realised that Cúchulainn must be dead and went up to him. Lugaid, avenging the death of his father Curoí mac Dáire, cut off Cúchulainn's head after arranging his hair about his shoulder. Then they went away, bringing with them Cúchulainn's head and also his right hand.

The death of Cúchulainn was avenged within twenty-four hours by Conall Cernach,* with whom Cúchulainn had had a pact. His death marked the end of the dominant influence of the Red Branch Knights and their power based at Emain Macha* but, as a central figure in history/mythology he remains a major force in the Irish imagination.

> A hero there in that chariot: a black thick head of hair: smoothness of it on him: I should imagine it is a cow that licked it. A grey jerking eye in his head. A purple blue tunic about him of borders of all white gold. . . . A brooch of red gold on his breast: it extended over each of his two shoulders. A white hooded cloak about him, with a flashing red border. A sword of gold hilt in arrangement of rest on his two thighs. A broad grey spear on a shaft of wild ash in his hand. A sub-sharp aggressive dart near it. A purple shield with an even circle of silver, with loop-animals of gold above his two shoulders. I should think it was a shower of pearls that was flung into his head. Blacker than the side of a black cooking-pit each of his two brows: redder than ruby his lips.[18]

Cúroí mac Dáire   Cú Roí means hound king (also known as *rí in domain* — king of the deep). A divinity, also supposed to have been a king of Munster at the time of Conchobar mac Nessa.* His fortress has been associated with Caher Conree, Co. Kerry. 'In a field near the foot of the Caher Conree Mountain lies a low cromlech. . . ; it has the name on it of a man called Cú Rí in its early genitive form of Conu Rí'.[9]

Cúroí, a magician and master of illusion, was one of those sought by the heroes to act as arbitrator of the covenant over the champion's portion in the Fled Bricrend (*see*: Bricriu*).

46

Cúroí was a habitual traveller, always moving east, which has led some to believe that his fortress may have been either Wicklow or Wexford. He appears as a *baclach*° (churl) in the Fled Bricrend.

When it turned out that his judgment was not acceptable, he was portrayed as having 'ravenous yellow eyes, portruding from his head, each of the twain the size of an ox-vat. Each finger as thick as another person's wrist'.[9] When the covenant had been completed and Cúchulainn* given sovereignty of the heroes of Ireland, Cúroí vanished. His presence at this event was in fulfilment of a promise earlier given to Cúchulainn. Cúroí had helped Cúchulainn storm and take a fortress on the Isle of Man; this expedition was against Echde Horse-mouth, a king of the Fomorians.* The booty from this raid was a cauldron, cows, and Bláthnat or Bláithíne (wife of Cúroí) and, when Cúchulainn failed to repay him for his help, Cúroí kept the booty for himself. (The cows from this booty were known as three magic cows, 'the spotted ones of Echde'; each day they filled a copper cauldron with sixty pints of milk.) He later embedded Cúchulainn up to his armpits in the earth and shaved off his hair.

Later Cúchulainn went to Fort Cúroí (Caher Conree?) to recover Bláthnat. He saw the waters turning white and he recognized this to be the signal from Bláthnat that he could enter unopposed. This he did and, finding Cúroí asleep on Bláthnat's lap, cut off his head. He brought Bláthnat to Ulster, but he was followed by Ferceirtne, Cúroí's servant. At a spot bordering on a high cliff, Ferceirtne clasped Bláthnat and jumped with her over the cliff so that they died together. Fort Cúroí is a castle by the sea but, in keeping with the Otherworld* spirit, it is not an ordinary one. 'In what airt soever of the globe Cúroí should happen to be, every night o'er the fort he chanted a spell, till the fort revolved as swiftly as a millstone. The entrance was never to be found after sunset.'[9]

Cúroí is enigmatic, seeming to change quite a lot, and being seldom at home, whether that be Sliab Mis,° Wicklow or Wexford. It is said of him that since he took up arms he never reddened his sword in Ireland nor did the food from Ireland pass his lips. His whirling castle and his title of 'king of the world' give Cúroí a more universal setting. He is mentioned in the poem 'Elegy of Curoi', from the Welsh *Book of Taliesin*. Here the sea is treated as 'Curoi's wide well' and the poet is taken aback by Cúroí's death wail.

> The death wail of Curoi has startled me;
> *cold* the deed of him of rugged passions,
> whose crime was one which few have heard of.

Daire's son held a helm on the southern sea,
sung was his praise before his burial.

In mythology, Cúroí stands apart. Less interested in the opinions of those around, he is more a luminary with close associations to water, constant movement and shape changing. Cúroí's origins would appear to be in a pre-Gaelic race whose myths were assimilated in a slightly distorted way by the Gaels, just as Celtic myths were often presented in a slightly distorted way by the Christians. 'But the gods do not easily die, neither does the spirit which gave them life'.

Dagda   The full title of the Dagda is Dagda mór mac Eladan or Dagda mór mac Eithenn. The chief of the Gaelic pantheon of gods, he is the Irish equivalent of Zeus, Jupiter and Odin. Known also as Eochaidh Ollathair° (father of all), the Dagda is also referred to as Ruad Rof-hessa° (lord of perfect knowledge). *Fiss* (the modern Irish *fios*) has the special sense of 'occult knowledge'. Knowledge of what was hidden or was to come was the highest kind of wisdom. The Dagda had powers of wizardry and led the Tuatha Dé Danann* into Ireland against the Fir Bolg.* Nora Chadwick[21] says the 'Irish gods do not emerge as gods in

The entrance to the Great Chamber at Newgrange beside the Boyne
(before restoration)

48

the usual meaning of the term. They are neither worshipped nor sacrificed to. They are supernatural beings with magical powers. . . . The greatest of the gods is the Dagda, "the good god", not good in a moral sense but "good at everything".'

Professor Chadwick[21] describes associations with the Dagda, such as his cauldron: 'a stupendous porridge is prepared for him in his cauldron . . .; another tradition has it that the porridge was to be eaten from a huge hole in the ground'. This last reference can be expanded by reference to the Samain,* when the Dagda came south from the river Unius in Donegal. Here on the eve of 1 November (Samain) a fertility rite occurred between the Dagda and Boand,* in this hole in the ground, after he had finished eating his porridge from the cauldron. The home of the Dagda may have been Grianán Ailigh° in Donegal. He later became lord of Bruig na Bóinne° after ousting Nuadu.* Aengus* Óg was the offspring of his relationship with Boand.

The Dagda took part in the battles of Mag Tuired* (plain of weeping) against the Fomorians.* He is associated with a club which was so weighty that it had to be borne on wheels. The Dagda is a warrior god in the heroic mould. In the account of the Tuatha Dé Danann preserved in the *Book of Lecan* it is stated that Dagda Mór 'Great God Fire, so called from his military ardour' was king of Ireland for eighty years.

The Dagda was killed at the battle of Mag Tuired. A woman named Ceitleann cast a sling shot at him and he died from the 'bloody missile'.

He had three sons, Aengus, Aed and Cermad, who are buried with their father at Bruig na Bóinne. The mound there called Síd an Bhróga was raised over them as a monument. However, it is also written that he is buried at Leithet Lachtmaige in Murlough Bay, Co. Antrim, between Tor Point and Fair Head. Reference to the Dagda is omitted in the index to the *Annals of the Four Masters*. This omission reinforces Professor Chadwick's[21] reference to 'Christian censorship'. It can be noted also that there is no reference in the Annals to the Dagda's daughter Brigit,* goddess of fertility. These omissions seem to imply on the part of the Franciscan scribes not merely a transcriptual role but a censorial one as well.

Ancient bronze cauldron in the RIA collection

49

Dál nAraide   This is the name given to the Cruthin people who survived in Ireland, mostly in Co. Down. The Cruthin came to Ireland from Scotland, but originally they were the inhabitants of Britain. Strabo described them as the Priteni; he said that they never stayed long in one place; 'they paint their faces with woad which gives them a blue colouring . . .; they wear their hair long but otherwise shave, except for a head and upper lip'. Caesar referred to them as the Priteni Interiore and to the Fir Bolg* or Belgae as Priteni Mare.

The Cruthin were the earliest inhabitants of these islands. They were in Ireland before the Fir Bolg and the Gaels. The Cruthin were the Dál nAraide; the Fir Bolg were the Ulaid; and the Gaels, perhaps the Gauls from Galicia in Spain. In east Ulster the kinsmen of the Dál nAraide were the Uí Echach or Horse people. Lough Neagh is the lake of the horse, and it is around Lough Neagh and Strangford Lough (Loch Cuan) that these people lived. To the east of Lough Neagh the Cruthin became independent and became the state of Dál nAraide.

There were two types of Picts. The northern Picts settled in the north-western isles of Scotland and were pirates and seamen and used curraghs. Like the Irish they had been little touched by the Roman invasion of Britain. The southern Picts were agriculturalists.

Both O'Rahilly and Watson state that the Chruthin in Ireland were not Picts. However, Picts were simply the Celtic and pre-Celtic people of Scotland defined as Picts because they painted themselves. Some sources say that they were naked and painted their bodies blue, that they had been in these islands since the Bronze age and that they were head-hunters. Conall Cernach*, the warrior and famous head-hunter, is an ancestor deity of the Dál nAraide.

The Dál nAraide practised divination by means of the flight and cries of birds:

> The honouring of sneezes and omens, choice of weather, lucky times, the heeding of the voices of birds they practised without disguise.[32]

The Cruthin were a matriarchal people; eligibility for kingship depended on the candidate's mother being of the royal line. An example of this matriarchal succession is Conchobar mac Nessa*, who owed the title to his mother Ness. The matriarchal succession of their kings shows that their social structure differed from that of the succeeding Gaelic order.

Some upright stone slabs have been found in Scotland, which have sculptured symbols in low relief upon them. The following incised animals have been associated with the symbols: the fish, serpent, duck, bull, hound, stag, boar and deer. Many of the symbols are of an abstract design, such as a V rod, a Z rod, and a double disc. In their writing the Picts have left a number of inscriptions in the ogam* character; these have never been interpreted.

In Ireland the kingdom of the Dál nAraide extended from Slemish mountain to Newry. A notable king of the Dál nAraide was Suibne Gealt*, the inspiration of Ulster poets. The battle of Mag Rath in AD 637 may have marked the end of their independence.

Some placenames in Ulster preserve the name of these ancient peoples — for example, Drumcroone, the ridge of the hill of the Cruthin, and possibly the old ruined church in Mountstewart demesne in the Ards, Co. Down, called Templecroone, or the church of the Cruthin.

Dealbaeth   Son of Ogma* and king of Ireland in the year AM 3451 (1747 BC). After being king for ten years he was killed by his own son, Fiacha mac Dealbaeith, who then became king.

Dealgnat   Wife of Partholón, she came to Ireland in AM 2520 (2678 BC). This was the twenty-first year of the reign of the biblical patriarch Abraham, the twelfth year of the reign of Semiramis, empress of Assyria, and two hundred and seventy-eight years after the Flood.

Díchorb   Son of Oilioll Olum,* killed at the battle of Mag Muccrama in Co. Galway along with his six brothers and his uncle Art, son of Conn.

After the battle of Mag Muccrama, Oilioll Olum recited the following verse:

> Mac Con has slain my seven sons;
> Pitiful is my bitter, grievous cry,
> Eoghan, Dumbhmearchon, Mogh Corb,
> Lughaid, Eochaid, Díchorb, Tadg.

Díthorba   Son of Deman and king of Ireland in AM 4477 (721 BC). The *Annals of Clonmacnoise* tell about this period that there were 'three kings of Ireland at once. All were kinsmen (Aed Ruad, Díthorba and

Cimbaeth). In order to preserve peace each of the contending kings would rule Ireland for seven years, one after another, without impediment of any of the rest. There were seven magicians, seven poets and seven principal lords of the Ulster nobility, chosen to see that the agreement was finally kept. The magicians for their part would (using their art), work against anyone breaking the agreement; the poets would chide and scold at them in their rhymes and writings, with as great a disgrace as they could invent, the seven principal lords to follow and prosecute the violator with fire and sword. But all this was not necessary, for the preservation of their agreement, for they did agree without any square at all, till at last Aed Ruad was drowned in Easroe, leaving no issue but one only daughter Macha* Mongroe — Macha of the Red Hair.'

Druids

> In cech diamair-dhán draoidechta . . .
> (in every occult art of the druids).

An ancient caste whose origins and functions are open to debate. Herodotus states that they were a tribe of the ancient Celts who emigrated from the Danube towards Gaul and Britain. Said to have traced their origin to Japhet, son of Noah, they derived their philosophy from Pythagoras, who flourished around 500 BC.

Pliny said that the druids held the oak in high esteem, adorning it with flowers before every religious ceremony and worshipping the tree as a symbol of Jupiter. Tacitus says that for the druids it was unlawful to build temples to the gods or to worship them within walls or under roofs.

Caesar speaks of druidic schools[87] where great quantities of verse were memorized in a training that often lasted twenty years. They did not wish writing to become common property 'as it tends to relax the diligence of the student', and consequently they taught by purely oral methods. Their learning involved astronomy, including the size of the universe and of the earth and the influence of the gods. It also included moral philosophy. Many lessons were uttered in the form of riddles. Caesar states that they regarded the day as starting in the evening and that they followed a lunar calendar, observing *saeculae*, ages or generations of thirty years.

He held that druids used sacrifice as part of their ceremonies. Some of these ceremonies involved human and animal victims being placed in large wickerwork figures and set on fire. While it seems that druids did participate in such rites, whether they occurred in Ireland or not is a moot point. The fact that no written evidence bears testament to such sacrifices is perhaps not sufficient to refute the possibility that they did take place.

Diodorus Siculus wrote of a similarity between the druidic idea of an afterlife and the Pythagorean doctrine of metempsychosis. This is equivalent to the doctrine of transmigration of souls, which holds that the spirit at the time of death passes into another body of either similar or different species. However, unlike the Pythagoreans, the druids did not believe in the expiation of sin after death or the idea of retributive justice in the next world. The Otherworld* was simply seen as a certain time spent in a happy or blessed place. Lebor na hUidre* makes reference to the occult art of the druids ('in cech diamair-dhán draideachta').

In Irish legend it is said that the early colonizer Partholón* arrived with three druids called Fios, Eolus, and Fochmarc (intelligence, knowledge, and inquiry). There is no record of any druidical acts or auguries of these three, but druidic influence is recorded among many of the early colonizers of Ireland. The Milesian druid Caicher is said to have foretold to his people that Ireland was their ultimate destination.

The Tuatha Dé Danann,* confronted with the Milesians' arrival at Tara* and protesting that they were caught unawares, persuaded the Milesians to return to their ships and move back out to sea the distance of 'nine waves'. The Tuatha Dé Danann druids then worked spells, creating storms to drive the Milesians away. These efforts were, however, unsuccessful.

After the Milesian settlement in Ireland, their druid Mide lit a fire at Uisneach,* believed to be the first druidical fire lit in Ireland. According to legend this burnt for seven years and it was from here that every fire in Ireland was lit. Mide and his successors were entitled to a sack of corn and a pig from every house in Ireland. When the other druids disagreed with this, Mide had their tongues cut out. He burnt the tongues in the earth at Uisneach and sat over them, to which his mother said, 'It is proudly (from *uaisne*, pride)° you sit there this night.'

The Irish druid divined by means of ogam* carved on wands of yew. A druidical charm was to pronounce an incantation on a wisp of hay or straw, throw it into a person's face and thus cause him to go mad and become an unsettled wanderer. This was called *dlaí fulla* (magic wisp of straw). The druids interpreted omens from the flight and cries of birds. They decided which days were good for carrying arms from these interpretations. Thus Medb delayed her attack on Ulster in the Táin* until the druids deemed the time appropriate.

Druids were held in esteem as soothsayers and, as such, practised the Teinm Laeda,° a particularly druidical verse of incantation, believed to confer upon the druid or poet everything proper to say. With this ability the druids were often asked by kings to forecast the future. Daithi, nephew of Niall of the Nine Hostages* and king of Ireland, was in Ess Ruaid° near Ballyshannon settling territorial disputes. As it was the eve of the Samain* he consulted his druids to ascertain his future. They told him the main incidents that would happen to him until the eve of the next Samain. Dogra the chief druid took Daithi and his companions to Rath Achaill,° near Screen in Co. Sligo, where the

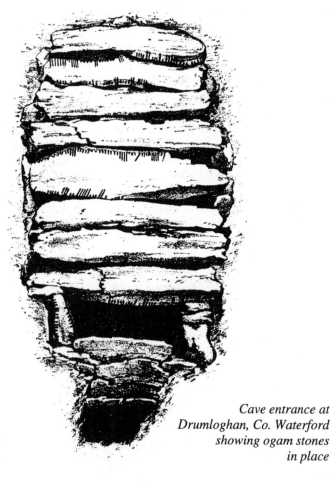

Cave entrance at Drumloghan, Co. Waterford showing ogam stones in place

druids' altars were. At sunrise in the morning Dogra went into the king's bedroom and told him he would return to Tara and that there he would convene a gathering of provincial kings and decide on an expedition to Scotland, Britain and France. Dogra said he had consulted 'the clouds of the men of Érinn' and that Daithi would do these things as had his uncle Niall and his grandfather Crimthann Mór.

The druids were described by John Toland[88] as wearing short hair with long beards. They wore long habits and over these a white surplice when they officiated religiously. In Ireland they wore white colours in their robes. (Colours in clothing, said to have been introduced by Tigernmas,* denoted rank and status, with only the king and queen wearing seven colours.) He states that all dues had to be paid to the druids by the Samain, else the 'cairn fires' could be used against the offender's property. These fires are described by Toland: '. . . . it was customary for the Lord of the place, or his son, or some other person of distinction, to take the entrails of the sacrificed animal in his hands, and walking barefoot over the coals thrice, after the flames had ceased, to carry them straight to the druid, who waited in a white skin at the altar. If the noblemen escaped harmless, it was reckoned a good omen, welcomed with loud acclamations; but if he received any hurt, it was deemed unlucky both in the community and himself. Thus I have seen people running and leaping through the St John's fires in Ireland, and . . . proud of passing unsing'd. . . .'[88]

Many places in Ireland, Britain and France still bear placenames associating them with the druids, as does Dreux, the place of their annual meeting in France. Kerig-y-Drudion, or druid-stones, is a parish in Denbighshire, so called from some remaining altars there. In Anglesey there is the village of Tre'r Driu, the town of the druid. Close by is Maen-y-Driu or druid's stone and also in Wales is Caer-Dreuin, the city of the druids, in Merionethshire. The druids in Anglesea (Mona) were rounded up and butchered by the Romans under Suetonius in AD 61. This brought an end to druidism in Roman dominions.

Among the many famous druids are Trosdan, 'who found an antidote against the poisoned arrows of the British invaders'; Cabadius, grandfather to Cúchulainn* (Cúchulainn is said to have been given 'a drink of oblivion' in order that he forget the fairy woman Fand); Tages, father of Muirne, who was mother of Finn mac Cumaill;* Dadera, who was killed by Eoghan, the son of the Munster king Oilioll Olum*; Lámderg, (bloody hand), was said to live enchanted in the mountain between Buncrana and Fathan in Co. Donegal; Lucad the Bald, druid to King Laoghaire, was burnt at Tara during the time of St Patrick. Ida and Ono, druids of Corcachlann near Roscommon, are said to have presented their house to St Patrick. This house or fortress, known as Imleach Ono, is said to have been converted by Patrick into the religious house of Elphin. (Ailfinn, meaning white stone, was a vast obelisk that stood by a well in Elphin until it fell down in the year AD 1675.)

The cromlech in the Druid's Glen, south Co. Dublin

Legend describes certain places as being 'druidic houses'. A fine example is that on the island of St Kilda off western Scotland. Reputed to have belonged to a druidess, the conical-shaped structure is arched, open at the top and with fireplace in the centre. Up to the nineteenth century it was the custom to respect such places by walking three times round them from east to west, following the course of the sun. This walking is called deiseal or *deas soil°* (right hand to the sun).

Popular folklore in Ireland still widely refers to megalithic remains such as dolmens as 'druids' altars'. Recumbent stones in stone circles are popularly considered to be sacrificial stones once used by druids and the notion of druids generally as ancient priest-magicians is widely held.

Duach Dallta Deadad   The son of Cairbre Lusc, king of Ireland in AM 5032 (166 BC). Keating[4] states that he was called *dallta* (blinded) because he blinded his brother Deadad lest he aspire to the kingship.

But O'Flaherty[20] states that he was called Dallta Deadad, foster son of Deadad. Deadad was son of Sen, of the Erneans of Munster. According to the *Annals of Clonmacnoise*, Duach remained king for seven years and was slain by Faghtna Faghagh about the same time as Julius Caesar was assassinated. Duach's death took place at the battle of Ardbrestine in Co. Carlow.

Duach Finn   Son of Sédna Innarig, he was king of Ireland for ten years. He fell in battle at Mag (precise place not identified). His killer, Muireadach Bolgrach, was in turn slain by Énda Dearg, son of Duach.

Duach Ladrach   Duach the vindictive, or 'quick avenger of wrongs'. He was the son of Fiacha Tolgrach and slew Airgetmar to become king. After ten years as king he was slain by Lugaid Laigde, who had joined with him in the killing of Airgetmar. Aed Ruad, the grandson of Airgetmar, then slew Lugaid Laígde.

Eadan   The son of Uighe, Eadan was a Milesian chieftain who slew Fódla* wife of Mac Cuill, in the battle of Tailtiu. Coming from Spain, he took part in the slaughter of the Tuatha Dé Danann*. In the distribution of territory by the sons of Míl,* Eadan is believed to have been allotted land in Sligo, Eadan established a fort called Rath Righbaird in Muiresc. This is situated near the hill of Knocknarea.

Eadan and his brothers Un and En were slain later by Éremon,* another son of Mál, at the battle of Comhraire in Meath. This place is now called Kilcomreragh, near the Hill of Uisneach* in Westmeath.

Éber   One of the sons of Míl* who arrived in Ireland, with a fleet of one hundred and twenty men, in the 2nd century BC.

After the battles of Tailtiu and Sliab Mis, Éber and his brother Éremon* divided Ireland into two parts. Éber erected the following mounds during the kingship: Rath Uamain (fort of the cave), now probably Rathowen in Wexford; Rath-Árda-Suird,° about half a mile from the old church of Donaghmore, near Limerick city, the site now occupied by the ruins of a castle; and the mound of Rath-Úin, now Rahoon, Co. Galway. A dispute arose between Éber and Éremon about territory, leading to a battle in which Éber was slain. It is said that this was fought at Argatros,° near the River Nore. According to O'Rahilly[2] the name Éber means 'Irishman', Eberus and Ebernus being Hiberno-Latin forms of *hibernus*. The Macnamara family (clann mac Con Mara) are said to be sprung from Éber.

Echdae   Known as Echdae Horsemouth of Scotland. He was raided by Cúchulainn and Cúroí mac Dáire. The carried off his three magic cows known as 'the spotted ones of Echde', who fill with their milk each day the copper cauldron containing sixty pints of milk which is called their 'calf'.

Eithrial   King of Ireland in the second century BC. After a reign of twenty years he was slain at the battle of Raeire by Conmael, son of Éber. Raeire is situated in the modern barony of Tinnahinch, Co. Laois. During the reign of Eithrial the following plains were cleared: Mag Lugad in Louth; Tenmag in Connacht; Mag Belaig in Uí Tuirte (Uí Tuirte being the name of a tribe in Antrim); Mag Geisille in Offaly (this being the ancient name of a plain included in the present barony of Geshill in Offaly); Mag Ochtair in Leinster; Lochmag in Connacht; and Mag Rath near the modern village of Moira, Co. Down.

Élim   The son of Conra, Élim was king of Ulster for twenty years in the first century AD until slain at the battle of Achall° by Tuathal Techtmar.* This battle was fought on the Hill of Skreen near Tara* in Co. Meath. Élim was one of the provincial kings who killed Fiacha Findolad. Fiacha's son Tuathal Techtmar thus avenged his father's death by killing Élim.

Élim Oillfínsneachta   Monarch of Ireland, his name arises from the legend that snow (*sneachta*) with the taste of wine fell in the year he was slain by Giallchaid, son of Oilioll Ollchaín.

Ellén Trechenn   Anciently '*in tEllén Trechend*'° (triple-headed Ellén), a destructive deity from the Otherworld.* This god emerged from the cave of Cruachain* on the eve of Samain* (Hallowe'en), laying waste to the land. O'Rahilly[2] associates the word E*llén* with Aillén mac Midgna, who used to burn Tara* every Samain until slain by Finn mac Cumaill.* It is also said that it was Amergin, father of Conall Cernach,* who slew this triple-headed, life-endangering monster. Many creatures who emanated from Cruachain, apart from devastating the land in general, seem to have had a special enmity for either Emain Macha* or the Hill of Tara. It is thus that these malevolent gods issuing from the Otherworld of Connacht are often slain by the heroes of Ulster or Tara. The word *ellén* may be a derivative of Ailill, which stands for Aillill, identical with the Welsh *ellyll* (spirit, elf).

Eochaid   The son of Erc (a son of the king of Tara), Eochaid became king of the Firbolgs* in the 3rd century BC after slaying Foidbgen the previous year. After ten years as king, he himself was slain by the victorious Tuatha Dé Danann* at the battle of Mag Tuired,* in Conmaicne Cile Tolad° in Connacht. Eochaid was, according to the *Annals of Clonmacnoise*, the last of the kings of the Firbolgs.

According to the *Lebor Gabála*,[15] fleeing from this battle, Eochaid was overtaken and killed on the strand at Tráigh Eochaile° near Ballysadare in Sligo. His cairn, described in the *Book of Ballymote* as one of the wonders in Ireland, still exists here. Though not high above the strand, it is believed that the tide can never cover it.

It is said that when Eochaid mac Eirce was king 'no rain fell, but only the dew; there was not a year without harvest; falsehood was banished from Ireland in his time, he was the first to establish there the rule of justice'. Here we see the ancient association between the king's justice and the fertility of the soil, 'which is the very formula of the magic of kingship'.[49]

The site of the battle of Mag Tuired is between the villages of Cong and Neal in Co. Mayo. Here, according to the *Annals of Clonmacnoise*, the Firbolgs were overthrown and 'one hundred thousand of them slain, with their king Eochy Mac Eirke, which was the greatest slaughter that was every heard of in Ireland at one meeting'. Sources referring to this battle make it clear that great numbers were slain, but certainly not as many as mentioned in the Annals, highly influenced as they were by romantic accounts.

The death of Eochaid mac Eirce marks the end of the reign of the Firbolgs in Ireland. Their nine kings had reigned for a total of thirty-seven years.

Eochaid Mugmedón   Father of Niall Nóigiallach* (of the Nine Hostages). His epithet Mugmedón (slavelord) is derived from the fact that he made raids on Roman Britain and brought back slaves. He made one of these, Cairenn,* his wife, and she, reputedly the daughter of a Saxon king, was to become mother of Niall of the Nine Hostages. Eochaid Mugmedón was slain at Dub Commair° (the modern Drumeague, Co. Cavan) by his grandsons, the Three Collas. Dub Commair was the pre-historic pagan centre of ancient Ireland. Eochaid was the protector of this ancient Celtic religious centre and his murder by the Three Collas marks the end of the old theocratic order and the further progress of Christianity.

St Patrick was in no doubt that the Irish did worship a sun god. Eochaid may mean 'the lightning god' or 'he of the sun god'. Eochaid Mugmedón was the defender of the theocratic constitution which for many centuries was the protector of the numerous tribes of Leth Cuinn, the northern half of Ireland.

Eochaid Mugmedón was defeated in battle by Eanna Cinnsealach, king of Leinster, at the battle of Cruachan Claonta (the moat of Clane, Co. Kildare). His druid, Ceadnathach, was killed by a spear, flung from Eanna. Eanna was paid a yearly tribute of white bronze from Leth Cuinn.

Thomas Barron,[10] an historian from Co. Cavan, says that there was until the nineteenth century a curse on the hill at Dub Commair on account of some vile 'crime' committed there. This crime may have been that of the Three Collas and may have caused the adjective *dub* (black) to become part of the name Dub Commair.

Eochaid Mugmedón was king of Tara for eight years, his territory presumably extending across Meath and into Cavan. His reign took place towards the end of the fourth century AD, he being reputedly the earliest historical king there. He was in a direct descent from Conn Cét Chathach, the 2nd century king of Ierland. The Uí Néill trace their line back to Eochaid Mugmedón through his son Niall Noígiallach. And the Connachta trace theirs back to his other sons, Ailill, Bríon, and Fiachra. According to Keating[4] St Finbar of Cork was the greatgrandson of the greatgrandson of Eochaid Mugmedón.

Eóganacht A race of southern Gaels* who trace themselves back to their ancestor deity Eóghan Mór. The leading power in Munster, they formed alliances with the peoples known as the Osraige° and the Ciarraige.° Based in Cashel, Co. Tipperary, the Eóganacht dynasty became established around the fifth century AD. They are also associated with west Munster, particularly around Knockainey in Limerick and Co. Clare. The Eóganacht and the Múscraige defeated the Érainn, a large tribe, in a battle of Cenn Febrat (or Abrat), in the hills between Kilmallock and Doneraile in Co. Cork.

Éremón One of the sons of Míl,* he was leader of a Milesian expedition which left Spain for Ireland. Landing at an estuary in Co. Kerry, probably Kenmare river, they proceeded north to Sliabh Mis, and from there to Tara.* The date of their arrival varies between 1498 BC (*Annals of the Four Masters*),[5] 1342 BC (Philip O'Sullivan, antiquarian to Philip IV of Spain) and 1029 BC (*Annals of Clonmacnoise*), although it is generally now held that they arrived between the 2nd and 3rd centuries BC.

On their northeasterly trek the Milesians fought two battles. The first was at Gleann Faisi, a valley in the Slieve Mish Mountains of Co. Kerry, and the second at Tailtiu, now Telltown, in Co. Meath. Their victories left the Milesians rulers of Ireland. Éremón's brother Éber insisted on a partition and the country was divided into two equal parts, Éber taking the south and Éremón the north.

After a year and another battle, Éremón became sole ruler of Ireland, but the struggle between north and south was maintained by the followers of the two brothers. The Gaelic ancestry of Ireland is traced back to Éremón, who is regarded by the genealogists as the major ancestor of the Irish.

> Since the rule
> of Éremón, the noble man of grace,
> there was worshipping of stones,
> until the coming of Good Patrick of Macha.
> *(The Dinnsenchus of Mag Slecht)*

> The princedom of Éremón the perfect, the youthful,
> dug was his grave after the time of his death,
> in the land of silvery Argatros,
> on the same chariot-land.
>
> *(Lebor Gabála)*

Ériu Queen of the Tuatha Dé Danann,* Ériu was slain by Suirge at the battle of Tailtiu (now Telltown, Co. Meath). At this battle in c. 200 BC the Milesians defeated the Tuatha Dé Danann, killing all their chiefs and queens, and afterwards slaughtered the Tuatha Dé Danann wherever they were overtaken.

Ériu represents the earthy or geographical aspect of Ireland. Ériu is the original name of Éire which, in modern Irish, means Ireland. The meaning of *Ériu* (regular traveller), implies that she was a sun goddess. 'Elatha, when he came to mate with Ériu, wore a shining brooch of

61

gold (*delc n-óir*)° on his breast, and on his back were five wheels of gold'.[2] The goddess is thus traditionally described as wearing rings or circlets, symbolic of her connection with the sun or moon.

In the *Lebor Gabála*[15] we read:

> Cethor pleasant, fair his colour, free was he;
> Ériu his wife, a generous woman she, sun his god.

Ériu, Banba* and Fódla* were the three daughters of Fiachna, grandson of Ogma.* Ermas was mother of these three sisters as well as being mother of Fiachna. Ériu was married to Cethor, also named Mac Gréine. When the Milesians attacked Ireland, Ériu said to their leader Amergin* that his cause in conquering Ireland was an unjust one. When Amergin replied that they had come to conquer Ireland, Ériu asked, 'Then at least grant me one thing . . . that this island shall be called by my name'. 'It shall be', replied Amergin.

Eterscél Eterscél was the son of Eógan, grandson of Oilioll Olum, and king of Ireland for five years. He was slain by Nuadu Necht at Ailenn. Ailenn is a large fort, Knockaulin (Cnoc Ailinne),° near Kilcullen in Co. Kildare.

Fer Diad A warrior of the Domnainn, a tribe settled in north-west Mayo. In the Táin* he is called Fer Diad mac Damáin. He is also known as Fer Diad Conganchness ('of skin-like horn'). According to O'Rahilly[2] he belongs to the tradition of the Érainn° (a race associated with Munster and Ulster). He trained as a warrior under Scathach* in Scotland where Cúchulainn* was his junior. In the Táin he is baited by Medb* to engage in single combat with Cúchulainn. As the great Connacht warrior Fer Diad, he goes to fight the Ulster warrior, his former friend and gillie,° Cúchulainn, with reluctance. He put on his famous horn-skinned battle dress and fought till sunset. They then kissed and parted and exchanged food and medicinal herbs. On the fourth day Cúchulainn killed Fer Diad with the Gaé Bolga.* He carried him to the bank of a river and laid him on the Ulster side saying, 'Yesterday he was greater than a mountain; today he is less than a shadow'.[1] The modern town Ardee in Louth is called Áth Fhirdia.° It is situated on the river Dee, and legend has it that here this most famous of all Irish single combats took place.

Fergus mac Roich (also known as Fergus Ro-ech or Fergus 'great horse), king of Ulster in the first century BC, his palace being at Emain Macha.* He wished to marry Nes,° daughter of Eochaid Sálbuide° and mother of Conchobar mac Nessa.* Nes agreed on condition that her son be made king for a year. Fergus thus became the foster-father of Conchobar and husband to Nes, but he never regained the kingship, as Nes successfully schemed for Conchobar to remain king.

Fergus brought the Sons of Uisnech* back from Scotland where they had fled with Deirdre, whom Conchobar had wanted for himself. Fergus acted as pledge for their safety, but when they returned he was obliged to obey a *geis** and attend a banquet for three days. During this time Conchobar, who had vouched for their safety, had the Sons of Uisnech put to death.

Incensed at the dishonour of Conchobar, Fergus returned to Emain Macha and burned it down. He then went with his followers to Cruachain Connacht,* the kingdom of Ailill and Medb.*

During the Cattle Raid of Cooley (the Táin* Bó Cualgne) Fergus went with the Connacht warriors under Medb to attack the Ulaid. However, because of old friendships and the fact tht he had been their king, he sent a warning to the Ulstermen, leading his army on a great detour south in order to give his opponents time to assemble. Fergus did, however, keep the Connacht king Ailill informed about the names and strengths of warriors opposing, and fought against them, killing hundreds with his famous sword. This sword was named In Caladbolg,° a two-handed lightning sword. He fought in the last battle of the Táin and with In Caladbolg Fergus 'carved a gap of a hundred men in the ranks'.[22] Fergus was stopped from killing Conchobar, the cause of his exile, by Cormac Connlonges,° Conchobar's son. Then, to give vent to his fury, Fergus is said to have struck the tops off three hills in Co. Meath with In Caladbolg.

Fergus was Medb's lover. Coupled with the fact that he had received succour at Cruachain Connacht after his banishment, this may have accounted for his allegiance to her during the battles. His relationship with Medb led to his death. One day Fergus and Medb were swimming in Findloch.° 'Medb was on the breast of Fergus with her legs entwined around him'.[1] Jealousy siezed Ailill. 'It is delightful what the hart and the doe are doing in the lake', said Ailill to Lugaid, a warrior who never missed his aim. 'Why not kill them?' Lugaid said. Ailill replied 'Do thou have a cast at them'. Then Lugaid threw his lance so that it passed through the breast of Fergus and out through his back.[1] Fergus died by the side of Findloch.

Seanchán, chief bard of Ireland, instructed his fellow bards to wander until they discovered and were able to repeat the tale of the Táin to perfection. They wandered until eventually they came to the grave of Fergus mac Roich and induced his spirit to reveal the Táin to them.This he did after three days of invocation, when 'the shade of Fergus, high, mighty as in life'[23] issued from his mound and told the heroic legend.

Finn mac Cumaill   The central character in the Ossianic Cycle of Tales. A major hero of ancient Ireland, stories concerning him are collected in the *Duanaire Finn*, translated as the Lays of Finn[36] (in Scottish legend Finn is called Fingal).

Origins of Finn

Many authorities state that Finn was a real historical person who lived in the 3rd century AD Keating, writing in the mid-seventeenth century[4] asserts that Finn and his followers, the Fiana, really existed, while admitting that some of the tales were romantic fiction. O'Donovan[5] also held that 'Finn mac Cumaill was a real historical personage, and not a myth or a god of war'. Eugene O'Curry[34] writes that 'it is quite a mistake to suppose Finn mac Cumaill to have been a merely imaginary or mythical character'. Windisch,[74] whilst agreeing with these writers, was sceptical about the dates assigned. Zimmer felt that, though he was real, his origins were to be found in the Norseman Caittil Find, slain in Munster in AD 847.

On the other hand, Alfred Nutt[39] states that 'the Ossianic saga is romantic rather than historical'. J.A. MacCulloch[25] says of the saga that 'little historical fact can be found in it; whether personages called Finn, Oisín, Diarmuid or Conán ever existed, what we know of them is purely mythical.' T.F. O'Rahilly[2] states bluntly that 'Finn and his followers . . . never existed. Finn is ultimately the divine hero, Lug or Lugaid, just like Cúchulainn'.

Regardless of its veracity or otherwise, it is indisputable that the Fenian epic has been for many centuries the chief hero-lore of the Gaelic-speaking races of Ireland and Scotland.

Finn's Ancestors

The *Book of Genealogies* compiled by Dubháltach mac Fir Bhisigh gives six different pedigrees for Finn. Two of these trace his descent

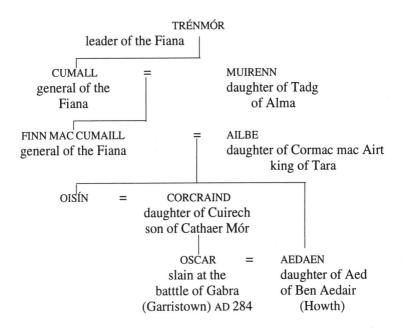

```
                        TRÉNMÓR
            leader of the Fiana

   CUMALL          =              MUIRENN
  general of the                  daughter of Tadg
     Fiana                          of Alma

FINN MAC CUMAILL       =          AILBE
general of the Fiana              daughter of Cormac mac Airt
                                      king of Tara

  OISÍN    =         CORCRAIND
                  daughter of Cuirech
                  son of Cathaer Mór

                    OSCAR      =     AEDAEN
                  slain at the      daughter of Aed
                  batttle of Gabra  of Ben Aedair
                  (Garristown) AD 284  (Howth)
```

The genealogy of Finn mac Cumaill

from Nuadu Necht, the god Nuadu,* regarded as ancestor of the royal line of Leinster, thus claiming Finn as a Leinsterman and attaching him to the ruling race. Other pedigrees connect him to Munster, with the Orbraige of Druim Imnocht (a sept of this race is retained in the name of the barony of Orrery, Co. Cork) and with the Úi Fidgente, a tribe in Co. Limerick.

All accounts state Cumall to have been Finn's father. He was, according to Kennedy[23] king of Leinster and head of the Clann Baoiscne. Cumall ruled the Fiana under the high king, Conn of the Hundred Battles.* After refusing an order to attend a meeting at Tara,* Cumall's leadership of the Fiana was promised by Conn to Goll mac Morna.* Whilst preparing for battle over this, Cumall met Muirne, daughter of the druid Tadg of the Luminous Side. Muirne became pregnant by Cumall, and Tadg, whose fortress was Almu (Hill of Allen), vowed that Cumall would die in the battle.

On the eve of battle Cumall sent word to Muirne: 'When my son is born, flee away with him, and let him be brought up in the most secret places you can find. Conmean the druid has foretold his fortune, and that under his rule the Fiana of Érinn shall much exceed what it enjoys under mine. Entreat the forgiveness of the Golden Haired Muirrean for me. Farewell.'[23]

The battle took place at Cnucha, the modern Castleknock, Co. Dublin, Cumall being killed by Goll mac Morna.

The Destiny of Finn

Apart from the mythological elements, a main theme in the story of Finn is the blood feud between him and the Clann mac Morna. It was the destiny of Finn to follow his own private war in the form of this inherited vendetta. The duty of avenging his kinsman's blood would eventually lead to his own death. However, between the pivotal points of the death of Cumall, the death of Goll and the death of Finn are a myriad of tales. Feasting, destruction of monsters, expeditions over sea and supernatural encounters are described.

The Naming of Finn

Finn was brought up in a cavern on Slieve Bloom by Boghmin, Cumall's female messenger. Finn's name then was Deimne. His foster-mother took him to Tara to participate in games. Conn of the Hundred Battles, impressed by his athletic performance, asked what was the the name of this 'pairte Finn' (dear member of the Fiana). 'I thank you, Conn, for conferring a name on him', Boghmin replied; 'Finn he is and Finn he shall remain'.

The Salmon of Knowledge

A druid called Fionn lived on the Boyne where he occupied his students, among them Finn, then called Deimne, in catching salmon. It was the druid's intention to secure 'the salmon of knowledge', whose taste would make him conscious of everything happening in Ireland. The pupils caught the salmon, cooked them and served them to the druid. One day Finn saw a blister on the side of the fish in the pan. He pressed it down with his thumb and, as it burned, he licked the thumb and became aware of what was happening in the courts of Tara,* Emain Macha* and Naas. He mentioned what had happened to the druid.

'I know by my art that the salmon of wisdom has to be tasted by a Fionn', said the druid,' I am Fionn and you are Deimne'.

'Ay, but I am Finn also', replied Finn, 'thus named by Conn of the Hundred Battles'.

'Well, well', said the druid, 'keep yourself out of the power of the High King for a while; when the opportunity arrives, acquaint him with your newly acquired faculty, and he will make you commander of the Fiana'.[23]

However, the wisdom only became available to Finn when he chewed his thumb. (Some accounts attribute Finn's wisdom to his once having jammed his thumb in the door of a *síd*.) According to O'Rahilly[2] 'an essential part of the divinatory rite . . . given the name of *imbas forosnai** was the chewing of a piece of the raw flesh of an animal sacrificed to the pagan gods'. Thus Finn's chewing of his thumb could be said to be modelled on the rite of the pagan diviner. From this chewing also arose the notion that Finn possessed a special 'tooth of wisdom' (*dét fis*).°

With this power of second sight, Finn the warrior hunter and human hero foretold the coming of the Danes and the coming of Diarmuid mac Murrough.

> The Leinstermen are first to suffer bondage,
> (sad to my heart that it should come to pass),
> having no king but a black earl,
> having no warrior bands to protect them.

Many stories deal with Finn in relation to the high king, Cormac mac Airt.* One tells how a dispute broke out between Finn and Cormac during a feast at Tara, when 'the drinking went to Cormac's head'.[36]

Cormac challenged Finn to battle, saying that he would make him pass under the fork of the cauldron. Old antagonisms were revived, Finn being reminded of the battle of Cnucha and his father's death. 'They slew my worthy father', he said, to which the response was that Cumall his father was to blame for having taken Muirne his mother away by force.

Garad, the son of Goll mac Morna, described the death of Cumall: 'We were sixteen men of the house of Morna; to tell the truth, we thrust every man his spear into the side of Cumall the champion'. Oscar, Finn's grandson, then challenged the house of Morna to single combat, and this was accepted by Cairbre, son of Goll. At this point Ciothruaidh sang a song, quietening all before they took up their weapons. On the following day sixteen of the Fenians went on a foray against Cormac. First they went to Emain Macha and then to Aengus Óc* who guided them in their raid on Tara.

We threw ourselves like men across the trail,
we routed the hosts of Tara, we wounded Cormac
of the feasts, and we captured skin-white Cairbre.[36]

To secure the release of Cairbre, Cormac had to go under the fork
of the cauldron in view of the men of Ireland. Finn himself went under
the fork at the other end and thus was peace restored between them.

Ghosts and Phantoms

Fiachna, son of Eoghan of Munster, presented Finn with a fast black
horse. Finn and Caoilte* and Oisín went for a long ride with the new
horse across the mountains of west Munster, over Druim Caoin and
Druim Dha Fhiach. In the evening Finn saw a house with a fire in a
valley ahead. Caoilte said he had never seen this house before, 'though
I know this yew glen well'. On their way into the house they were met
with screeching, wailing and shouting, and inside was a grey haired
churl (an *aithech*). 'Rise up ye folk that are within', said the churl, 'sing
a song for Finn'.

At this, nine headless bodies rose up from one side of the room, nine
heads from the other, each making a horrid screech. The churl answered
each in turn and the headless bodies sang, their song described thus;

> The song they sang for us would have wakened dead men out
> of the clay; it well nigh split the bones of our heads; it was not
> a melodious chorus.

The churl then killed the horses of Finn, Oisin and Caoilte with his
axe, cut them up, put them on spits at the fire. He then served Finn with
his own horse's meat on spits of rowan. Finn refused, 'Horse-flesh have
I never eaten'. At this the churl became incensed and everyone went
for their swords. The fire was quenched and they found themselves
fighting in darkness. They fought all night, and in the morning when
the sun came in the window 'a black mist' entered their heads and they
passed out.

When they awoke the house and all its inmates had vanished. These
nine phantoms in the yew glen with whom they had fought had been
seeking vengeance for their sister Cuilleann, who had been slain by
Finn in the cave of Céis Chorainn.

The Dwelling of Céis Chorainn is another tale in which three women
seeking vengeance against Finn tie up the Fiana in bewitched lengths

68

of yarn. They then carry them into the cave where the warriors are powerless. Goll mac Morna slays these witches, releasing Finn and his men.[7]

The Battle of Ventry Harbour

This story is one of the many associating Finn with south-west Ireland. He and his friends were swimming and fishing in the Shannon when word came from the warden of Finntráigh (White Strand, Ventry, Co. Kerry) that the king of Rome, Dáire Donn, together with a vast army, was in the harbour ready to land. He had been led to the Skelligs by a renegade member of the Fiana.

Alerting the clans throughout Ireland, including a remnant of the Dé Danann settled at Conall Gabra in Co. Limerick, Finn and the Fiana gave battle. After a year and a day they were victorious, although Gall from Ulster had worked himself into such a fury fighting that he lost his senses and fled to Gleann na nGealt (the madman's glen) in Co. Kerry.

The Lay of the Smithy

Finn and the Fiana found themselves on Sliab Luachra in Co. Kerry. A huge one-footed warrior with three arms, approached them. His face was the colour of coal and he had one eye in his forehead. 'The shadow of his hand and his gloom were sufficient danger for us'. This was Lon mac Liomtha, a teacher of smiths for the king of Lochlann in Bergen in Norway. He spoke to the Fiana: 'A *geis* and the pangs of a woman in travail be upon you, ye leaders in every strait, if eight of you do not follow me to the door of my smithy'.[36]

The giant leaped away over the mountain tops, the Fiana following. They went after him into the cave of Céis Chorainn, where he had a forge. There, with Daolgus, one of the Fiana, the smith made a fine sword. To each of them then he gave spear and 'a blue blade of true fierceness'. Altogether they got seven swords and nine spears. (Mac an Luin was the name of Finn's sword, 'which caused the flesh of men to suffer'.) Next day when the sun rose the Fiana found themselves back at Sliab Luachra with the smith's weapons.

Finn and Goll mac Morna are bonded by friendship and marriage ties throughout most of the stories. Finn's daughter Caince was mother of Goll's children and together they controlled the Fiana throughout the five provinces. (The Connacht Fiana were under Goll's command.) However, when Finn killed Goll's son Feadha 'through pride', the old enmity reappeared. Fighting broke out, resulting eventually in Goll being slain by Finn. Thus Finn finally avenged the death of his father.

This re-emergence of conflict between the Clann Morna and Finn's Clann Baoiscne led to many skirmishes and battles. In AD 283 Finn was killed in a skirmish with a rebellious member of the Fiana at Áth Brea (the ford of Brea) on the Boyne.

> Finn was killed, it was with darts,
> with a lamentable wound;
> Aichleach, son of Duibhdreann, cut off
> the head of the son of Mochtamuin.[5]

His death took place in the sixteenth year of Cairpre, son of Cormac mac Airt.[5] Elsewhere it is stated that:

> Finn mac Cumhaill, the celebrated general of the Irish militia fell by the hands of Aichleach, son of Duibhdreann, a treacherous fisherman who, fired with the love of everlasting notoriety, slew him with his gaff at Rathbreagha, near the Boyne, whither he had retired in his old age to pass the remainder of his life in tranquility.[57]

Athleach was soon after himself beheaded by Caoilte mac Ronáin, a relative and faithful follower of Finn.

The Fiana

The nineteenth century historian Pinkerton[90] put forward the idea that the Fiana were an imitation of the Roman legions. Macalister[16] developed this notion.

> Cormac had ample opportunities of becoming acquainted with Roman methods of government, and with the machinery of empire. He organised a standing army — a thing till then

unheard of in Ireland. So deep was the impression produced by this innovation that the general entrusted with its organisation has dominated the country's folklore ever since, in the person of the gigantic Find Mac Cumhaill.[16]

O'Rahilly disputes these ideas,[2] saying that the question of the historicity of the Fiana is 'bound up with the historicity of Finn and Goll; if these are mythical figures, so too are the Fiana who have no existence apart from them'.

The Fiana, whether modelled on Roman standing armies or not, did not have knights in the Teutonic sense. The members of the Fiana were *laochs* (heroes, the German *helden*). When grouped together in a military order they were *curaid*, warriors.

A free man seeking admission would have to undergo a series of tests. A typical one involved him, while armed only with stick and shield, having to guard himself from spears thrown by six men from a distance of 'nine ridges'. Another involved him having to run through a wood, getting out uncaught at the other side by the same six warriors. (A group of six warriors was a *fian*,° the basic unit of the Fiana.) If he passed his tests he was obliged to swear loyalty to the high king. His near relations were obliged never to seek *éiric*° (retribution) for his death but to leave the defence of his honour to his brothers-in-arms.

References to Finn and the Fiana

Folklore has it that the Fiana made their meals in what are called ovens of the Fiana. These small circular cavities, paved with stones and surrounded with low stone walls are found throughout the countryside, both in Ireland and the Scottish Highlands. Also, many stone alignments throughout Ireland are known as the fingers of Finn.

Many places are associated with Finn and his name. The river Blackwater in Co. Meath used be called the river Finn. The river Finn in Co. Donegal flows into the Loch Finn. Hubert Butler[45] suggests that the former river Finn in Meath is connected with the Finn tribe. He states that the Veneti, a Gaullish tribe from Brittany, were originally related to this Finn tribe, their largest concentration being in the north-west and south-west of Ireland. Butler says that Finn came from Sliab Ban Finn (Sievenamon) in Co. Tipperary and that he died at Cill Finn in Perthshire. Generally, there is no shortage of places throughout Ireland with which he is associated: 'A lake is explained as a hollow made in the land by him when he scooped out a handful of earth to throw at an enemy. A long grassy spot on a rough mountainside may be said to have once been his bed'.[56]

While Cúchulainn has his famous statue by Oliver Sheppard in the General Post Office in Dublin, Finn has no major work of art associated with him. However, James Joyce's *Finnegans Wake* has many allusions to Finn, both in title and throughout the book. Anna Livia's monologue towards the end of *Finnegans Wake* says: 'Who'll search for Find Me Colours now on the hilly droops of Vikloefells?'

When asked by St Patrick was Finn mac Cumaill a good lord, Caoilte replied:

> Were but the brown leaf,
> which the wood sheds from it, gold,
> were but the white billow silver,
> Finn would have given it all away.

And what was it that maintained you living thus?

> Truth that was in our hearts,
> strength in our hands, and
> fulfilment in our tongues.[56]

Fir Bolg   Historians differ as to the origins of the Fir Bolg people and the meaning of the name. O'Rahilly[2] avers that there cannot be any doubt that the Fir Bolg of ancient Ireland were in origin an offshoot of the Belgae, a tribe of continental Celts, but Macalister[15] rejects this theory; O'Flaherty writing in 1685[20] came to the same conclusion as O'Rahilly. . . . But Rhys writing in 1884[26] concurs with Macalister. Other commentators suggest that the Fir Bolg were 'weavers of breeches' and as such were amongst the 'lower orders' or the plebian races who had each leg separately clothed. Other accounts have them as 'men of bags', meaning a caste of bagmakers, or, again, as slaves in Greece who used bags to gather earth to spread on stony ground. The Fir Bolg worshipped an ancestor god named Bulga or Bolga, meaning a god of lightning.

If the Fir Bolg were identical with the Belgae, as such, they were a body of pre-Gaelic invaders of Ireland who are associated with many placenames around Ireland, e.g., Aghabulloge, Co. Cork and Caherbullog, Co. Clare.

They were a vast tribe of Celts, originally from north of the Marne and Seine, sometimes referred to as Teutonic Celts, due to the fact that

Caesar was informed that they had previously lived on the right hand side of the river Rhine. They first came to Ireland in the 3rd century BC. However, a large number came after Caesar defeated them in the marshes of Aisne, north of Rheims and southwest of the Ardennes in 58 BC. From Gaul they went to Cantium (Kent) in England. Caesar regarded the Fir Bolg in Britain as the most civilized tribe there, differing little in culture from the Gauls. They were an agrarian people with a warlike aristocracy. They introduced monarchy to Ireland as well as the iron spearhead. They established the principle of association between the king and the earth; this is exemplified by the statement from Arthurian legend that 'Arthur and the earth are one'.

The Fir Bolg landed on the east coast of Ireland; Malahide (Inber Domnann) is associated with one of their communities namely the Fir Domnann.

The *Book of Invasions*[15] says that the Fir Bolg brought five chieftains with them to Ireland — Gann, Genann, Rudraige, Sengann and Sláinge,* the five sons of Dela. These brothers partitioned the country into five provinces — Ulster, Leinster, Connacht and the two Munsters. According to P.W. Joyce[27] the Fir Bolg colonised Ireland *c.*250 BC. The Fir Domnann,° the Gálioin* and the Érainn communities are said to be from Fir Bolg stock.

The Fir Bolg reigned for thirty-seven years until the great battle of Mag Tuired* in Conmaicne, Connacht. This battle, near Lough Arrow in Co. Sligo, was fought between the Fir Bolg and the victorious Tuatha Dé Danann.* Eleven hundred Fir Bolg were slain, the survivors going to Rathlin and the Aran Islands. Eventually they came under the protection of Medb* and Ailill but were crushed by the Ulaid in their various battles with the Connachta.

Fódla or Fótla was one of three sisters who came to symbolize Ireland. Fódla represents the warrior aspect of Ireland. Together with her sisters Ériu* and Banba* she was slain at the battle of Tailtiu in Co. Meath in *c.*200 BC. Fódla died at the hands of Edán* the Milesian.

Fomorians A race of sea-robbers who came from Lochlainn (Scandinavia). They are associated with the north- west coast of Ireland and particularly with Tory Island off the Donegal coast. They harassed the Nemedians (*see*: Nemed*) according to some sources, as early as the year 2300 BC. This conflict resulted in a terrific battle on the strand near Tory Island where nearly all the Fomorians fell. Retreating Fomorians were supposed to have been drowned by a tidal wave which occurred during the battle. The Fomorian leaders were Bres* and Balor.*

The mythical Tuatha Dé Danann,* rulers of Ireland, were later challenged by the Fomorians. This led to the famous battle of Mag Tuired* in which Balor was killed by Lug,* champion of the Tuatha Dé Danann. This battle marked the defeat of the Fomorians.

Both McNeill[24] and Macalister[15] have suggested that the ancient Irish believed in two divine races. The Tuatha Dé Danann were lords of life and light, and the Fomorians lords of darkness and death. There are two corresponding Otherworlds* for these two divine races — the happy otherworld of the Tuatha Dé Danann and the dwelling place of the Fomorians.

'The rulers of Elysium are always members of the Tuatha Dé Danann or the síd-folk and never a Fomorian like Tethra'.[25] The Fomorians are associated with the malevolent god, but O'Rahilly[2] says that no real distinction can be drawn between the two groups. For example, Lug is Balor's grandson and Tethra is a king of the Fomorians. And the people of Tethra are said to belong to the people of the Happy Otherworld.

The Fomorians' name is derived from two Irish words meaning 'under the sea' according to Rhys.[26] They are given characteristics which the Celts associated with the sea — vastness, darkness and a cradle for monstrous beings. Perhaps the Fomorians represent an older time in history associated with water and moon worship, whereas the Tuatha Dé Danann represent a worship of the earth and the sun.

Froech   The son of the sister of Boand, the divine Bé Find, is often mentioned as being the most beautiful of Ireland's heroes. He was loved by the daughter of Medb* and Ailill, Findabair.* However, because Froech would not pay the bride price asked for, and because Medb and Ailill feared that other kings would attack them if the betrothal took place, they plotted Froech's death.

A particular rowan tree grew on an island in a lake, with a snake or dragon (*péist*°) coiled about its roots. Bearing fruit every month, the juice of this tree prolonged life and healed illnesses. Ailill asked Froech to get a branch from the tree whilst swimming in the lough. One version of the story has it that Froech killed the *péist* but died from his wounds, whilst another has it that the monster guardian of the tree attacked Froech. He called for his weapon and when Findabair leapt into the water with it, Ailill threw a 'five-pronged spear' at her. Froech caught this and flung it back. He then chopped the head of the monster off.

Severely wounded from this encounter, Froech was borne by 'one hundred and fifty of the Síd clad in crimson with green head dresses'. They returned with him the next day and he was fully recovered. Findabair was then betrothed to Froech on condition that he join in the Cattle Raid of Cualgne (the Táin*).

Gabhra   Gabhra (Garristown, Co. Dublin) is the site of a famous battle fought in AD 285, which brought to an end the power of the Fiana in Ireland. King Cairbre, wished to marry his daughter, Sgéimh Solais (beauty of light), to a prince; the fiana were gathered at this time at Clane by the river Liffey. They wanted Sgéimh Solais for one of their own men or, failing that, a ransom of twenty ounces of gold. When Cairbre refused these requests the fiana advanced on Tara. They met the men of Tara at Garristown (on the present-day borders of Dublin and Meath). The field in which the battle took place is since known as the black acre. At Gabhra the king of Tara,* Cairbre, son of Cormac mac Airt,* defeated the Fiana under Finn's grandson Oscar. The body of Oscar was taken from the battle-field on a bier. Cairbre himself died here. To commemorate the slaughter of the fiana here a Celtic cross was erected in the 'black acre' in the last century. This has since blown down in a storm.

Gaé Bolga   Legend has it that the god Ailill Érann, also called Bolga, invented the missile spear. Gaé Bolga is translated as 'Bolga's spear' and also translated as 'a harpoon-like javelin'.[28] Sometimes referred to as 'lightning weapons', these weapons had their origin in the Otherworld* where they were forged by the divine smith. In mythology one finds the weapon wielded by the Hero. The lightning weapon used a lightning stroke or thunderbolt which was always fatal. In Scandinavian mythology Thor, son of Odin, wields the lightning hammer, Mjollnir.

The Gaé Bolga has been translated from the *Book of Leinster* as a 'gapped spear'.[29] It is also called a 'forked spear' and a 'two-fold spear.'

John Rhys[26] regards Gaé Bolga as meaning 'the spear of the goddess Bolg'; in other words it was a spear associated with the Fir Bolg.* There have been many attempts to figure out how this spear was used and what its particular characteristics were. It would appear to have been multi-headed and used in the water 'shot from underneath'. The word *bolg*, apart from references to the names of gods, can also be simply translated as 'bellows' or 'bladder'. Thus, the spear was held in the *bolg* and, when pressure was exerted by pressing with one's foot, the spear

shot out. In the Ulster Cycle of stories the Gaé Bolga belongs to
Cúchulainn.* He obtained it in Scotland (Alba) from Áife or from her
double, the goddess Scáthach.* He killed Fer Diad* by casting the Gaé
Bolga at him from underneath. 'Cúchulainn caught it in the fork of his
foot and sent it casting towards Fer Diad and it went through the deep
and sturdy apron of twice-smelted iron'.[22]

Gaels   A race from Gaulish Europe, different sources offering widely
different dates for their arrival. The *Lebor Gabála*[15] gives dates in the
second millenium BC, the Four Masters[5] give 1700 BC, but O'Rahilly[2]
suggests that they came much later than the Iron Age, which began
about 500 BC, adding that the reason earlier sources give earlier dates
was to support theories concerning the origins of the Irish people.
Whatever about that, the smiths of the Gaels are said to have smelted
iron which produced the particular flange-hilted bronze swords of the
early iron age.

The Gaels are the race to whom the ninth century historians gave a
dominant position. For example, all kings traced their pedigree back
to Éremón, son of Míl* (a Gael), whose sons led the Milesian invasion
from Galicia in Spain.

In Ptolemy's time the Celtic spoken in Ireland was of the Brythonic
type, that which linguists refer to as P-Celtic, as opposed to the later
language Q-Celtic. According to O'Rahilly[2] the pre-Gaelic races were
P-Celts and the Gaels, the latest of the Celtic invaders, were Q-Celts.

There were many pre-Gaelic societies in Ireland before the time of
Míl, including the Fir Bolgs,* the Lagin and the Gálioin.* Míl's wife
was Scota,* assumed to be related to the peoples called Scotti or
Scythians. The Gaels are said to have come originally from Scythia,
north of the Black Sea in modern day Ukraine. The ancestors of the
Gaels include Gaedel Glas and Fénius Farsaid.

Gálioin   A pre-Gaelic race of invaders of Ireland, according to O'Rahilly,[2] the Gálioin were associated with north Leinster. The territory of
Dál Mesi Corb in Co. Wicklow was also known as Dún nGálion.
Historically linked with the Lagin of Leinster, and with the Domnainn
of Malahide, their leader was Sláinge,* who is said to have died at
Duma Sláinge or Dinn Ríg on the Barrow river. Legend has it that
druidic chants were cast against the Gálioin and many of them perished.
Some were assimilated into a larger tribe and Tuathal Techtmar* is
reputed to have slain the remnant.

Later, known as the Gailing or the Gailenga, the Gálioin were employed as soldiers by the Gaelic kings of Tara* and are associated with east Cavan and Sliab Guaire (known as the Highland of the Gods) in that county, They are also associated with Dál mBuinne in Co. Antrim. They fought for the Gaels of Tara in the battle of Crinna in Connacht, and for this were awarded territory in Co. Mayo in the present day barony of Gallen.

In the Táin* it is recorded that, before the cattle raid, Queen Medb* observed the three thousand strong Gálioin. Noting their prowess, she felt it would be a mistake to include them in the battle as they would get all the credit. On the other hand, they could not be left out of it or they would (according to Medb) destroy Connacht whilst she was at war. So, she instructed that they should be wiped out. However, her husband Ailill objected, and Fergus mac Roich* suggested that they be integrated into the general army, scattered among the other battalions. Thus they survived and fought in the Táin.

Geis   A *geis* (pl. *geasa*), is an ancient injunction, prohibition or taboo against performing an act, or an obligation to do an act. The breaking of geasa often results in death. 'From a literary point of view, the unconscious infringement of geasa is the motif of some of the very finest scenes in the heroic romances'.[30] Diarmuid ua Duibhne, by killing the boar of Ben Gulban broke his *geis*, and consequently died. In Diarmuid's case the *geis* placed upon him from infancy by Aengus* of the Brug was that he must not hunt boar. Examples of *geasa*, some of which were hereditary and binding on all kings:

The kings of Leinster must not drink by the light of wax candles in the palace of Dinn Ríg.

The monarch of Tara* was enjoined that 'the sun should not rise upon him on his bed at Tara'.

The king must not go to Mag Breg (Bregia, Co. Meath) on a Wednesday; nor traverse Mag Cuillin after sunset; nor go against North Tethbe (Teffia), Co. Longford on a Tuesday; nor be in a ship on the water the Monday after Bealtane (first of May); nor leave the track of his army upon Áth Maigne (Co. Westmeath) the Tuesday after Samain (Hallowe'en).

There was a *geis* on Cúchulainn* not to eat the flesh of a hound because it was his namesake, *cú* being the Irish for 'hound'.

King Conchobar mac Nessa was never to pass judgement nor was he permitted to enter battle. He did, however, take part in the battle of Rosnaree and the siege of Howth.

Aífe laid three *geasa* upon her son Conlaí (whom she had by Cúchulainn), when Cúchulainn left her for Emer. The first was that he was not to turn back, the second that he was not to refuse a challenge, and the third that he was never to tell his name. So it was that Caonlaí failed to avenge his mother and died by his father's hand.

'A good number of these *geasa* may be ascribed to precautions, another series to early ideas of morality and a large number to primitive notions of honour'.[30] Many of the taboos were prescribed by druids at birth. A *geis* prohibited Fergus mac Roich* from refusing a feast, which in turn led to the death of the Sons of Uisneach. Diarmuid was placed under *geasa* by Gráinne* to elope with her and, as no hero could break a *geis* placed upon him by a woman, he fled from Tara with her.

On the night that Cormac Connloinges (son of Conchobar mac Nessa) was born, the druid Cathbad* laid the following taboos upon him: to be borne by horses yoked with an ashen yoke; to swim at one time with the birds of Loch Lo; to pass dry foot over the Shannon; to be accompanied by women over Áth Mór; for his hounds to pursue the swift hare of Mag Sainb. To break these laws meant death. When Cúchulainn's mother Dechtire offered him a cup containing a special drink advantageous to victory, the contents changed into blood. This happened on each of three occasions he was offered it. Cúchulainn said to his mother, 'Lady, as regard thyself there is no fault; it is that my geasa are destroyed, and my life's end is near'.[31]

Giolla Decair   The story of the Giolla Deacair is preserved in the title of Imtheacht Deacair or the pursuit of the Giolla Deacair and his horse, an Irish Fenian romance, one of the many romances associated with the fiana of Finn mac Cumhail.*

The fiana* were hunting one summer around Knockainy in Co. Limerick; they had their hounds with them to rout the deer and badgers from the coverts. Finn asked Finn bán mac Bresal to climb the hill of Knockainy and to report on the chase.

After a while Finn bán saw a warrior of great size coming from the east towards the hill, leading a horse. He had 'thick lips, and long, crooked teeth, and his face was covered all over with bushy hair'. His weapons were rusty and slovenly looking; he had an iron club which he dragged with him. His horse was equally ugly, with tangled black scraggy hair, and all the points of his big bones protruded through his skin. Finn bán brought this warrior to Finn mac Cumhail. Finn asked him his name, to which he replied: 'My name is the Giolla Deacair; I have come to ask you to take me into your service for one year; and at the end of that time I shall fix my wages according to my custom'.

This was agreed, but then the Giolla Deacair's horse ploughed into the horses of the fiana, causing havoc. Conán Maol of the fiana tried in vain to calm the horse, but he and fourteen of the fiana were taken by the horse to Tír-fo-Thuinn (the land beneath the waves). On his way to the oceanic Otherworld* the horse passed the barony of Connello, in Co. Limerick; it went up Slieve Loughter, a celebrated mountain near Castleisland, in Kerry, through the long peninsula lying west of Tralee and including Dingle and on to the Slieve Mis mountain range and to the village of Cloghan on the north coast of the peninsula. At Cloghan (formerly Cloghan CinnCait), the Giolla Deacair's horse with fourteen fiana on his back and Conán Maol hanging on to his tail, plunged into the waves of the Atlantic.

In pursuit of the Giolla Deacair and his horse, Diarmuid Ó Duibne ends up in Tir-fo-Thuinn which he arrives at, at the bottom of the well. The fiana and Finn eventually catch up with them and they rescue those taken away. They also become involved in internecine warfare between a king and his brother and help to resolve the conflict. By this time the Giolla Deacair has changed into a kind, gentle king called Abarta. Conán Maol, the satirist of the fiana, felt that Abarta should get a dose of his own medicine. So he asked him to change back into the Giolla Deacair and put fifteen of his men on the horse and he would have to hold on to his tail. The Giolla Deacair held on to the horse's tail until they reached Cloghan CinnCait and then he ran alongside the horse until they reached Knockainy; there the Giolla Deacair pointed to where his horse had laid waste the horses of the fiana. When the fiana looked to where the Giolla Deacair was pointing, all they saw were horses grazing peacefully inside the fence. When Finn and the others turned round to question the Giolla Deacair about this, both he and his horse together with the fifteen heroes from the land of Promise had disappeared.

Glas Gaibhleann   A grey cow from Donegal, owned by a local chieftain named mac Cinn Fhaolaid from Rath Finan. Noted for its inexhaustible supply of milk, legend has it that if the Glas Gaibhleann slept in a field the grass would be luxuriant and milk-producing. An old Irish saying refers to rich pasture thus: *Chodail an Ghlas ghaibhneach ann* (the glas gaibhleann slept there).[28]

The cow was so productive that it was coveted by all the neighbours, and Balor* greatly wished to possess it. One day mac Kinelly brought the cow with him while he was having some swords forged. By a trick

79

Balor got the halter into his hand and brought the cow to Tory Island. The place where he dragged the cow is today called Port na Glaise (harbour of the grey cow). Distracted by all this mac Kineely consulted a local druid on the problem. He was told that the animal would not be recovered so long as Balor was alive, for Balor with his basilisk eye would petrify anyone that approached. The cow was recovered after Balor's death.

The Glas Gaibhleann, which some legends connect with Goibniu* is said to lie buried in Duma na mBó (mound of the cows) west of the Mound of the Hostages at Tara.*

In the Burren in Co. Clare around Slievenaglasha at Knockans there are many places associated with the cow and her owner in Clare, the smith Lon. These sites include Tobar na Glaise (the well of the cow), Mothair na Ceártan (the thicket of the heifer), Leaba na Glaise (the bed of the glaise) and Glasgeivnagh Hill.

Goibniu *Seachtain briochta ban agus gabhann agus druadh* (Beware of spells of women, smiths and druids).

Goibniu was the Irish smith god. In the genealogy of the Tuatha Dé Danann* he is described as being in the company of Nuadu* Argatlám and as one of the three craftsmen of the Tuatha. He is one of the Aos Dána (people of skill, poetry etc.), or poets. In the *Book of Invasions*[15] he is named as one of the seven chieftains of the Tuatha and also as one of the four sons of Esarg, son of Nét, the other three being Luchta, Credne and Dian Cécht. Another genealogy describes him as one of the seven sons of Ethliu, his illustrious brothers including the Dagda,* Credne, Luchte, Nuadu Argatlám and Lug* mac Céin. These seven brothers are the chieftains of the Tuatha Dé Danann who conquered Ireland under their leader Bethach.

Together with Luchta the wright and Credne the worker in bronze, Goibniu the smith is one of the three gods of craftmanship. Collectively the are known as na Trí Dee Dánann.° According to Ross[32] they are the 'three gods of Danu'.

The weapons for the second battle of Mag Tuired * were forged by the Trí Dee Dánann and were given to Lug so that he might win. Goibniu provided spear-points which would slay all they touched.

Goibniu forged the 'lightning weapon which Lug sent through Balor's* eye. O'Rahilly[2] states that Balor the sun god and Goibniu the smith god are ultimately the same. This may mean that, like Balor, Goibniu is a god of fire and thunder and it is with his thunderbolt that Balor is overcome. O'Rahilly further states that 'Goibniu, whose name is a derivative of *goba* (gen. *gobann*), "smith", is primarily the Otherworld* god in his capacity as artificer'.

Goibniu was Lord of the Otherworld-Feast (*see*: Dagda,* and Manannán's* pigs), it being named Fled Goibnend, meaning 'Goibniu's Feast'. He supplied the food and drink, and those who partook were preserved from age and decay.

As a healer Goibniu is invoked in an old Irish charm against the prick of a thorn: *Todaig rogarg fiss goibnen aird goibnen menaird goibean ceingeth ass* (Very sharp is the goad [awl] of Goibniu, let Goibniu walk away from it).[33]

In the second battle of Mag Tuired, between the Tuatha Dé Danann and the Fomorians,* Lug, a young warrior, joins the Tuatha and becomes their chief. He calls for the three artificers, the Trí Dee Danann, and asks what aid can be given. Goibniu answers, 'Though the men of Érinn should continue the battle for seven years, for every spear that falls off its handle and for every sword that breaks, I will give a new weapon in place of it; and no erring nor missing cast shall be thrown with any spear that is made by my hands, and no flesh into which it will enter shall ever taste the sweets of life after'.

Ruadán, son of Bres,* chief of the Fomorians, and of Brigit,* daughter of the Dagda, entered the camp to spy for the Fomorians. He had easy access, as his grandfather the Dagda was chief of the Tuatha. He related to the Fomorians the performances of the smith and was told to kill him. Intending to do so he returned to the camp of the Tuatha and asked the Trí Dee Dánann to make him a spear. This they did and Ruadán threw the spear at Goibniu and wounded him. Goibniu took the spear from his own body and killed Ruadán with it.

Goibniu's forge was situated in the depths of the forest of Glenn Treicím, near the hill of Mullagh Mast.[34] It was called Cerdcha Ghaibhnenn (the forge of Goibniu), in a glen east of Mullagh Mast in the northern part of Co. Wicklow. This area was known to abound in copper ore, of which metal the ancient swords and spears were made. (At a later date this forest on the east side of the river Liffey was used by Tigernmas* for the smelting of gold and the manufacture of vessels and trinkets.)

The importance of the smith's craft is expressed in the triad: 'the three renovators of the world: the womb of a woman, the udder of a cow, the moulding-block of a blacksmith'. Another triad stated: 'three things which confer status on a blacksmith: the cooking spit of Neithin (chief smith of Tara), the cooking pit of the Mórrígan*, the anvil of the Dagda'*).

Closely associated with the Goibniu is the Welsh smith and brewer,

Gofannon or Govannan. The Roman god Vulcan is strongly associated with the thunderbolt and the sun, like Goibniu. Also, Vulcan's son is reputed to have been born in a forest near a forge, reminding one of Goibniu's forge in the forest of Glenn Treicím. The Greek Hephaestos served the gods with drinks as did Goibniu. Also, Hephaestos suffered from a wound, as did Goibniu. The Norse Voelund was, like Goibniu, a smith and a seer and was invoked. There is a mound in England near the Vale of the White Horse called the Mound of Wayland Smith.

In a more popular context the smith becomes the Gobán Saor, who is reputedly from Turvey Strand, probably the modern Fairview Strand, Dublin. His father threw an axe towards the beach to stop the incoming tide. The Gobán Saor has enriched the storytellers' folklore and is generally held (in fanciful stories) to have been the builder of the round towers of ancient Ireland and of the Castle of Ferns associated with the kings of Leinster. He is also included in folktales from the Aran Islands,[104] where he has nine daughters and builds castles as far away as Italy.

The death of Goibniu occurred at the battle of Mag Tuired* and is recorded in the following verse of the *Lebor Gábala*:[15]

> Marba de thám thregtach trá,
> Dian Cecht ocus Goibnend Goba
>
> Now of painful plague,
> died Dian Cecht and Goibnenn the smith.

The following passage from *Lebor na h-Uidre*[35] describes Goibniu and other heroes: 'I saw a couch with three large heroes on it; three dark grey 'lenas' (shirts or smocks) on them; each limb of theirs was rounder than the body of a man. They had great large swords; each of them larger than the leg of a weaver's loom; they would split a hair on water. A large vessel is placed in front of them — large as a caire colbhaige (a communal meat boiler); in it a hideous liqer. A large vessel is placed in front of them — large as a caire colbhaige (a communal meat boiler); in it a hideous liqer. A large vessel is placed in front of them — large as a caire colbhaige (a communal meat boiler); in it a hideous liquid. The spear is plunged from its haft so that you would think there is a fiery pit in the top of the house . . . These three are the valour holding heroes of Ériu, namely Sencha the beautiful, son of Ailill, Dubthach Dael Ulad and Goibniu son of Lurgnech.'

Goll mac Morna   The chief of the Clan Morna, Goll mac Morna was the leader of the Connacht Fiana. He is sometimes referred to as one-eyed Goll mac Morna. After the battle of Cnucha (Castleknock), when the Clanna Morna together with the Lagin defeated the Clanna Baoiscne under Cumall mac Trénmár, Goll became the leader of the Fiana throughout Ireland. He had previously held the command of the Fiana under Conn Cét Chathach* but had been banished to Scotland by Cumall and the Gálioin* race, who were a pre-Gaelic community living in Leinster. He had then been brought back to Tara* to join in Conn's plans to attack the Leinster Fiana. At the battle of Castleknock he slew Cumall in what may have been a form of covenant, that is, Goll and his fellow chieftains all cast their blades into him.

Thirty-nine verses of the *Duanaire Finn*[36] describe the 'wild rush' of the Clanna Morna in which 'five thousand six hundred and twenty-six of the children of Baoisgne died'. These events occurred over many battlefields, including Tonn Tuaidhe, Tonn Chlíodhna, Howth and Castleknock. As leader of the Fiana at this time Goll was fighting to defend the Ard-Rí, Cormac mac Airt,* against Clanna Baoiscne.

The night before he died Goll was driven in battle onto a rocky promontory of the sea. His wife stayed by him, although Goll exhorted her to leave and marry a man worthy of her. She, 'daughter of Conall of Cruachain',* would not leave, and said, 'Where might I find west or east thy equal for a bedfellow. . . . Thou hast not shown me a harsh mind. . . . From this night out I will not be light-minded. . . . I will belong to no man on the surface of the earth'. Goll had not eaten for thirty days and his wife then suggested to him that he eat the flesh of his dead assailants and drink the milk from her breasts, but his *geasa* forbade him to do so. And so Goll spent his time waiting for Finn, hungry and talking of former times when 'I stained my shafts right well in the bodies of the house of Trénmór.'

Goll was then killed by Finn with the Corrbolg or lightning weapon which had previously been in his own possession.

> Dost thou bear in mind, bright Goll,
> against the son of Cumhall of Almhain, how
> thou wert killed there on the rock and
> parted from thy soul.[36]

Much later when Finn himself had died, Goll is reputed to have gone to hell with Daighe, Conán and his son Art, to rescue Finn from the 'demons of the blue host', this in spite of the fact that Finn had been responsible for his death.

Gráinne   The daughter of Cormac mac Airt,* high king of Ireland. Her enclosure at Tara* can still be seen today. In his old age Finn mac Cumaill* solicited Cormac for Gráinne's hand in marriage. Cormac agreed and invited Finn to Tara. Finn accepted, but he then had to obtain the consent of Gráinne herself, 'which was necessary in such matters in those days'.[34]

Finn went to Tara with a *fian*° including Oisín,* Oscar and Diarmuid Ua Duibhne. It was the custom at great feasts at that time for the lady of the house to fill a goblet with her own choice of liquor and have it sent by a maid to the chief guest and then in turn to all the guests present. However, when Gráinne distributed the goblet, Diarmuid and Oisín were excluded. The liquor had been drugged and those who had drunk fell asleep. Gráinne then sat between Diarmuid and Oisín and said that she was too young for such a war-worn man as Finn, Oisín's father. She would gladly go with either Oisín or Diarmuid, but as Oisín would not dishonour his father 'she conjured Diarmuid by his manliness and his vows of chivalry' to take her away and be her mate. 'I put you under ancient bonds to bring me forth from this ruined revelry. I choose. I put you under loving bonds in peril, in darkness, to love me, defend me, Diarmuid O'Duibhne.'[37]

Agreeing to the elopement, Diarmuid left Tara with Gráinne. This is the start of the ancient story of the Pursuit of Diarmuid and Gráinne, in which Finn and the Fiana hunt all over Ireland for the lovers. The impact of the romantic associations of the tale is testified by the number of so-called 'beds of Diarmuid and Gráinne' around Ireland. One of these is the cave on the Hill of Howth, another is on Ben Bulben, Co. Sligo. Dozens of places are called after the famous couple, many cromlechs being erroneously described as their 'love beds'.

Some stories refer to Diarmuid as having had a *ball seirce* (love spot). The sight of this spot would cause the viewer to be strongly attracted to Diarmuid. Diarmuid's spot is variously described as having been on his forehead or his shoulder. In either case the spot was covered, either by hair or clothing. A story related how Gráinne saw it while watching Diarmuid playing hurling.

The Pursuit of Diarmuid and Gráinne is one of the greatest of all the Irish love stories. It is undoubtedly pre-medieval in so far as it is generated by the earthy instincts of Gráinne rather than the later romantic ideas of 'pure love' and courtly behaviour. In Gráinne's time, and before it, it would appear that a woman of her standing had a right to unrestricted sexual licence. She used this right by placing *geasa* (*see*: geis*) on Diarmuid to be her lover.

84

'O where is Gráinne, the golden, the beautiful?'
And like the flowing of sea waves others cried:
'O where is Gráinne, the golden, that was wed
yet was not wife?' And a sad voice replied:
'Lo! Gráinne, the golden, the beautiful, is dead
and her red lips are dust'. The warriors sighed,
bowed as if they sank in sleep. Arose
Gráinne, the sweet voiced, spake out laughingly,
'O men, Ye pale as poplars when wind blows
rainly! Ye drowse and grow afraid
of dreams!'[37]

Grian   The goddess who dwelt in the *síd* of Cnoc Gréne, a hill near Pallas Green, about seven miles from Knockainey, Co. Limerick. She is represented as daughter of Fer Í (man of yew), son of Eógabal. It would seem that Grian and Áine* are the same goddess under different names. The placename Knockainey is derived from the Irish *cnoc Áine* (hill of Áine). Grian was a sun goddess and was associated with Co. Clare. Loch Gréne or Lough Graney in the east of the county is called after her.

Imbas forosnai   A pagan ritual practised by *filid* (seers) to acquire supernatural knowledge. A *fili* chewed a piece of raw animal flesh and chanted an incantation over it, offering the flesh to the gods whom he invoked. He then slept and, whilst asleep, the knowledge was transmitted to him.

Cormac, the king-bishop of Cashel in the tenth century, details the ancient rite. *Imbas forasnai* is the knowledge that enlightens, i.e., it discovers everything which the poet likes and which he desires to manifest. Thus is it done: the poet chews a piece of the flesh of a red pig, or dog or cat, and puts it afterwards on the flag behind the door, and pronounces an incantation on it, and offers it to idol-gods, and afterwards calls his idols to him. . . and pronounces incantations on his two palms, and calls again his idols to him that his sleep may not be disturbed, and he lays his two palms on both his cheeks, and in this manner he falls asleep; and he is watched in order that no one may interrupt or disturb him until everything about which he is engaged is revealed to him'.[6] Thus revelation whilst asleep was the fruit of this rite of pagan divination. Patrick abolished the *imbas* and adjudged that anyone who practised it should have neither heaven nor earth, because it was renouncing Baptism.

Finn* mac Cumaill speaks through *imbas forosnai*, and Scáthach* prophesies through *imbas forosnai* in the wooing of Emer. In the Táin* Bó Cualgne, Queen Medb* asks the *banhfili* or prophetess Fedelm whether she has acquired *imbas forosnai* (see under Medb).

Imram   *Imrama* (pl.)were voyages that famous adventurers made to the Otherworld,* also known as Mag Mell (the plain of honey); *imram* means 'rowing about'. This type of voyage was voluntarily undertaken, as distinguished from the longer journeys of 'voyages of exile'.

Some of these adventures in the Otherworld are among the oldest stories preserved today. The most celebrated include the Imram of Bran,* the Imram of Laegaire mac Crimthainn* and the Imram of Mael Dúin.* Alwyn and Brinley Rees[8] state the function of the *imram* is to 'teach the "craft" of dying and to pilot the departing spirit on a sea of perils and wonders.'

Probably an ancient rite practised before death: the person would go out to sea towards the Otherworld* in a small boat or coracle. Famous Imrama have been preserved in early literature and they are subsequently mentioned. The sea was believed to 'fall down' at the horizon of the 'flat earth'; thus the Otherworld was not too far away and entrance to it was fairly sudden. This custom was also used as a form of punishment: 'if a woman commits murder or arson, she is put into a boat with one paddle and a vessel of gruel, and is set adrift on an off-shore wind.'[98] Whether this punishment was introduced by Christianity or not, it is difficult to say. It was prescribed by St Patrick for mac Cuill who later became bishop. It occurs as a punishment in the Imram Snédgusso agus maic Ríagla.

A nineteenth century coracle

Imram Brain   The voyage of Bran is a tale found in the eleventh century *Lebor na hUidre*.* Placed among the oldest survivals of Irish story-telling, the noted linguist Kuno Meyer felt that it may have originally been written in the seventh or eighth century.

Bran mac Febail was an Irish king who one day was enchanted by the sound of pleasant music and fell asleep. When he awoke he saw a branch with white blossoms and took it into his house. Inside there was a woman who is known in the tale as 'the Woman from Unknown Lands'. She sang to him, describing the Otherworld:*

> Cróib dind abaill a hEmain
> dofed samail do gnáthaib,
> gésci findargarrait fora,
> abrait glano co mbláthaib . . . .

> A branch of the apple tree from Emain
> I bring, like those one knows;
> twigs of white silver are on it,
> crystal birds with blossoms.[39]

Before leaving, the woman from unknown lands instructed Bran:

> Do not fall on a bed of sloth,
> let not thy intoxication overcome thee,
> begin a voyage across the clear sea,
> if perchance thou mayst reach the land of women.

Bran set out on the *imram* the next day with a band of twenty-seven men. On the voyage he met Manannán mac Lir,* who told him he was on his way to Ireland to father a child by Caintigern, wife of Fiachna, king of Ulster. Their meeting is described in some of the most lyrical and colourful poetry in the Irish mythological tradition.

> Cáine amre lasin mBran
> ina churchán tar muir glan
> os mé im' charput di chéin,
> is mag scothach immaréid.

> Bran deems it a marvellous beauty
> in his coracle across the clear sea:
> while to me in my chariot from afar
> it is a flowery plain on which he rides about.

In the end, Manannán prophecies that Bran will arive at Emne, 'Island of Women', before sunset:

Fossad airsin imraad Bran,
ni chían co tír inna mban,
Emne co n-ildath féle
ricfe ré fuiniud gréne.

Steadily then let Bran row,
not far to the land of women,
Emne with many hues of hospitality
thou wilt reach before the setting of the sun.

When they arrived, Bran was addressed by the leader of the women: 'Come hither on land, O Bran son of Febal! Welcome is thy advent!' He did not want to go ashore but the woman threw a ball of thread over his face and, caught up in it, he was pulled to land.

Bran and his men were coupled with the women and, provided with beds and a permanent supply of food, they lost their sense of time. Eventually however, when Nechtán mac Collbrain, one of the company, became homesick, Bran left with his people. The woman warned that if they left they would never again touch land.

They sailed until they arrived at Srub Brain. There are two places with this name in Ireland, one now called Stroove or Shruve Brin, at the entrance to Lough Foyle, and the other in the south west of the country. Kuno Meyer believes that, as Mag Mell was supposed to be in the south west, the latter is where Bran arrived.

Awaiting there was a gathering, inquiring who they were, to which Bran replied, 'I am Bran, son of Febal'. They told him that the voyage of Bran was in their ancient stories. Nechtan mac Collbran, he who had been homesick, leapt from the coracle and became a heap of ashes. The others stayed in the boat from where Bran told them on the shore of his wanderings. He then left, and from that time his wanderings are not known.

Both Bran and Manannán have Irish and Welsh mythological associations. Bran is an Irish king and a king from Wales. The Irish Bran meets Manannán. The Welsh Bran is the Welsh Manawydan's brother. Manannán mac Lir and Manawydan Son of Llyr are synonymous. They are the Celtic Neptune whose *síd* is the Irish Sea; after him the Isle of Man is named.

Imram Laegaire meic Crimthain Laegaire was the son of Crim-than, king of Connacht. One day, while he was on the Plain of Two Mists (Mag Dá Cheo), at the modern day Loch Naneane in Co. Roscommon, he was approached by Fiachna mac Retach of the men of the *síd*. Fiachna's wife had been carried off by Goll mac Dolb and he had come to Laegaire to seek the help of a mortal.

Laegaire agreed to help the Otherworld* chieftain and, accompa-nied by fifty of his fighting men, he dived down into the Lough. They went to the fort of Mag Mell, where Fiachna's wife was imprisoned, and rescued her. However, she, the daughter of Eochaid the Dumb, lamented her rescue:

> Hateful day on which weapons are washed
> for the sake of the dear dead body of Goll mac Dolb!
> He whom I loved, he who loved me.
> Laegaire Liban — little he cares!

> Goll I loved, son of Dolb,
> weapons by him were hacked and split,
> by the will of God, I go out
> to Fiachna mac Retach.

After the rescue, Fiachna's daughter was coupled with Laegaire and fifty women from the síd with his fifty warriors. After a year's stay Laegaire wanted to temporarily return home. Fiachna told him to travel by horse and, if he wished to come back, not to dismount.

Laegaire and his companions returned to Connacht where he found his people mourning him. 'Approach us not', he said, 'we are here but to bid you farewell'.

Crimthann, his father pleaded with him to stay, 'Leave me not; the royal power of the three Connachts shall be thine, their silver and their gold, their horses and their bridles, their fair women shall be at thy will, only leave me not.'

Laegaire replied to his father:

> Noble the sweet sounding music of the síd!
> From kingdom to kingdom one goes
> drinking from burnished cups
> holding converse with the loved one.

> A marvellous thing, O Crimthann Cass,
> I was master of a blue sword,

one night of the nights of the *síd*,
I would not give for all thy kingdom.

Laegaire then returned to the *síd* below Loch Naneane and there became joint master with Fiachna mac Retach.

Imram Mael Dúin   Mael Dúin set out on a voyage to avenge the death of his father Ailill at the hands of coastal raiders. Advised by a druid, he built a boat from three skins and set off with seventeen companions. His three foster-brothers swam out and were taken aboard, thus going against the *geis** of the druid, and leading to later misadventure.

The voyagers visited thirty-three islands,[40] where various adventures befell them. They met fabulous beasts, including one who could turn its skin round like a mill. (A similar feat is associated with stories of Cúchulainn.*)

At one island they had stones thrown after their currach as they made their escape. At another, the Island of Smiths, the smith threw a red hot iron bar after them which caused the sea to boil Many of the adventures are similar to those occurring in Imram Brain* and echo those in classical mythology. For instance, on the Island of Laughter and the Island of Weeping, Mael Dúin encountered a primal chorus which drew in travellers against their will.

Surreal imagery is employed in the story to give an Otherworld* illusion. Silver columns and silver nets, and an island with a pedestal with a door at the base, and one with a revolving rampart of fire, inside which people bore vessels of gold, and the air filled with music. On one island a cat jumped through one of the foster brothers, reducing him to ashes. Mael Dúin gathered the ashes and threw them over the sea cliff.

On the Island of Women, the queen and seventeen daughters welcomed Mael Dúin and his seventeen men. (Just as, in the story of Imram Brain, Bran and his men were welcomed on their Island of Women.) Here they were feasted and induced to remain forever, in this world of perpetual pleasure and eternal youth.

After three months they returned to their boat, but the queen threw a ball of thread after them, preventing them from leaving. They stayed three months more, attempting to leave three times, each time being brought back by these *femmes fatales*. However, on the fourth attempt the thread caught on the hand of one of Mael Dúin's companions, Diuran, a crewman; they cut off the hand, and they escaped.

They then met the Monk of Torach, who asked Mael Dúin to forgive the slayer of his father. This he did and in due course reached the island of the former enemies, where he was made welcome. Here they related the story of their wanderings and after that they returned to Ireland.

Iuchair and Iucharba   Sons of Tuireann, together with their brother Brian they slew Cian, father of Lug.* Their story, generally called the Fate of the Children of Tuireann is one of those known as the Three Sorrowful Tales of Erin.

Cian was in Bruig na Bóinne° (the Boyne Valley) assembling the Tuatha Dé Danann* in preparation for the battle of Mag Tuired.* He saw the three armed brothers approaching him. There was an enmity between Cian and the sons of Tuireann and, outnumbered, he changed his shape into a pig and joined a nearby herd of pigs.

However, Brian had spotted Cian before his shape changed. Iuchair and Iucharba had not, and Brian changed them into hounds, setting them on the pigs. When the magic pig was separate from the herd, Brian speared it. His brothers returned to human form and wanted to save Cian's life . . . but Brian refused. Cian asked that he be changed back to human form before death and his request was granted. Cian was slain and later an *éiric*° (blood fine) was imposed upon the brothers. This involved obtaining the 'spear of Assal', which was the spear of the king of Persia, bringing back three apples from the Garden of the Hesperides . . . , getting a chariot and two horses, the property of the king of Sicily . . . , getting the seven magical pigs from King Easal of the Pillars of Gold . . . the hound-whelp from the king of Iceland . . . the cooking spit from the Women of Inis Fionnchuire at the bottom of the sea between Ireland and Scotland . . . , and getting the pig skin of Tuis, king of Greece, which had the power to heal all who touched it and to turn a stream of water into wine for nine days. The final task was to give three shouts from Miodchaoin's hill in Lochlainn.

They succeeded in all until they came to the final task when Brian was challenged by Miodchaoin, who was watching. Miodchaoin was killed by Brian, but his sons avenged him by mortally wounding the Sons of Tuireann. Dying, they made their way home, and asked Lug if they could have the pig's skin to heal their wounds. The request was refused, the sons died, as did Tuireann shortly after. A poem written by Flann Mainistrech *c.* AD 1056[41] says that Cian met his death at the hands of Brian, Iuchair and Iucharba.

The story of the Children of Tuireann occurs before the battle of Mag Tuired and many of the tasks set forth by Lug would have helped him in battle. With such treasures as the spear of Assal and the chariot and horses of King Dobhar of Sicily, Lug was better equipped for battle against Balor* and the Fomorians.*

Labraid Loingsech   The progenitor of the Lagin, the Leinstermen, twenty-fifth in direct line from Éremán,* ancestor of the Gaels.* Also referred to as Labraid Lorc and as Labraid Moen, he is said to have been born at a place called Ath Laegaire which, according to O'Rahilly[2] was possibly in Co. Kildare on the river Liffey. Kuno Meyer supposes him to have been 'a living king in Ireland at the time of the Roman invasion of Britain'. For the Lagin he was their ancestor deity, *ardu déib doén*, 'a man higher than the gods'. In the *Dindshenchas*[42] he is the father of the god Nechtan. He is described[41] as being one of those in the pedigree of the kings of the Dál nAraidi.°

Labraid is the hero of the tale Orgain Denda Rég (the Plunder of Dinn Rég), mentioned in an early manuscript.[43] This story, occurring elsewhere[41] tells how Cobthach Coel killed his own brother Loegaire Lorc as well as Loegaire's son Ailill, who was Labraid's father. After this battle Labraid went to Gaul, and when he returned he slew Cobthach, becoming king of Ireland. The Lagin are said to have got their name from the *laigne* or spears with which Labraid equipped his forces on his return from banishment.

> Labraid Longsech lór a lín.
> ro hort Chobhthach i nDind Rig.
> co slúag láignech dar lind lir.
> dib ro hainmnigthe Lagin.

> Labradh Loingsech with his ample force
> slew King Cobthach in Dinnrigh,
> with a lance-armed host from the sea,
> from him are named the Laighean.

The story of Labraid is the earliest tale of the Lagin. According to O'Rahilly[2] the names Lagin and Gálioin* did not exist until Labraid came from Gaul. He summarises from the *Book of Leinster* one version of the Orgain Denda Ríg as follows: 'Cobthach Coel Breg, king of Ireland, slays his brother Loegaire Lorc, and poisons Ailill Áine, Loegaire's son. Labraid, Ailill's son, is banished "out of Ireland" by Cobthach; and accompanied by Craiphtine and Ferchertne, he goes westward to Scoriath, king of the Fir Morca, in Munster. Moriath, the

View of the main chamber of Cairn L at Lough Crew
(Slieve na gCaillighe — Witches' Hill), Co. Meath

king's daughter, falls in love with Labraid, who wins her by means of Craiphtine's music, which sends her watchers to sleep. Thereafter Labraid with an army of Munstermen marches to Dinn Ríg. Craiphtine's music sends the garrison to sleep; the fortress is captured and the garrison slaughtered. Labraid is now king of Lagin and lives in Dinn Ríg. There he builds a house of iron. He invites to a feast, Cobhtach, who comes with thirty other kings; and, confining his guests in the iron house, Labraid burns them all to death'.[2]

This roasting to death in an iron house also occurs in Mesca Ulad,[o] and in the Mabinogion (the Welsh cycle of stories) in the tale of Branwen, daughter of Llyr. Other versions of the story tell how Labraid goes to Armenia and comes back with three hundred ships arriving at the Boyne and going south to attack Dinn Ríg. Elsewhere it is told how he receives help from the Franks, arriving in Wexford before the battle. Various dates are given for the overthrow of Cobthach by Labraid, 307 BC being given by the *Book of Leinster*. In all versions he marries Muiriath, daughter of the king of Fir Morca of West Munster.

The overthrow of Cobthach and the occupation of the royal seat by the Lagin under Labraid is a significant date in early Irish history. It established a precedent for seeking foreign aid in times of crisis. At a later date the descendants of the Lagin, the Leinstermen under Diarmuid mac Murrough used the pattern established by Labraid to maintain his kingdom. Dinn Ríg, an ancient centre of power of Leinster, today quietly exists without signpost beside the main road on the river Barrow near Leighlinbridge, Co. Carlow.

Popular folklore still has it that Labraid Loingsech had horse's ears. He told this secret to a tree; the tree was cut down and made into a harp, and the harp revealed the secret. There are similarities between this story and that of Midas in Greek mythology, he having asses' ears and his secret being made known. Sigmund Freud[44] suggests a relationship between 'ears' and testes; the story of Labraid, the progenitor, can thus be seen describing him as a potent fertile male.

Lebor na hUidre   The oldest of the parchment manuscripts extant, the earliest compilation being dated *c.* AD 1100 and containing 134 folio pages. The name means 'The Book of the Dun Cow', being named from the hide of a famous pet cow of St Ciarán of Clonmacnoise.

The manuscript is in the Royal Irish Academy in Dublin, having been purchased along with 212 other MSS in 1844 for 1200 guineas. *Lebor na hUidre* fills three large folio volumes and is catalogued in the RIA as number 225 in the Hodges and Smith Collection. Prior to being in the hands of these booksellers, Hodges and Smith, its whereabouts were unknown.

It was apparently written by the culdee° Mael Muire mac Célachair in the twelfth century. An insertion made in AD1245 states this, including the relations of the scribe. In the fourteenth century it was carried from Donegal to Connacht. In 1347 the book was renovated by Sigraid Ó Cuirrndín, a poet of Bréifne. It was brought back to Donegal by Aed Ruad in 1470. In its present state it consists of sixty-seven leaves of vellum measuring eleven by eight inches. A facsimile copy was made by Joseph O'Longan and published by the RIA in 1871.

Altogether the book contains sixty-five items, many of them incomplete. There is a fragment of the Six Ages of the World as well as a fragment of *Lebor Bretnach*, a history of Britain. Also included is Mesca Ulad° (the Intoxication of the Ulstermen), Táin Bó Flidais (the Cattle Raid of Flidais), and the epic Táin* Bó Cualgne (the Cattle Raid of Cooley). There are the stories of the Feast of Bricriu and the Voyage of Maeldúin and others, most of the tales belonging to the Ulster Cycle.

Lia Fáil   The Stone of Destiny stands on Tara* Hill. This was the stone upon which pagan kings stood at inauguration. It was supposed to have roared when stood upon by Milesian kings. According to the *Dindshenchas* the origin of the word *fál* can be related to *Fo ail*, meaning 'the under stone', i.e. the stone under the king.

It was called 'the stone under the king', because tradition has it that the king-to-be stood on top of the stone pillar, and it 'roared' when stood upon by a rightful man. The roaring of the stone was caused by a 'bull-roarer'; this was a slab of wood attached to a string and swung round so as to make a hissing or roaring sound. This apparently was done out of sight of those attending the inaugural ceremony.

In the ancient maps the Lia Fáil is located by the side of Dumha na nGiall, the Mound of the Hostages, a little way from its present site. It was moved after the rebellion in 1798 to the Rebels' Plot, then known as 'the croppies' grave', commemorating those slain at Tara in that year. Petrie[48] cites an earlier researcher as saying that the stone was removed from Tara to Cruachain Connacht* in earliest times. He relates also that it failed to emit its roar after it was profaned by Cúchulainn's* inauguration of his friend Fiach, an usurper.

Petrie states that the stone was not in fact taken to Connacht, the story merely being a fabrication to support the Connachta's claim to the kingship of Ireland. The origins of the story lay in a dream of

Cormac mac Airt.* Thus from early sources Lia Fáil is clearly identified with the stone of Tara.

However, it is held by Scottish historians, from Boetius down to the present time, that the 'stone of fate' was sent from Ireland to Scotland in the fifth century for the coronation of Fergus mac Erc, the first king of Dál Riada. It is said that this is the stone that was later taken by Edward I to Westminster. Despite recovery by Scots in modern times, it was repossessed by the English and still remains under the coronation chair of their monarchs.

Petrie[48] maintains that, other than Geoffrey Keating[4] writing in the seventeenth century, no Irish accounts support the above contention. It is noted that, whereas the Irish accounts state that the Lia Fáil was brought to Ireland from Northern Germany by the Tuatha Dé Danann,* the Scottish states it as having being brought to Ireland by the Milesians from Spain.

The identification of the Lia Fáil as the present-day stone at Tara is supported by Petrie, pointing out that the Irish writers of the tenth, eleventh and twelfth centuries located the Lia Fáil at the very position occupied up to 1798 by the large pillar stone in a prostrate position. He notes that this stone was a monument of antiquity, an idol stone, as the Irish writers described it, which seems evident from its form and character. In the nineteenth century it was popularly known as Bod Fhearghais, meaning the 'Penis of Fergus'. 'It would be difficult', Petrie states, 'to find a monument of antiquity with which so many national associations can be connected'.

The actual stone itself is of granular limestone. It stands five feet above ground, its total height being about eight feet. No granular limestone actually exists in the particular district, but whether the Lia Fáil is of Irish or foreign origin is not known.

Loegaire   The son of Niall Nóigiallach*, Loegaire became king of Ireland in AD 428 and remained so for thirty years.[35] He was never Christianised by St Patrick. However, he allowed Patrick and his followers freedom to move and to convert. At the battle of Athdara in Co. Kildare he was defeated by the Lagin, from whom he had demanded *bórama* (tribute); he then gave guarantees to the Lagin, 'by the sun and moon, water and air, day and night, sea and land', that he would never again demand *bórama*. His word was accepted.

It was prophesied to Loegaire that he would die between Ériu and Alba (Ireland and Scotland) and thus he never went to sea. However, breaking his guarantees to the Lagin, he again attacked them, demanding tributes. When he was between two hills called Ére and Alba in Mag Liphi, near Naas, he was killed, by the sun and the wind it is said, and by the earlier guarantees, 'for no one dared dishonour them at the time'.

> Násad fir na ndula de
> issed ro marb Loegaire.

> The just vengeance of the sacred elements
> it was that killed Loegaire.[35]

Loegaire decreed that he be buried in his own rath south of the royal enclosure; and that he be buried in a standing position with his own shield, facing the Leinster men. Loegaire's fort is south of the royal enclosure on the Hill of Tara.

Loegaire Buadach   Loegaire the Triumphant was son of Cornad mac Ilíach and one of the Ulster warriors in the court of Conchobar mac Nessa.* He was a noted member of the legendary Craeb Ruad° or Red Branch Knights from Emain Macha.* Loegaire is the same person as Loegaire Bern Buadach,[2] the ancestor deity of the Érainn.
Loegaire was praised by Bricriu* in Fled Bricrend.

> A balc bullig Breg, a brúth bullig
> Midi, a bethir breóderg, a búaid n-oc nUlad!

> Thou mighty mallet of Bregia, thou hot hammer
> of Meath, flame red thunderbolt, thou victorious warrior of
> Ulster.[9]

Queen Medb* describes Loegaire on his arrival at Cruachain:*

> Compeer of kings, an old disposer of conquest,
> a fury of war, a fire of judgment,
> a flame of vengeance; in mien a hero,
> in face a champion, in heart a dragon;
> the long knife of proud victories which
> will hew us to pieces;
> the all-noble, red-handed Loegaire;
> his the vigour that cuts the leek with the sword edge
> the back stroke of the wave to the land.[9]

Loegaire met his death in defence of a poet called Aodh mac Ainninn, who was accused by Conchobar mac Nessa* of carrying on an intrigue with his wife, Maghain. Conchobar ordered that Aodh be drowned in a lake called Loch Loegaire (now Loch Mary, two miles west of Newtownstewart, Co. Tyrone). Loegaire went to the aid of Aodh but hit his head against the upper door post of Aodh's house; he succeeded in rescuing Aodh but died later close to the house.

Longes mac nUsnig The Exile of the Sons of Uisneach is one of the 'three sorrowful tales of Ireland', the others being the Fate of the Children of Lir (Oidheadh Cloinne Lir)* and the Fate of the Children of Tuireann (Iuchair and Iucharba).*

The story is told in the *Book of Leinster* and the *Yellow Book of Lecan. The Book of Leinster* version, generally regarded as being from the eight or ninth centuries and thus older than the twelfth century book itself, was translated by Ernst Windisch in 1880. The story falls into the Ulster Cycle of Irish sagas.

The story, set in the time of Conchobar mac Nessa,* high king of Ireland, begins in the house of his storyteller Feidlimid mac Daill. Feidlimid's wife was pregnant, and as she passed the Ulster Warriors (the Ulaid), the child cried out in the womb, being heard throughout the house. Cathbad* the druid was asked to explain this. He put his hand on the woman's body and said, 'Truly it is a woman child who is here. *Fír ar se ingen fil and agus bid Derdriu a hainm, agus biaid olc impe:* Deirdre shall be her name, and evil woe shall be upon her'.

Later, some days after the child's birth, Cathbad again prophesied that she would bring ruin. The Ulaid called for her death, but Conchobar said he would have her reared and, when grown up, he would take her for a wife. She was thus brought up alone as in the case of Rapunzel, with no one allowed to see her except foster-parents and Lebarcham, a female satirist (*ban chainte*).

Deirdre once saw her foster-mother skinning a calf in the snow and a black raven came to drink the blood. She said to Lebarcham, 'That man only will I love, who hath the three colours that I see here, his hair as black as the raven, his cheeks red like the blood, and his body as white as the snow'. E.G. Quin[56] states that this incident of the three colours is commonly found in folk and fairy tales and that in this story it may be considered 'as the trigger which releases the whole action'.

The three sons of Uisnech were Noíse, Ainnle and Ardán. Noíse found himself alone on the ramparts at Emain Macha;* here he was approached by Deirdre. In their conversation Deirdre said that she would choose him, rather than Conchobar to whom she was promised.

'I would take myself a younger bull', Deirdre said. Noíse tried to avoid her advances as he feared the prophecy of Cathbad.

'Sayest thou this as meaning to refuse me?', said she.

'Yea indeed', he said; and she sprang upon him, and seized him by his two ears. 'Two ears of shame and mockery shalt thou have', she cried, 'if thou take me not with thee'.

'Release me, O my wife!', said he.

'That will I'.

Deirdre and the Sons of Uisneach set out for Assaroe near Bally-shannon in Co. Donegal. They then travelled to Howth in Co. Dublin but, continually pursued by the Ulaid, they eventually sought refuge in Scotland, then known as Alba.° Here, protected by the king of Scotland, they offered military services in return. However, as the Scottish king desired Deirdre for himself, Scotland became unsafe for the Sons of Uisneach.

Deirdre uttered this farewell to Scotland:

Glen Lay!
There I used to sleep under a shapely rock.
Fish and venison and badgers fat,
That was my portion in Glen Lay.

Glen Massan!°
Tall is its wild garlic, white are its stalks:
We used to have a broken sleep
On the grassy river-mouth of Massan.

Glen Etive!°
There I raised my first house,
Delightful its house! when we rose in the morning
A sunny cattle-fold was Glen Etive.

Glen Urchain!°
That was the straight, fair-ridged glen!
Never was man of his age prouder
Than Naoíse in Glen Urchain.[105]

They returned to Ireland. Fergus mac Roich,* who was their surety, was made attend an ale feast far from Emain Macha at the connivance of Conchobar. The Sons of Uisneach went to Emain Macha accompanied by Fergus's son Fiacha.

At this time an old enemy of Conchobar's, Eoghan mac Durthacht, had come to make amends with the high king and Conchobar ordered him, as the price of peace, to kill the Sons of Uisneach.

> The Sons of Uisneach stood upon the level part of the meadows, and the women sat upon the ramparts of Emain. And Eogan came with his warriors across the meadow, and the son of Fergus took his place by Noíse's side. And Eogan greeted him with a mighty thrust of his spear, and the spear broke Noíse's back asunder, and passed through it. The son of Fergus made a spring, and he threw both arms around Noíse, and he brought him beneath himself to shelter him, while he threw himself down above him; and it was thus that Noíse was slain, through the body of the son of Fergus. Then there began a murder throughout the meadow so that none escaped who did not fall by the points of the spears, or the edge of the sword, and Deirdre was brought to Conchobar to be in his power, and her arms were bound behind her back.[95]

A battle followed the murder of the Sons of Uisnech and when Fergus mac Roich returned he burnt Emain Macha, later seeking shelter with Medb and Ailill in Connacht.

Deirdre then lived for a year in Conchobar's household, in a state of deep unhappiness. 'She raised not her head from her knee'. One day Conchobar said to her, 'Of all you see what do you hate most?' 'You', she replied, 'and Eoghan mac Durthacht'. 'Then you shall be a year in Eoghan's company', said Conchobar.

The following is the Gaelic version of the death of Deirdre from a fifteenth century Irish MS now in Edinburgh and known as MS 56:

> Agus ar mbeith ag triall dhoibh do bheireadh sí súil ar Eoghan roimpe go fíochda, agus súil ar Chonchubar ina diaigh; óir ni raibh dís ar domhan is mó dh'a ttug fuath no iad ar aon. Mar do mhotaigh umorro Conchubar ise ag silleadh fa seach ar féin agus ar Eoghan, a dubhairt sé tré abhacht: 'a Dhéirdre, ar se,' 'is súil caorach idir dhá reithe an tsiul sin do bheire orm-sa agus ar Eoghan'.
>
> Ar mo chlos sin do Dhéirdre, do ghaibh boidhga leis an bhréithir sin í do thug baoithléim as an ccarbad amach, gur bhuail a cceann ar charrtha cloiche do bhí roimpe go ndear-

maid mise míonbhrighte d'a ceann, gur ceann, gur ling a hinchinn go hobann aiste; go ro amha sin tainigh bás Dhéirdre.

And as they were journeying onward [*in a chariot towards the fair at Emain Macha*], she would give a look fiercely at Eogan in front of her and a look back at Conchobar behind her; for there were not two men in the world whom she hated more than them both. But when Conchobar noticed her looking alternately at himself and Eogan, he said in sport, 'Deirdre, the look of a ewe between two rams is that look thou givest me and Eogan'. When Deirdre heard that she took fright and made a wild leap out of the chariot, so that she struck her head against a pillar-stone that was before her, and made small fragments of her head so that her brain suddenly leapt out; (and) in that wise occurred the death of Deirdre.[79]

> I am Deirdre, the joyless,
> for short time alive,
> though to end life be evil,
> 'tis worse to survive.

Finally four lines to conclude this heroic romance of Ireland:

> The sons of Uisneach, who like shields their friends protected well,
> by might of hosts on battle-field to death were borne and fell;
> and each was white of skin, and each his friends in love would hold,
> now naught remains for song to teach, the Third of Griefs is told.[95]

The death of Deirdre for love of her dead Noíse must surely put the lie to those who claim that Ireland lacks a romantic tradition or that the women are either *femmes fatales* like Gráinne or fearful sexual war goddesses like Badb* or the Mórrígan.* The story of Deirdre and the Sons of Uisneach must stand beyond all others as a testament to the capacity of love to transcend its more usual associations with power, sexuality and acquisition.

> And Deirdre dishevelled her hair and began kissing Noíse and drinking his blood, and the colour of embers came into her cheeks, and she uttered this lay:

101

That I should remain after Noíse
Let no one in the world suppose!
After Ardan and Ainnle
My time would not be long.
O man that diggest the tomb
And that puttest my darling from me,
Make not the grave too narrow,
I shall be beside the noble ones.[105]

Lug   One of the principal gods of the Tuatha Dé Danann,* Lug is both the Gaulish and Gaelic sun god, the god of genius and light. He was the son of Cian and Eithliu and the grandson of Balor.* He is the divine father of Cúchulainn.*

Hubert Butler[45] links Lug with St Moling, the Lingones and the Ligurians. He also associates St Molua or Mo Lua mac Oiche with Moling. He notes that Clonfert Molua in the Slieve Bloom mountains may also be associated with Lug. Another connection between St Molua and Lug is the fact that St Molua's feast is celebrated on 1 August, which is Lugnasa.* St Molua's well at Emlygrennan was earlier associated with Lug.

Butler connects the name Lug with many tribes. The Lugii and Lygii in Eastern Europe, the Ligyes near Cadiz, the Lugones in Asturias, the Lougi on the Moray Firth. He mentions the Ligurians, a tribe from the Gulf of Genoa, associated with Lucca, which once extended as far as Spain and Britain. This tribe fought against Hercules in Spain. The word Liger, Butler suggests, may be an older name for the Loire. The Ligurians, Butler feels, may be associated with Lugudunum, the ancient name of Lyons, with Lugdunum the old name for London, and also with Luguvallium or Carlisle. In Ireland there is a wide selection of Lig-Lug tribes. Lug is regarded as being an ancient pan-Celtic god. He is attached to dozens of ancestor names, e.g., Aedlug, Caemlug, Cindlug etc.

A popular story concerning Lug tells of Nuadu* holding a great feast at Tara.* On his arrival Lug was refused entrance by the doorkeeper as 'no one without an art enters Tara'. Here begins a long series of questions and answers outside the banqueting hall.

'What is your craft?'
'I am a carpenter'.
'We have one here already, he is Luchtna'.
'Question me, I am a smith'.

'We have one already, he is Goibniu'.
'Question me, I am a champion'.
'We have one already, his name is Ogma'.
'Question me, I am metal worker'.
'We have one already, his name is Credne Cerd'.

The dialogue continues, describing all the artists, druids, warriors and the general social configuration of the banqueting hall during the reign of Nuadu.

Finally, Lug asked the doorkeeper if there was any man present who had all the skills mentioned. The doorkeeper went to enquire and then Nuadu invited Lug in. He asked this *samildánach* (master of all the arts) to play *fidchell*° with his best player. Lug won with a move called 'Lugh's Enclosure', and thus gained entrance to the hall at Tara, sitting at the seat of the sage.

Ogma* and the harper both challenged him. Lug met these challenges successfully and was given the king's seat at Tara. Nuadu then sought his help in the struggle against the Fomorians.*

Lug called on the deities for specialised help in the forthcoming battle. This battle, known as the second battle of Mag Tuired,* is regarded as fictional, being related to the real battle fought near Lough Arrow, Co. Sligo. The deities said that they would lend their support. Dian Cécht the physician would heal anyone provided his head was not cut off nor his spinal marrow hurt. Goibniu* would provide all the weaponry for seven years if needed. The Mórrígan* would pursue them that flee from the battle, 'For I always catch what I chase'.

The story of the second battle of Mag Tuired may be connected to the struggle between Lug and his Fomorian grandfather Balor. Here Balor, a Celtic sun god, was overcome by a divine hero personified by Lug.[2] Lug killed Balor of the Evil Eye by hurling a spear, made by Goibniu, through his eye. This battle is said to have occurred at Dunlewey, Co. Donegal.

Lug and the Dagda* and Ogma then pursued the Fomorians who had carried off the Dagda's harp and harper named Uaithne. They eventually found the harp. It leapt from the wall where it had been placed and came to the Dagda.

In the story of Baile in Scáil,[46] Lug is a king of the Otherworld* visited by Conn king of Tara. He prophecies to Conn the names of the kings who will succeed him at Tara. Lug tells Conn that a festival will be held at Tailtiu as long as Tara remains the centre of the high king.

Lug was killed by Mac Cuill, Mac Cécht and Mac Gréine, sons of Cermait, whom Lug had slain through jealousy for his wife. Lug and the sons met at Uisneach* to talk peace, but the sons were determined on vengeance, and Mac Cuill thrust a spear into Lug's foot. He escaped to Loch Lughborta, where he drowned. A cairn close to this lake is reputedly Lug's grave.[42]

Lugaid Réoderg   Son of the Trí Finds Emna, the three Fair men of Emain. He was a foster-son of Cúchulain.* His epithet *réoderg* means of red stripes. He had three red stripes, one for each of his fathers. His head resembled Nár, his chest resembled Bres, and from his waist down he resembled Lothar. He acceded to the kingship of Tara as a result of an old ritual known as the Tarbfes.* Before going to Tara he received a set of regnal instructions from Cúchulainn. These precepts or moral instructions are known in old Irish as the Bríatharthecosc Con Culaind. Some of these are as follows: Be not seeking combat or doing base things. Be neither fierce, churlish or arrogant. Be neither fearful, violent nor suddenly rash. Do not descend to wealth, which ruins and confuses.

Lugnasa   A festival held in August in connection with Lug.* The original harvest-festival was held in present-day Telltown, Co. Meath, in commemoration of Tailtiu, Lug's foster-mother.

> . . . after Tailtiu died in Tailtiu, her name was imposed on the place, and it is her grave which is north-east from the seat of Tailtiu; and the games were made every year by Lug, a fortnight before Lugnasa and a fortnight after Lugnasa (1 August). Lugnasa, the assembly of Lug, is the name of the games.[15]

A commemorating game or fair, called *nasad*, i.e., a festival or game of Lug mac Ethlenn, was celebrated by him at the beginning of autumn.[6]

> About the Calends of August she (Tailtiu) died, on a Monday on the Lugnasa of Lug; round her grave from that Monday forth is held the chief fair of noble Erin . . .[42]

Lugnasa came to be generally held on the last Sunday in July, this harvest-associated festival taking many names — Garland Sunday, Colcannon Sunday, Rock Sunday and (in Co. Westmeath) Lough Sunday (this latter because assemblies were held at Loughs Owel and

Ennell). In the west coast Irish-speaking areas it is known as Domhnach Chroim Duibh.

At the more popular places — Aenach Carmen in Kildare, Aenach Tailtenn in Westmeath — the harvest festival included games, matchmaking and horse-racing. In many districts the first new potatoes were dug on the first Sunday in August.

It would appear that Lugnasa was regarded as the sun god's day, being celebrated in many of the places specifically associated with Lug i.e., Leyden in Netherlands, Lyon in France and Carlisle in England.

In Ireland these summer festivals were originally associated with the kingdom of Meath, at the ancient sites of Tailtiu, Tlachtga and Uisnech.* As time went on they became a feature of life throughout the country. Eventually Lugnasa and the assemblies took on a Christian flavour, the ancient site becoming associated with a saint and the assemblies in effect being pilgrimages associated with the local patron saint. Notable among these are the mountain pilgrimages at Croagh Patrick and Mount Brandon.

Máire mac Neill[47] records a Lugnasa festivity in the Gortahork area of Donegal. On that day the young people went up the hills of Beltany and Carn Treuna, bringing 'flatcakes of oatmeal and milk'. They would spend the day there, picnicking and wandering about. The boys gathered bilberries and with these made bracelets for the girls, competing with each other to make the best and prettiest for his own girl. They would sing, tell stories and recite verses and dance. Before going home the girls would take off their bilberry bracelets, leaving them behind on the hillsides.

This account was related in 1942 by an old woman, then eighty-five, who herself had heard it from her mother: 'It is a long time since people stopped going to Carn Treuna for the bilberries. An odd one here and there used to go until about thirty years ago, but the old people consider that it is between eighty and a hundred years since they went up in crowds'.[47]

Macha The daughter of Aed Ruad, a Milesian chief, and wife of Cimbaeth, King of Ireland. Árd Macha, meaning the Hill of Macha, the modern Armagh, is called after her as is Emain Macha (Navan Fort), the seat of the Ulster warriors. Legend has it that Macha first traced the outline of Emain Macha with her brooch. Macha appears in a number of stories associated with different times and there are thus understood to be a number of different Machas.

In one of the stories Macha went to the house of Cruind, an Ulster

105

farmer, and, after circling three times on the flagstone in front of his house, went in and entered into his bed. She became pregnant and, later on, Cruind boasted to the king of Ulster that she could outrun any horse. The king demanded to see this regardless of her pregnancy. Macha's plea to delay the race was not accepted and she raced the horses. After she won she died whilst giving birth to twins. (Emain Macha literally means the twins of Macha.) With her last breath she cursed the Ulstermen for nine generations, saying they would be subject to pains in time of stress. This story has associations with primitive beliefs (*see*: Cess Noínden Ulad*) and may further show Macha as a deity associated with the horse. In Corleck Hill, Co. Cavan, she is remembered as a whitehorse.

Together with Badb* and the Mórrígan* she makes up the Mórrígna, a trio of war-fertility goddesses, who often appear in animal or bird guise as crows or ravens and are associated with battles where they often play a decisive part. Their appearance is usually mentioned within the older Mythological Cycle, and the Ulster Cycle, of Irish legend.[49] Macha's 'fruit-crop' is stated to be 'the heads of men that have been slaughtered'. Macha can here be compared to Kali, her equivalent from Indian mythology, with her 'necklace of human skulls'.[92]

Although Macha is related as being wife of Nemed,* it is as daughter of Aed Ruad that she is best recorded. In this context she is known as Macha Mong Ruad, Macha of the red tresses.

Aed Ruad assumed the kingship of Ireland in *c.*300 BC.[5] His domain was most probably confined to Ulster and perhaps Connacht. He and his two cousins Cimbaeth and Díthorba* were children of three brothers, Bodarn, Deman and Fintan. In order to maintain harmony, the brothers had imposed injunctions (*see:* geis*) to the effect that the kingship was to be rotated from one cousin to the next until the end of their lives. Poets, magicians and chiefs were to ensure that the injunctions were kept. The arrangement operated successfully for over forty-five years until Aed Ruad was drowned in the river Erne at Assaroe, Ballyshannon. When Macha, taking his turn, assumed sovereignty, Díthorba and Cimbaeth said they would not allow the position to be held by a woman. In the war that resulted Macha was the victor. Díthorba was expelled to Connacht where he died at Corann in Sligo. Macha married Cimbaeth and gave him the kingship. She then went to Corann, captured the sons of Díthorba, and brought them in fetters to Ulster. Holding them in servitude, she made them build the fort at Emain.

Under Macha, this fine ring fort became the royal centre of Ulster, the home of the Ulaid or Ulster warriors. The founding of the fort is variously dated as between 666 BC and 450 BC.[5] Contemporary archaeologists date it at around 330 BC.

Macha succeeded Cimbaeth after his death in c. 300 BC.[5] She reigned for seven years until she was slain by Rechtaid Rigderg, son of Lugaid Loígde, who had been killed by Aed Ruad. Thus, although the kingship returned to the line of Lugaid, the *éiric*,° or blood-fine, continued, Ugaine Mór slaying Rechtaidh Rigderg twenty years later in revenge for Macha who was his foster-mother.

The attempt by Bodarn, Deman and Fintan to introduce an equitable society based on trust and understanding was disrupted. With Macha there returned to Ulster the right of conquest and the *éiric*.

Sjoestedt[49] sees different elements in the three Machas. Two of these elements contain the notion of fertility — the maternal reproductive element in Macha the wife of Cruind and the agrarian element in Macha the wife of Nemed. Nemed cleared a plain for her 'so that it might bear her name'; finally the warlike element compounded with the sexual in Macha as daughter of Aed Ruad. All the elements joined together to form a war-fertility goddess who exists in Macha as one of the chief mother-goddesses of Ireland.

Mac Con   Also known as Lugaid mac Con. When Cúroí mac Daire's uncle or brother, Conganches mac Dedad, was dead and buried, there issued from his head three dogs; their names were Trí Con and from them were named Lugaid mac Con, Lugaid Muman and Lugaid mac Trí Con. The dog whom Cúchulainn slew is said to have been one of these hounds. All of the above personages have hound or wolf in their name and bring us back to a possible hound or wolf god. In the case of the word *cú* or *con* it seems to associate itself with pre-Gaelic tribes (whether these hounds or wolves represent ancestor gods or not, it is difficult to say). Mac Neill[99] states that in the 16th century mummers appearing at traditional festivals wore paper masks representing animal's heads.

Legend has it that Mac Con got his name from playing with a hound as an infant in the house of Oilill Olum*, king of Munster. Mac Con was a king of Ireland (AD 207-237) in the early historical period. His ancestry has been included in the Gaelic pedigree of kings back to Galicia; this has been seen by some[2] as a ploy to discredit the Érainn as having preceding the Gaels in Ireland. Mac Con is regarded as being of Érainn stock, the Érainn emanating from the Fir Bolg* or Belgae.

Prior to succeeding to the kingship at Tara, Mac Con fought a battle at Cenn Abrat, 'in the hills between Kilmallock and Doneraile', against Eógan of the Eóganacht and a section of the Érainn who had been subsumed into the Gaels by marriage. Mac Con lost this battle and was banished. He went to Scotland. He fought the people from Orkney at Kintyre. He was friendly with the king of Scotland, Béinne Briot, and he attacked the Irish king at Tara, Art mac Aonfir, with soldiers from Argyle.

Mac Con's mother was Sadb, daughter of Conn Cet Chathach.* After her husband died she married Oilill Olum* and bore him nine sons. Seven of these were to die at the battle of Mag Muccrama, the plain which extends westward from Athenry in Co. Galway. This significant battle of the early third century resulted in the defeat of Art, king of Tara. It gave the Fir Bolg temporary kingship of Tara, under Mac Con. After this Tara returned to the Gaels under Cormac mac Airt.*

Whilst Mac Con was king at Tara, Cormac mac Airt* was in fosterage there. One day Mac Con passed judgment[98] on a woman whose sheep had grazed the woad garden of the queen. Garden woad (*Isatis tinctoria*) was extensively cultivated for the blue dye, prepared from its leaves. Mac Con judged that the woman should forfeit the sheep. The woman was distressed and Cormac said to her that the judgment was in error. He said that the judgment should have been 'one shearing for another', that the sheeps' wool should have been sufficient for the grazed woad. When Mac Con saw that he had made an error in the 'king's justice' (*fír flathemon*), he resigned. This may say something of early Irish law and of the power of 'true judgment'. After this Cormac mac Airt became king of Tara.

The Érainn came from Britain; some sources say that they were the dominant power in Ireland *c.*325 BC. They settled in Munster. Mac Con is recorded as being king of one of the two Munsters. His territory was south of the Bandon river to the sea. He is buried on Corran Hill between Balineen and Clonakilty.

Mag Slecht The Plain of Prostration, in Co. Cavan. This was an ancient ceremonial site where the corn god Crom Cruach* was propitiated by human sacrifice, in order to obtain corn and milk. There are similarities between these primitive agricultural sacrifices and those of the Dionysian cult of ancient Greece. People gathered at Mag Slecht around the time of Samain.* It is related that, in worshipping Crom, people rubbed their noses against the idol until the skin was worn away to the bone.

Here used to be
a high idol with many fights
which was named the Crom Cruach.
It made every tribe to be without peace. . . .
To him without glory
they would kill their piteous wretched offspring
with much wailing and peril,
to pour their blood around Crom Cruach. . . .
to him
noble Gaels would prostrate themselves,
from the worship of him, with many slaughters,
the plain is called Magh Sleacht.[42]

Mag Tuired   Situated west of Lough Arrow in Kilmactranny parish, Co. Sligo. It can be translated as the Plain of Reckoning or the Plain of Weeping. Legend has it that the Tuatha Dé Danann* fought two battles here, and according to O'Rahilly[2] the first battle was an historical fact. In this battle, according to the *Book of Leinster*, the Tuatha Dé Danann came from Ulster to Sliab Conmaicne Réin in Leitrim, and from there, westward to Mag Tuired. The battle resulted in a great defeat for the Fir Bolg* in Connacht.

Sir William Wilde[50] felt that the site was between Lough Mask and

The 'Eglone', Moytura

109

Lough Corrib at Cong, a view perhaps supported by references in later texts describing the battle site as Mag Tuired Cunga.

> The battle was fought on the plains of Moy Turey, in Co. Sligo, where Nuada Airget Lám, the king of the Tuatha Dé Danann completely routed the Belgae or Firbolg, a vast number of whom are said to have been slain; and on that battle field, the Marathon of Irish history, we have still remaining the tumuli or barrows erected over the remains of our early pagan progenitors.[50]

O'Rahilly[2] states that it was not the Tuatha Dé Danann but in fact the Lagin who defeated the Fir Bolg at Mag Tuired: 'In order to lend some verisimilitude to the mythical Tuatha Dé Danann as conquerors of Ireland the *Lebor Gabála* compilers represented these instead of the Lagin as victors in the battle'.[2] After the battle the Fir Bolg are said to have fled to the islands of Islay, Arran, Man and Rathlin.

The second battle of Mag Tuired is the source of one of the great tales from the Mythological Cycle of stories. After the first battle Nuadu* gave up the kingship of the Tuatha Dé Danann to Bres.* Bres, who was son of the Fomorian* king Dealbaeth,* had been adopted by the Tuatha. However, under him the Fomorians demanded the *bórama* or cattle tribute from the people.

Thus, the stories say, the gods were reduced to servility, Ogma* to carrying firewood and the Dagda* to building and digging trenches. The Tuatha Dé Danann society was beginning to crumble until one of their poets, Cairbre mac Étain, displeased with his treatment by the Fomorians, prophesied ill luck for Bres:

> Without food quickly on a dish:
> without a cow's milk whereon a calf grows:
> without a man's abode in the gloom of night:
> without paying a company of storytellers, let that be Bres's condition.
> let there be no increase in Bres.[51]

Bres reigned for seven years, after which the kingship returned to Nuadu. He held a war council to overcome the bondage suffered under the Fomorians; in this he was aided by Lug* and the Dagda. Lug, Ogma and the Dagda were given the plan of battle by the three gods of Danu and then spent seven years preparing for it. The Dagda met the Mórrígan* along the river Unius in Corann and they slept together. She foretold that the Fomorians would land at Mag Scétne, saying that she would kill Indech, son of the Fomorian king, by 'depriving him of the blood of his heart and the kidneys of his valour'. Later she gave two handfuls of that blood to the Dé Danann before the battle.

After each day's fighting the weapons were renewed by Goibniu* and the wounded treated by Dian Cécht in the well of Slane, east of Lough Arrow. The Tuatha were led by Lug, the Fomorian chiefs were Balor,* Bres, Indech and Elatha: 'Abundant was the stream of blood there over the white skin of young warriors mangled by hands of eager men. . . . The battle was a gory ghastly melee, and the river Unius rushed with corpses.[51]

The Mórrígan appeared, encouraging the Tuatha Dé Danann to fight harder and the Fomorians were beaten back to the sea. Ogma fell at this battle, as did Indech, son of Dia Domnann, king of the Fomorians. Bres was spared for telling the Tuatha Dé Danann how to plough, sow and reap. Then the Mórrígan proclaimed victory for the Tuatha Dé Dannan throughout Ireland.

Manannán mac Lir He may be seen as the Irish Neptune, or sea god. His name means son of the sea (*lir*). Often represented as riding through the waves on horseback, he is thus encountered by Bran (*see:* Imram Brain*). Manannán was then on his way to Ireland to sire a son by the wife of Fiachna, king of Ulster (*see:* Mongán*). Manannán is recorded as having come to Fiachna's aid in battles in Scotland against Saxons.

Manannán is also a sun god. His daughter Áine,* sometimes referred to as his wife, is also a sun goddess. The sun god was at times seen as having the form of a horse. A French riddle asks, 'What runs faster than a horse, crosses water and is not wet?' To which the answer is 'the sun'.[52]

P. W. Joyce[53] recorded an oral tradition prevalent in the Isle of Man and the eastern counties of Leinster that Manannán had three legs on which he rolled along on land, wheel-like, always surrounded by 'a magic mist'. This image is the origin of the three-legged Manx symbol, a wheel with three legs, which may be seen as a sun-symbol suggesting movement.

Cúchulainn* fell in love with Manannán's wife Fand, living with her for a month. He returned to Cenn Trachta near Newry and Manannán appeared to Fand in a 'magic mist'. When she recognised him she said:

When Manannán the great married me

I was a wife worthy of him.
A wristband of doubly tested gold
he gave me as the price of my blushes. . . .

Fand left with Manannán who shook his cloak between her and Cúchulainn so that they might never meet again in time.

Manannán has associations with birds, with hounds and with pigs. It is said that his pigs were such that although eaten today they are alive and ready for slaughter again to-morrow. Manannán was in possession of a bag, made from the skin of a crane. This bag, known in legend as the Crane Bag, contained all the treasures of the Tuatha Dé Danann.* Its contents included such things as the shirt and knife of Manannán, the king of Lochlainn's helmet, a smith's hook and the bones of Asal's swine.

The origin of this story is that Aífe, daughter of Delbaeth,* had been turned into a crane by Luchra out of jealousy for a lover. It was her skin that had been made into 'the crane bag'.

A good vessel of treasures will be made of thy skin —
no small event; its name will be — I do not lie —
in distant times the crane bag.[36]

Manannán is often regarded as overlord of the Tuatha Dé Danann, and as the god who distributed all the síde among the Tuatha, so that none was left for him. This is why he is always moving from síd to síd, and why he dwells beyond the *síde* in Eamain Ablach (Emain of the apple trees). Manannán makes an agreement with the farmer Cian, that he will come to his aid in retrieving his cattle in return for half of his booty. After many adventures Cian returns with a son, which he has had by Balor's* daughter. Rather than give 'half of his booty' to Manannán, Cian gives him the boy and Manannán calls him Ioldánach or master-craftsman. This Ioldánach is Lug's* nickname, thus Balor's grandson becomes Manannán's adopted son and champion of the Tuatha Dé Danann.

Legend has this popular overlord of the Celtic pantheon bringing Cormac mac Airt* into the Otherworld,* where Manannán is in charge of the feast of the Lords, which feast made the Tuatha lords invisible. It is he who institutes the Fled Goibnend, which gives the Tuatha Dé Danann eternal life, and it is his pigs which give the warriors eternal food washed down with the ale of immortality. It is said that with his magic he concealed from human eyes the above feasting which took place in the fairy hills or *síde*. Legend has it that as a shape shifter

112

Manannán appeared in various forms at a famous feast at Ballyshannon, east of Donegal Bay in the 16th century. The host at this feast was the historical Black Hugh O'Donnell, who died in 1537.

The 20th-century writer James Joyce has Manannán in *Ulysses*, rising chin on knees from behind a coal scuttle. A cold seawind blows from his druid mantle. Above his head writhe eels and elvers. He is encrusted with weeds and shells. He 'wails with the vehemence of the ocean, "Aum! Baum! Pyjaum! I am the light of the homestead. I am the dreamery creamery butter".'[101]

Medb Belongs to the ambiguous goddesses of dawn and dusk, found allied at one time with light, at another with darkness'.[26] The name has been related to the English 'mead' and the Sanskrit *madhu*, meaning 'honey, or sweet drink'. In India *madhu* is also one of the Daityas, a clan of demons. The queen of the fairies in Shakespeare is Mab. The old Irish word *medb* is translated as strong and also intoxicated.

The Táin describes Medb as a 'beautiful, pale, longfaced woman with long flowing hair, having a crimson cloak fastened with a brooch of gold over her breast, a straight ridged spear flaming in her hand'.[22]

Many scholars regard Medb as an historical queen of Connacht. Both Heinrich Zimmer and Kuno Meyer felt her to be, and Eoin MacNeill felt that she reigned at the beginning of the Christian era. Eugene O'Curry agrees with this view, pointing to mention of her in documents from the eighth century onwards as evidence that she was a real personage. Alfred Nutt disagrees with these views, regarding the Cycle of Ancient Stories as wholly mythic, and T.F. O'Rahilly supports this interpretation, stating that 'leading characters in ancient Irish history such as Bricriu and Medb are euphemerised divinities'. Professor Mac Cana[55] states that 'Medb's legend is not an historical document, nor indeed is she herself the historical personage she purports to be'. Two other noted scholars, Nora Chadwick and Myles Dillon, writing in their book *Celtic Realms*,[38] agree to disagree even with each other on this subject. Whatever about all this, Medb as 'queen of Connacht' will long outlive scholarly wrangling.

Medb's father was Eochaid Fedlech, king of Tara,* and she had two sisters Eithne and Clothru. Medb killed Clothru, who was pregnant, with the son of Conchobar mac Nessa.* This child 'was taken out of her side with swords'.[9] With Ailill as husband, Medb took over sovereignty from Clothru who until then had ruled and administered the laws of Connacht on Inis Clothrand on Lough Ree.

As queen of Connacht, residing in her palace at Cruachain* with

Ailill, Medb appears in famous tales connected with the Ulster Cycle or the Cycle of Conchobar mac Nessa and his Red Branch Knights (Craebh Ruad°). She is a leading character in three of our most famous stories, the story of Mac Datho's Pig (Scél Mucce Meic Da Thó), the Cattle Raid of Cooley (Táin* Bó Cualgne) and in the Feast of Bricriu* (Fled Bricrend). In the Táin Medb, leading the expedition against the Ulstermen, meets Fedelm, a seer of Connacht (*banfaith*). Medb asks her to use her skill in *imbas forosna** to predict the outcome of her battle with the Ulaid. Fedelm replies that she sees 'red, red, red'.

The Feast of Bricriu is an ancient saga from *Lebor na hUidre.** In this the Ulster heroes are contesting the right to 'the champion's portion', i.e., the right to have first cut of a freshly roasted pig. Medb and Ailill are judges of the contest. She welcomes the warriors' arrival at Cruachain:

> Mná finna fornochta friú
> aurchíche aurnochta etrochta. . . .

> Women to meet them, in *déshabille*,
> full-breasted and bare and bonnie, in number weel,
> bring vats of cold water where wanting,
> beds ready for rest,
> fine food bring ye forth, and not scanty but of the best.[9]

After three days Ailill found he could not make the judgement. Medb said that, in that case, she could. The contenders were Loegaire Buadach*, Conall Cernach* and Cúchulainn.* She arranged events so that each felt he had been given the champion's portion.

Medb had a desire for Cúchulainn. When she was presenting him with the champion's portion she placed her arms around his neck and planned it so that the Ulaid remained at Cruachain. 'They slept there that night. The women were apportioned among them. Findabair, with a train of fifty damsels, was brought into the stead of Cúchulainn. . . . Other women went to the other champion's groups, whilst 'Medb herself was wont to resort to the stead of Cúchulainn'.[9]

Although Ailill was king of Connacht, Medb had the final say. She wished to be the first to enter the mead hall at Bricriu's Feast, thus affirming her position as first woman of Connacht and Ulster as well. Her wants dictated events; she could take as lover whomsoever she desired, 'each man in another man's shadow'; and she could dispose of anyone she wished. 'She used to have thirty men every day or go with Fergus mac Roich once.'

Medb, the most earthy of Irish queens, can be seen as a goddess of war and fertility, perhaps the greatest of Ireland's pagan queens. Although appearing in the stories as an historical character, there are some legends which give her divine characteristics: just as the urinating of Aengus's* horse is seen in legend as welling up to form Lough Neagh, so too the water passed by Medb during the tale of the Tá in welled up to form Fual Medba, meaning literally 'Medb's urine'. Medb's further connections with water can be seen in that a tree by a sacred or holy well is called Bile Medb. Also, she was under a injunction (*see:* geis*) to bathe every morning in a spring at the end of the island known as Inis Clothrand on Lough Ree. It was whilst bathing here in the early morning that Furbaide put a piece of cheese in his sling and hurled it at Medb. The cheese went through her forehead, into her head, killing her. Thus Furbaide, son of Clothru, avenged his mother's death.

Medb is said to be buried under a very large cairn at Knocknarea, Co. Sligo. For centuries it has been a custom to carry a stone and place it on top of this cairn. Another resting place associated with Medb is Knockma, Co. Galway.

Medb Leithderg   She was daugher of Conan Cualann and wife of Art Aoinfear who was the king of Tara and son of Conn Cét Chathach.* Art Aoinfear, however, lived with and had children by a dowered mistress, Echtach; Medb lived closely by at Rath Medb which is a large rath or ring fort about half a mile from the Hill of Tara. This rath is named after Medb Leithderg.

Mesroída mac Da Thó   A Leinster landowner living at the time of Conchobar mac Nessa.* The story known as the Pig of Mac Da Thó (Scel Mucce Meic Da Thó) belongs to the Ulster Cycle. Mesroida's hound Ailbe was desired by both Queen Medb* of Connacht and King Conchobar of Ulster, who both sent messengers with their request. This so upset Mesroida that he could not sleep for three days.

> Cú Mes Roida meic Da Thó,
> ba holc lathe etha dá. . . .[41]

> The hound of Mesroida meic Da Thó,
> evil was the day they came for him;
> many fair men will fall for his sake,
> more than one can tell will be the fights for him.[69]

Mesroída's wife suggested that both the rulers should be offered the hound, and so both the messengers of Medb and Conchobar were told that it would be given to their ruler. This resulted in the arrival of warriors and courts from the two provinces. One half of Mesroida's hostel was set aside for the Connachta, the other for the Ulaid.

Mesroída had his pig killed for the warriors and then the problem of the champion's portion presented itself. The theme is similar to that of Bricriu's Feast, and here it is Bricriu* himself who, when asked how the pig should be divided, suggested a contest of arms to establish the right of first cut.

Cet mac Mágach of Connacht raised his weapon above the assembly, took his knife in his hand, and sat down by the king. Conchobar of Ulster told his warrior Loegaire to stop Cet from carving the pig. However, Loegaire was reminded of a previous encounter with Cet and he sat down. Then, one by one, the Ulaid sat down when reminded by Cet of previous combats. Then Muinremur mac Gergind* stood up.

> 'Is that Muinremur?' said Cet.
> 'It is he', said the men of Ireland.
> 'It was I that cleansed my hands in thee, O Muinremur', said Cet. 'It is not three days since out of thy own land I carried off three warriors' heads from thee together with the head of thy first-born son.'[69]

Muinremur sat down at that, and Cet was lifting his knife to carve when Conall Cernach* arrived. He told him to get up from the pig, saying that he never slept without the head of a Connacht man under his knee. Cet accepted that Conall was a better warrior then he, but that if his brother Ánluan mac Mágach were in the house he would be a match for Conall. 'But he is', said Conall (*'Atá immurgu ar Conall'*).[69] He took Ánluan's head out of his belt and threw it at Cet's chest 'so that a gush of blood broke over his lips'.

After that Cet withdrew and Conall took his knife to the pig. The decision had been made, and Conall carved, surrounded by the shields of the Ulaid. As he gave less than a quarter of the pig to the men of Connacht fighting broke out and, according to the storytellers, fourteen hundred men died as a result.

As the fight continued, Cúroí mac Dáire* from Munster arrived and tore up an oak tree by its roots. Attacking all and sundry with it, he left with half of the pig on his back. Mesroída took out his hound Ailbe, which chose to side with the Ulaid and attacked the Connacht warriors. Ailill and Medb got in their chariot and left for Cruachain.* The hound gave chase, seizing the pole of the chariot. The charioteer dealt the hound a blow which removed its head from its body, the head remaining on the pole of the chariot. This was at Ibar Cinn Chon (the yew-tree of the hound's head), from whence it is said that Connacht takes its name. However, it is more generally recognised that Connacht takes its name from Conn Cét Chathach.

The theme of this story, the 'Curad-Mír', the champion's portion, is based on the right of the champion to first cut of the pig from the communal cauldron. Nora Chadwick[56] calls this story 'probably the most anciently attested of all Celtic stories'. Mentioned in the *Book of Leinster* and before that in a poem by Flannacán mac Cellaig (said to have been slain by Norsemen in AD 896), it was one of the chief stories which the *filid* or poets of ancient Ireland used relate to kings and chiefs.

Midir   One of the lesser gods of the Tuatha Dé Danann,* living among the *aes síde*° (people of the mounds) at Brí Léith in Co. Longford. Midir had lived in the fairy mounds for a thousand years with Étaín as his wife, but, through the jealousy and magic arts of her rival Fuamnach, Étaín was carried off to undergo a second birth as the daughter of Étar, king of Echrade.

Although Étaín, as a mortal, eventually married Eochaid Airem, king of Ireland around 134 BC, Midir sought to reclaim her. Midir met Eochaid at Tara,* challenging him to a board game (*fidchell*°). Eochaid won the first few games and demanded that Midir use his powers to clear Meath of rocks and stones, to build a causeway across the moors and to cut down the forest of Brega. Midir did all this.

In a later game, Midir insisted that the stake would be whatever the winner demanded. He won, and his wish was to hold Étaín in his arms and obtain a kiss from her. Eochaid forestalled this request for a month, and in that time he had Tara ringed with warriors in order to exclude Midir from the palace. However, Midir suddenly appeared in the palace in front of Eochaid and demanded Étaín for himself. He then carried her off through the smoke hole of the house. The warriors outside then saw two swans circling round Tara until they flew away in the direction of Síd ar Femen (the present-day Slievenamon), Co. Tipperary.

Eochaid pursued them there, where he began to dig up each of the mounds in an effort to find his wife. This led to war with Midir and the *aes síde*. When Eochaid and his army began to dig Midir's mound at Brí Léith, Midir sent out sixty women all in the shape of Étaín. Eochaid, deceived, took one of these women, believing her to be his wife. The woman was Mes Buachalla,° a daughter of 'the fairy mounds'.

117

At a later stage in the story, Eochaid returned to Brí Léith, this time recovering Étaín herself and returning with her in triumph to Tara. In the end Midir took her back again, Eochaid was killed, and his head taken to a fairy hill. This story, Torchmarc Étaíne (the Wooing or Courtship of Étaín), is one of the chief tales of the Mythological Cycle.

Midir has connections with both Aengus* and Mannanán mac Lir.* Like Aengus and Caer he encircles Tara as a swan before flying away. As with Manannán, Midir is associated with cranes. He is possessor of three mysterious birds. Midir was also foster father of Aengus whose help he received in recovering Étaín. Aengus and the Dagda* also helped Midir clear plains and make rivers.

Brí Léith is situated on Ardagh Hill, Co. Longford. This is one of the most famous *síde* in Ireland, having connections with Midir, Aengus and the Dagda. Legend has it that Midir lives in the centre of the hill.

Míl   The ancestor of the Gaels,* Míl came from Galicia in north-western Spain. His full name is Míl Espane or Miles Hispaniae (the soldier of Spain). Míl's wife was called Scota, a word which is the Latin for 'Irishwoman'. O'Rahilly[2] states that 'Scotti was assumed to be related to Scythi', showing that the Gaels may originally have come from Scythia, an area in present-day Ukraine.

The dates given for the arrival of Míl's people, the Milesians, vary between 1498 BC (*Annals of the Four Masters*), 1342 BC (Philip O'Sullivan) and 1029 BC (*Annals of Clonmacnoise*). According to Macalister[57] the Milesians arrived around 500 BC, these being the iron-age invaders who overcame the Tuatha Dé Danann* at Tara,* establishing themselves as overlords of the many older tribes settled before their arrival.

The list of kings in the *Book of Leinster*,[41] compiled by the poet Gilla-Coemáin, places Lugaid Luaigne as king of Ireland in 192 BC. Lugaid was great grandson of Míl and it may thus be inferred that between 350 BC and 250 BC is a more probable date for their arrival.

Nennius[58] states that the Milesians came to Ireland with a fleet of one hundred and twenty men. And it is generally held that they arrived in Kenmare, travelling across the Slieve Mish mountains to arrive eventually in Tara. The druid Caichér is said to have prophesied to Míl that Ireland was the land which his line was destined to rule.

In time, as the Milesian race became the dominant tribe, the bards or early genealogists traced all the kings back to Míl. The racial myth was further developed by the genealogists' tracing the ancestors of Míl himself back to Noah and Adam. A note in the *Book of Leinster*[41] states that 'he is no *fili* who does not harmonize and synchronize all the stories'.

Eoin MacNeill[36] states that the chief function of the *fili* was 'to reconstruct the early history of Ireland, and the central theory of its Irish history was that Ireland had been subject to the Milesian race for ages before the Christian era. The method of work was to make a study of the whole mass of popular mythological and heroic tradition, assigning to it a chronology which did not exist within it, and arranging all the events of tradition on a definite order of succession'.

Although there is no mention of Míl in the early Ulster or Connacht stories, with time the whole Irish aristocracy 'was grafted on a single genealogical tree'. MacNeill concludes his genealogical investigation by stating 'the authentic genealogies reach back only as far as AD 300' and that all the genealogical material from an earlier date, uniting earlier races to the Milesian stem, is the work of the harmonising and synchronising school.[36]

Mis Mis was the daughter of Daire Mór. When Daire Mór was defeated at the battle of Ventry, Mis went to the battleground to seek his body; when she found it, she began to drink the blood from the wounds. After this she went mad and fled to Sliabh Mis, where she stayed for three hundred years. He hair grew so long that it swept the ground behind her; she became wild. She ate animal and human flesh. The area where she lived (barony of Clonmaurice) became barren. A reward was offered for her alive; those who tried to capture her were killed, except Dubh Ruis, the harper to the king.

Dubh Ruis went to Sliabh Mis and played his harp to Mis. He stayed with her for two months, 'until the hair which had covered her body was all gone'. Her reason was restored then. Dubh Ruis was killed whilst collecting rent in the barony of Clonmaurice. Mis then issued a lament for her dead love. The story is known as the 'Lost Legend of Mis and Dubh Ruis'.

Mog Ruith Literally, servant of the wheel:

> The reign of nineteen successive kings
> was the life of Mogh Ruith with much fighting.
> From Roth son of Rioghall, great the fame
> To Cairbre Lifechair the strong.

Mog Ruith was the sun god symbolized by the wheel. He was the ancestor of the Fir Maige Féne, a tribe associated with the north-east of Cork, but particularly with Fermoy. He was said to have lost one eye; leaving him with one eye, this reminds us of Balor* the sun god.

Mog Ruith drove in a chariot made of white metal and of lustrous gems. The chariot represents the sun which moves across the heavens; thus for those who sat in this chariot the night was as bright as the day. Also associated with Mag Ruith is Roth Rámach or the 'oared wheel', and Roth Fáil or the 'wheel of light'. In a poem attributed to St Columcille the Roth Rámach is described as a huge ship which sailed across the sea and land. A 'remnant' of this wheel has been identified with a pillar stone at Cleghile, near Tipperary town.

Throughout Europe, the wheel-god is identified as the sky-god, Jupiter. In Gaul and the Rhineland many altars were dedicated to Jupiter; these included the wheel. Like Balor the name of Mag Ruith was used over a period of time by noted personages. This custom is called euhemerization. Thus in time Mog Ruith becomes a druid from Sliabh Luachra, who dwelt on Valentia Island, Co. Kerry, in the territory of Corcu Duibne. Mog Ruith is an ancestor deity of the Corcu Duibne.

When Cormac ua Cuinn, king of Tara, laid siege to Munster, the king, Fiachu Muillethan, sought help from Mog Ruith, who laid spells against the Tara men and defeated them at the battle of Druim Damgaire (now Knocklong), Co. Limerick. In reward for this victory, Fiachu granted Mog Ruith and his descendants the territory of Mag Féne, which extends from the Nagle Mountains to the Ballyhoura hills in north Cork. However, another version of this story is that Fiachu defeated Mac Con and the Corcu Loígde. Thus it was more a local battle within Munster between two local kings and between two local tribes, the Corcu Loígde and the Corcu Duibne.

As a sun god Mog Ruith was regarded as the chief enemy of Christianity. Thus the euhemerized Mog Ruith learned his magic from Símón Druí (Simon Magus) who attempted to show his superiority to St Peter by ascending into the air in a fiery chariot. (A 'remnant' of this wheel is the aforementioned pillar stone near Tipperary town.) As a result of this the wheel was seen as a weapon of destruction; it was said that before Judgment Day it would 'come over Europe' as a punishment for the way in which a 'disciple from each nation co-operated with Simon Magus in his opposition to St Peter'.[2]

In a late poem Mog Ruith is mac Seinfheasa, 'son of ancient wisdom'. Finally Anroth (glowing wheel) is the mythical ancestor of the Eoganacht and Mac Roth, the servant of Medg and Ailill, who circled Ireland in a single day.

Mongán   Sired by Manannán mac Lir,* Mongán's mother was the wife of Fiachna, king of Ulster. Whilst Fiachna was away fighting for King Aedan of Scotland, Manannán mac Lir visited his wife in his fortress in Rath Mór (Rathmore) of Moylinny, Co. Down. In common with many mythological characters, Mongán was known for his shape-changing.

> He will be in the shape of every beast
> both on the azure sea and on land,
> he will be a dragon before hosts,
> he will be a wolf of every great forest.[39]

Mongán's world is older than the narratives of battle and chivalry, possibly older than the Fenian Cycle. However, certain dates show Mongán in an 'historical setting'; stories about him have been regarded as being preoccupied with the 'bizarre and complicated'.[59] In keeping with this it is said that as Finn mac Cumaill* he brought about the death in AD 284 of Fothad Airgthech, king of Ireland. At a later date the *Annals of Clonmacnoise* state: 'AD 624 Mongán mac Fiaghna, a very well spoken man, and much given to the wooing of women, was killed by one Bicoir, a Welshman, with a stone'.

However, Mongán is not one to be contained by time and place; he is another 'traveller of the heavens', to use a chapter-heading of T.F. O'Rahilly.[2] Perhaps the earliest adventure recorded of Mongán was when Manannán mac Lir took him from Rathmore to the Land of Promise (Tír Tairngire).° This happened when he was three days old. He stayed in the Otherworld* until he was twelve. At sixteen he returned to Ulster. Mongán's father was killed by Fiachna Dub in AD 622[5] and Mongán avenged this by killing Fiachna. He then became king of Ulster, his home being the fortress of Rath Mór in Moylinny.

Mongán relates his adventures

Once, whilst at a gathering on the Hill of Uisneach,* a heavy shower of hailstones fell. Mongán's wife Fintigernd, (fair one), also known as Bréothigernd (flame-lady) reminded him that it was now seven years since he had promised to tell her his adventures. Now was the day to tell her of them. Mongán arose from the gathering with his queen and seven men, including his shanachie Cairthide. They came to a prominent fortress with a frontage of ancient trees and entered. Inside, Mongán had a frenzy (*buile*), and, during this frenzy he told Findtigernd of his adventures. Although appearing to be only one night, the telling of his story took a whole year. Afterwards, he found the fortress to be his own palace at Rathmore, Co. Down.

Mongán and Dub Lacha

Dub Lacha was the daughter of Fiachna Dub. Born at the same time as Mongán, she fell in love with him.

> She bared her breasts to Mongán and as he looked upon them, he beheld the great paps which were soft and white. And desire for the girl came upon him and Dub Lacha observed it.[39]

They became husband and wife but the king of Leinster, who had a commitment of 'friendship without refusal' from Mongán, requested Dub Lacha. She was given to the king, but Mongán continued to visit her. When the king found out about this Mongán was turned away. He fell into a wasting sickness.

After a year of longing Mongán sought the aid of the Cailleach* Cuimne. They changed shapes, Mongán into Aed, son of the king of Connacht, and the cailleach into Ibhell of the Shining Cheek. In this form they were entertained in the house of the Leinster King.

Mongán put a love charm into the cheeks of Ibhell, and the king desired her. He offered to exchange Ibhell for Dub Lacha. This was agreed, and they 'indulged themselves until they were drunk and hilarious'. The following day when he awoke the king of Leinster found lying in his bed the grey tall hag, Cailleach Cuimne, and nearby a dog with a twisted halter round his neck and a pack saddle.

> 'Art thou the grey-backed hag of the mill?'
> 'I am', said she.
> 'Pity that I should have a slept with thee, O Cuimne', said he.[39]

And Mongán with Dub Lacha had long since departed on fresh steeds with 'the swiftness of wind in them'.

> Cammán's daughter was Dub Lacha,
> The beloved of Mongán, their offspring was good. . . .[41]

Mongán and Eochu Rígéces

Although Mongán and Dub Lacha are said to have had children, as in

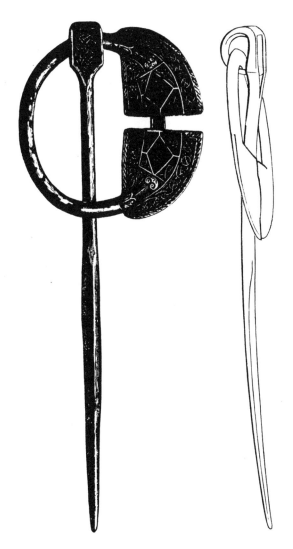

A brooch of white bronze,
found in Co. Roscommon
(actual size): 'It is not
right to put in that cloak
less than a brooch of
fine white bronze' (page 125)

the above story, the story of Mongán and Eochu contradicts this.

Eochu Rígéces was chief poet of the Ulaid but he feared the learning of the king's son Mongán. The companions of Mongán goaded him into showing up the ignorance of Eochu. This Mongán did by having some boys ask Eochu about the origins of six large pillar stones. He was unable to answer, not knowing that the Ulaid raised pillar stones to the number that they slew. Twice more Eochu was questioned and, failing to answer, he was put to shame. He blamed Mongán for his humiliation. Reproaching him, he said: 'The great sport thou hast made for thyself, thou shalt be without sport in consequence of it. Thou shalt have no issue . . . thou shalt not leave any great inheritance'.[60]

Mongán died, as noted in the *Annals of Clonmacnoise*, at the hands of a Welshman:

> Is fúar in geath dar 'ile,
> Dosfuil ócu Cind Tíre. . . .
>
> Cold is the wind across Ile,
> Which they have at Ceann-tire [Kintyre];
> They shall commit a cruel deed in consequence,
> They shall kill Mongán son of Fiachna.[5]

Mór Muman (Mór of Munster) Both a sun goddess (*tá Mór 'na suidhe*, the sun is up, *tá Mór 'na luighe*, the sun is setting;) and Sovereignty (*see:* Cailleach*), she was the daughter of Áed Bennáin, king of Irluachair (in Kerry) and of the Eoganacht* of Loch Léin (Co. Kerry).

Like Suibne Geilt* she had visions, heard voices from the air, and could leap or fly. She was for a while in a state of enchantment (*admilliud*) or exaltation or frenzy (*buile*). In this state she leapt over the ramparts of the fortress wherein she lived and wandered for two years throughout Ireland. '*Coro dubai fri gréin agus gáith hi certib agus lothraib*';[41] she was blackened by the sun and wind, [and dressed] in rags and fleeces. After this time she came to Cashel, Co. Tipperary.

She looked after the household stock like Mes Buachalla,° and like the latter ended up living with the king. One day she came into the royal house after the herd and the king's wife told him that he must sleep with Mór. Fíngen mac Áeda was the king. The queen made the bed for them and gave Fíngen her brooch to give to Mór: 'The maiden left the rags below and went to him in the bed. "Who are you, maiden?" asked Fingen. Then she told her name and her senses came to her. She remained with the king, wearing the queen's purple cloak and the queen's brooch in her cloak'.

A verse which seems apt here is translated by Kenneth H. Jackson from a fourteenth century Irish poem by Fearchar ó Maoilchiaráin: 'It is not right to put in that cloak less than a brooch of fine white bronze, or a marvellous brooch of goldsmith's work, my sweet-spoken red-lipped Mór'.[96]

Whilst she was living with Fíngen, as his wife, she bore him a son named Sechnasach mac Fíngin. Soon after this Fíngen died and Mór went from Cashel to Glennamain (in Kerry) where Cathal mac Finguinne was king. The kingdom of the Eoganacht rotated from Cashel to Glennamain and from there to Áine (in Limerick) and back to Cashel. That Mór Muman as sovereignty should be associated with these places is understandable as it was she who conferred the kingship. Thus it is that Cathal also is attracted to Mór: 'O woman there, do not pour out continuous lamentation for the dead man who has gone to the ground; love someone who will not cause you displeasure, until he himself dies'[41] (translated by Fergus Gillespie).

In Mór of Munster we find an earlier goddess living on in historical times. She with whom 'every noble woman in Ireland is compared', being particularly associated as mother-goddess to the Eoganacht kings of Munster.

Mórrígan *'Tri ingena aile dano Ernmais, Badb agus Macha agus Mórrigu.*[41] Ernmas (iron-death) had three daughters: Badb,* Macha* and Morrigu'.

The Mórrígan is often referred to as the great queen. She is the war fury par excellence. She is identified with Anu 'the mother of the Irish gods'; and she, Badb and Macha are known collectively as the Mórrigna, a triad of war/fertility sorceresses.

The Mórrígan met the Dagda* on the River Unius in Corann, Co. Sligo, at the great pagan feast of Samain.* She was washing herself, 'one foot on the south bank, the other on the north'. They conversed and then mated over water, this being part of the ancient fertility ritual. The 'Bed of the Couple' is the name of this place.

Afterwards she foretold to the Dagda the attack on the Tuatha Dé Danann* by the Fomorians.* Thus she prophesied the second battle of Mag Tuired,* telling the Dagda to summon the skilled men to meet her at the River Unius. The Mórrígan killed Indech, a Fomorian, giving handfuls of his blood to the waiting warriors.

Before the battle, the Mórrígan went with Badb and Macha to the

Mound of the Hostages at Tara,* and here they sent forth 'a cloud of mist and a furious rain of fire, with a downpour of red blood from the air onto the warriors' heads'. The Mórrígan then entered the battle, pursuing all those that fled. The battle won, she proclaimed victory to *dia síd cairib* (the fairy hosts) and to the 'gods of the high waters and to the gods of the rivermouths'. She then prophesied the end of the world:

> I shall not see a world that will be dear to me.
> Summer without flowers,
> kine will be without milk,
> women without modesty,
> men without valour,
> captures without a king. . . .
> an evil time![51]

Before the Cattle Raid at Cooley (the Táin),* the Mórrígan emerged from the *síd* at Cruachain.* She journeyed from Roscommmon to the Cooley Peninsula in Co. Louth, bringing a cow to the bull of Dáire mac Fiachna.

> . . . a chariot harnessed with a chestnut horse. The horse had but one leg and the pole of its chariot passed through its body, so that the peg in front met the halter passing across its forehead. Within the chariot one saw a woman, her eyebrows red and a crimson mantle round her. Her mantle fell behind her between the wheels of the chariot so that it swept along the ground. A big man went along beside the chariot. He also wore a coat of crimson, and on his back he carried a forked staff of hazelwood, while he drove a cow before him.[17]

On this journey the Mórrígan met Cúchulainn* who claimed ownership of the cows of Ulster. To this, she replied, 'I am a female satirist and the man is Dáire mac Fiachna of Cuailgne, I carry off this cow as a reward for a poem.'[17] Cúchulainn prepared to spring at her, but all disappeared. The Mórrígan had changed into a blackbird.

Later, prophesying the Táin she told Cúchulainn that the calf of her cow would still be a yearling when Cúchulainn would die. Then, during the Táin, she meets him, offering land and her love. He replies that he is fighting a battle and does not have time for 'women's behinds'. Angered, the Mórrígan threatens to kill him by various ploys. It is the Mórrígan who breaks the chariot wheels of Cúchulainn before his death. It is she who perches on his shoulder as a hooded crow.

The Mórrígan appeared before the battle of Mag Rath in AD 637, grey-haired, in the form of a lean, nimble hag, hovering and hopping about on the spears and shields of the royal army who were to be victorious. Her last recorded appearance was at the battle of Clontarf in 1014.

Mórrígan's name is associated with several places. In the present Co. Louth there is a district anciently known as Gort na Mórrígna or the Mórrígan's Field. The Dagda gave her this field. Fulacht na Mórrígna near Slievenamon in Co. Tipperary is an ancient 'cooking-place' known as the Mórrígan's Hearth. In the Boyne Valley there is Mur na Mórrígna, the Mound of the Mórrígan. Tirreeworigan, Co. Armagh, contains her name.

Comparisons exist between the Mórrígna, as Irish war goddesses, and the Valkyries of Norwegian and Germanic tradition. The Valkyries also often appear three in number, one of them often being the special companion of a particular hero, assisting him. However, unlike the Valkyries, the Mórrígna are never the direct cause of the hero's death. The Irish goddesses appear in the form of birds, especially that of a scald crow, while the Valkyries appear as swans. Similarities and links between these traditions bring us back to a time when the Rhineland Celts and the Germans mixed together.

Finally the town of Mainz, situated on the Rhine, was in Roman times called Mogontiacum after the goddess of light, Mogona. Mogona is also a mother goddess and Celtic, as is her Welsh equivalent Modron and the Arthurian goddess Morgain la Fée. The Mórrígán, Modron and Mogona would seem to be the same mother goddess originating in the warm, fertile lands of the Rhine.

Muinremur mac Gerrcind   A tribal god of the Mugdornaí, his name meaning 'fat-neck', Muinremur was a two-headed god, one the head of a bearded man, the other the head of a ram. He was one of the gods of Sliab na Trí nDé;° the original stone head now in the National Museum in Dublin, known as the 'Carraghy Head' from Co. Cavan, may be Muinremur. It is said that this head originated in Yorkshire, England.

Muinremur was one of the heroes of Ulster at the time on Conchobar mac Nessa.* It was he who claimed the honour of dissecting the pig of Mesroída mac Dathó.*

After Muinremur is named Loch Muinreamhair, now Lough Ramor, near Virginia, Co. Cavan on the borders of Co. Meath. One version of how he got his name is that the Connacht hero Cet mac Mágach cast a spear at him, striking him in the neck, causing it to swell up, thus becoming thick.

Nemed mac Agnomain Said to have come from Scythia on the northern shores of the Black Sea (Mare Euxinum), 'through the north-west side of Asia and the north-east part of Europe'. He gave his name to the Nemedians, one of the five successive colonies recorded as having arrived in Ireland.[15] His fleet consisted of thirty-four ships, each carrying thirty people. They sailed from the Black Sea, through the Bosphorus, across the Mediterranean, by the Straits of Gibraltar and then northwards to Ireland.

Four lakes are recorded[4] as having erupted during his time. These are Lough Loughall, Co. Armagh; Lough Ramor, Co. Cavan; and Loughs Derravaragh and Ennell in Co. Westmeath.

Nemed's wife was Macha.* She died after being in Ireland for twelve years and she was buried at Árd Macha, the present-day Armagh, named after her.

Nemed built two royal forts. Rath Chinn Eich, near Derrylee, Co. Armagh, and Rath Cimbaeith, near Island Magee, Co. Antrim.

During Nemed's time twelve plains were cleared, among them were Mag Cera, in the barony of Carra, Co. Mayo; Mag Cúile Toladh in the barony of Kilmaine, Co. Mayo; and Mag Luirc in Co. Roscommon.

Nemed fought and won three battles against the Fomorians* — at Slieve Bawn, Co. Roscommon; Rosneaghan, Co. Mayo and Murlough Bay, Co. Antrim.

In the battle of Camross, Co. Carlow, both Nemed's son Artur and grandson Lobcan were killed.

> During the battle of Cnámros [Camross], which was very
> > great,
> it is much there was of hacking of flesh;
> Artur and Lobcan fell there,
> although in it Gann was routed.[4]

Nemed and two thousand of his followers died of the plague in Oilén Árda Nemid or Great Island (Barrymore) in Cork Harbour. The Fomorians then imposed heavy taxes to be paid every year on the eve of the Samain.* This resulted in the Nemedians attacking the Fomorian stronghold at Tor Conaing (Tory Island), off Donegal. Defeated in this, the Nemedians left Ireland with the exception of a small number who remained under servitude to the Fomorians until the arrival of the Firbolgs.

A grandson of Nemed, Britán Mael, went to the north of Scotland, living there until the arrival of the Picts. It is said that Britain* is named after this chieftain; and thus Nemed can be considered ancestor of the Britons.

> Briotán went beyond sea, without stain,
> generous son of red-sided Fearghus;
> the Britons all, victory with renown,
> from him, without deception, they have descended.[4]

Niall Noígiallach   Niall of the Nine Hostages was son of Eochaid Mugmedón* and became king of Ireland in AD 379. His mother was Cairenn,* a Saxon princess taken hostage by his father.

As king of Tara,* Niall was distinguished for foreign conquest, leading a large invasion of Britain towards the end of the fourth century. Landing with a large fleet in Wales and carrying off plunder he was forced into retreat by the Roman general Stilicho. The Roman poet Claudian, praising Stilicho in a poem in which he speaks in the person of Brittania, says, 'By him was I protected when the Scot [Niall] moved all Ireland against me, and the ocean foamed with their hostile oars'.[53]

The extensive scale of these raids is indicated in the 'Confession' of St Patrick who says that he was brought captive to Ireland with thousands of men. The raids included attacks on Gaul and in one such raid Niall was assassinated on the banks of the River Loire, near Boulogne, by one of his own chiefs, Eochaid mac Énna Cinnselaigh. It was AD 405, the twenty seventh year of Niall's kingship of Ireland. His body was taken home and buried at Ocha (Faughan Hill), ten miles north-west of Tara.

> Westwards from Teamair went
> the band of his powerful retinue;
> then there was after sorrow,
> great lamentation of Niall's people.
>
> In high Ochan
> everyone bade farewell to the others,
> men of Leinster, of Munster,
> of Connacht, of Lí and of Lorg.[62]

Niall represents the Historical Cycle of Irish tales; his people, the Uí Néill, who may have been connected with the Connachta, rising fairly rapidly in power and influence. This sudden emergence of a new aggressive order causes even sceptical historians to accept that Niall most likely existed. However, his historical existence is interspersed with older mythological motifs occurring in such stories of Niall as the following:

Niall and his step-brothers, sons of Mongfhind, see a *cailleach** in a wood. She will only grant them the right to draw water from a well if they give her a kiss. Niall kisses and passionately embraces her and she changes into a young and beautiful woman. He asks her who she is and the *cailleach* replies that she is Sovereignty* and that Niall shall be king of Tara and his 'seed shall be over every clan'. The theme of sovereignty tales is that the hero must sleep with the earth goddess, for unless he does he shall not be king of Ireland.

Niall had fourteen sons, of whom eight left issue. Laegaire, ancestor of the O'Coindhealbháins or Kendellans; Conall Crimthainne, ancestor fo the O'Melaghlins; Fiacha, ancestor of the Mageoghegans and the O'Molloys; Maine, ancestor of the O'Caharny (now Fox), the O'Briens and the Magawleys.

All of the above tribes remained in Co. Meath, but Niall's other four sons settled in Ulster where they acquired extensive territories. Eoghan was ancestor of the O'Neills and Conall Gulban, ancestor of the O'Donnells. Cairbre's descendants settled in the barony of Carbury in Co. Sligo and in the barony of Granard, Co. Longford. Énda Finn's people settled in Tír Énda in Donegal and in Cinél Énda, near the hill of Uisneach* in Westmeath.

In a dirge for King Niall of the Nine Hostages, Torna (who took Niall as a child from the plain of Tara, where he was left to die) recited:

> Saxons will ravage her in the east,
> noble men of Erin and Alba,
> After the death of Niall, Echu's noble son —
> it is a bitter cause of reproach.

To which Tuirn, Torna's son, replied:

> Saxons, with overwhelming cries of war,
> hosts of Lombards from the continent,
> from the hour in which the king fell
> Gael and Pict are in a sore straight.

Nuadu Argatlám   Nuadu of the Silver Arm was king of the Tuatha

Dé Danann* for seven years before they came to Ireland.[15] In the first battle of Mag Tuired,* in which the Tuatha Dé Danann beat the Fir Bolg,* Nuadu's arm was hewn off. His physician Dian Cécht replaced it with a silver arm (*airgatlám*) 'with activity in every finger and every joint'. However, because of his disability, Nuadu was disqualified from sovereignty for seven years.

During this period Nuadu's cousin Bres* became king. After that, Nuadu reigned for another twenty years, his return to the kingship being celebrated at Tara* at a meeting which led to preparations being made for the second battle of Mag Tuired. At this battle Nuadu was slain by Balor* of the Mighty Blows, after which Lug* became king.

Nuadu had four sons, Tadg the Great, Caither, Cucharn, and Etarlam the poet. Nuadu was buried in the Grianán of Aileach, a tumulus at the base of the Inishowen peninsula between Lough Swilly and Lough Foyle in Co. Donegal.

> In Mag Tuired, it was through battle
> Nuadu Airgetlám fell:
> and Macha — that was after Samain —
> by the hand of Balor the strong smiter.[15]

Nuadu and Lug show certain features in common. Lug is connected to the Welsh Ludd who is called Lludd Llaw Ereint, Lludd of the silver hand or arm. The Irish Lug is Lug Lámfhota (long-hand). Both Nuadu and Lug are gods of the Tuatha Dé Danann, it being related that Lug took over leadership without conflict even while Nuadu was still alive. When Balor slays Nuadu with his 'evil eye', Lug slays Balor, and thus the Tuatha Dé Danann gods remain dominant over the Fomorian ones. Both Nuadu and Lug possess powerful weapons — Nuadu, the sword 'from whose stroke none could escape', and Lug, 'the invincible lance'. These were two of the four treasures brought to Ireland by the Tuatha Dé Danann.

The deities Nuadu and Lug occur throughout the British Isles in various related forms, e.g., Lug, Lludd, Nodons and Nuadu. The Welsh Lludd is connected to the British god Nudd.

The Irish Nuadu is identified with Nodons or Nodens, a deity whose chief sanctuary is the Romano-Celtic temple at Lydney Park, Gloucestershire: 'The sea monsters depicted in the mosaic pavements at Lydney Park have suggested that he was a sea-god; the "silver arm" conspicuous in his folklore being (rather fancifully) explained as a poetical description of a narrow strait of water between two islands'.[15]

The same source also says that Nuadu was a patron of wealth,

131

particularly in cattle, but goes on to say that there is a little substance in any of these theories. Ann Ross[32] says that the silver arm of Nodons may be the silver waters of the Severn, but she is doubtful of the connection. According to O'Rahilly[2] early accounts regard all the Irish as descended from Nuadu. Other accounts state that he was descended from Míl* and the Genealogical Tracts state that the Eoganacht,* the Dál Riata, the Ulaid, the Lagin and the Osraige descend from Nuadu.

Ogam A form of writing in which the letters are represented by combinations of parallel strokes in number from one to five, set in varied positions along a central stemline. It was originally intended for inscription upon upright pillar stones. The alphabet consists of twenty letters and five diphthongs; the letters were incised in groups of five, perhaps indicating some relationship to finger signs.

Ogam writing may well be pre-Christian in date. It seems to be of Irish origin, flourishing in Ireland between the fifth and eighth centuries AD (Some families of monumental sculptors used it as late as the early nineteenth century.)

Macalister[63] states that ogam derives from the Chalcidic form of the Greek alphabet, once current in northern Italy, in Cisalpine Gaul, the Roman side of the Alps, the present provinces of Piedmont and Lombardy. He states that it was used for secret communication, being part of the signalling or gesture system of 'druidic freemasonry'. However, other authorities generally hold ogam to be based upon the Roman alphabet.

Five foot high stone, at Drumconwell, Co. Armagh

132

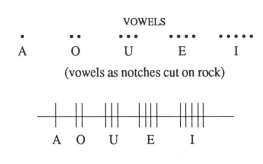

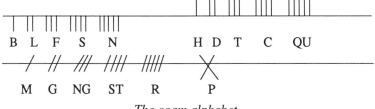

The ogam alphabet

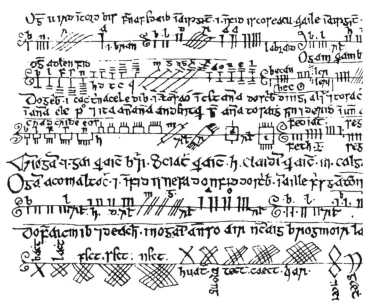

*Detail of a manuscript page showing ogam writing translated into
Old Irish*

Ogam in Ireland, according to Macalister, was used for magical or cryptical purposes. 'When paganism was waning the finger signs were used as a secret language and finally used for writing epitaphs'.

Ogam is the 'occult manner of writing used by the ancient Irish', according to the Highland Society of Scotland's *Dictionary of the Gaelic Language* (1828).

Charles Plummer[64] feels that there were uses for ogam stones other than as memorials to the dead, mentioning them as being used to show a border between two lands; the inscription on them being equivalent to a witness in determining territorial claims. O'Curry[65] states that a sale of land may have been recorded in this way.

The majority of ogam-inscribed stones are found in Kerry and Cork, a 1945 survey recording 121 and 81 respectively. This would appear to indicate that west Munster was the origin of the form. In Wales there are 15 ogam stones in Pembrokeshire, introduced by the Irish during their frequent raids there in the 4th and 5th centuries. In England there are 2 in Devon and 5 in Cornwall. Raftery[66] states that ogam writing was transferred to south-west Wales during migrations of the Dési.° Ogam characters are also found on the Isle of Man and in the north and east of Scotland. It is generally held that the Picts learned the script from the Irish settlers in Scotland.

An example of ogam is to be found at Cruachain,* where there are inscriptions on the lintel of the cave structure.

Could this be 'Froích son of Medb'? Froech* was the lover of Medb's* daughter Findabair,* and if, they were common law man and wife, he would have been Medb's son-in-law.

From Ballintaggart, near Dingle, Co. Kerry an early Christian inscription includes the following ogam:

translated as son of Efritt. Efritt was a monk who came from England to study in Ireland. The stone was a memorial to Efritt being in Ireland, rather than a headstone over his grave.

A nineteenth century ogam inscription in the graveyard of Ahenny, Co. Tipperary, written in two horizontal lines of Irish, translates as: 'Under this stone lies Mary Dempsey from Ballycranna'.

Ogma Son of Elathan and, with Lug* and the Dagda,* one of the three champions of the Tuatha Dé Danann.* Possession of all the *síde*° or mound-dwellings was divided among these three by the Dagda.

Ogma married Etan, the daughter of Dian Cécht, the god of healing. His sons included Tuirenn, whose sons in turn murdered Lug's father; this story is told in the saga, the Fate of the Children of Tuirenn (*see*: Iuchair* and Iucharba). Another son Cairpre became the poet of the Tuatha Dé Danann. Cairpre made what has been called the first satire in Ireland, on Bres* the Fomorian,* ending with 'May Bres's cheer be what he gives to others'. After this the Tuatha Dé Danann began to prepare for battle against their oppressors the Fomorians. At this time Ogma had a contest of strength with Lug which he lost, the contest involving the throwing of a flagstone out through the entrance to the fort or *lios*°.

During the second battle of Mag Tuired,* it is related[67] that Ogma slew Indech, a Fomorian leader. However, another version[15] has it that 'there fell Ogma son of Elada at the hands of Indech son of the Dé Domnann, king of the Fomoire'. It is also said that both Ogma and Indech were slain in this encounter. It could be that Ogma used the healing well of Dian Cécht and was restored to life by the magic spells of Dian Cécht's children.

After the battle of Mag Tuired, Ogma, with the other champions Lug and the Dagda, pursued the Fomorians to recover the Dagda's harp. Ogma's sword, it is told, related all the events of the battle and fighting. Ogma, thus, personifies the combination of warrior and orator. He is the patron of eloquence and literature and the fabled inventor of Ogam.* He is known as *Cermait* (honey-tongued). Ogma is also known as Ogma *Grianainech*, Ogma of the sun-countenance. Thus he may be traced back to the Gaullish god Ogmios. Anne Ross[32] tells of figures drawn on a piece of pottery from Richborough in Kent, England, where there is 'a deity with long curling hair with rays proceeding from his head'. This figure holds the whip of Sol Invicta, the Invincible Sun, and is accompanied by the name Ogmia. Lucian, the Greek poet, described Ogmios as wearing the skin of a lion and carrying a club. He states that the symbol of his power was a chain that fastened his tongue to the ears of those listening. Thus in Greek as well as Irish mythology Ogmios or Ogma is the god of eloquence or discourse.

A verse which connects Ogma with his *síd°* or Otherworld* resting place is as follows:

> Dead Nuada rests in the Grianan of Aileach;
> Ogma lies low in sídh Airceltrai;
> while the Dagda, thrust into the background by his
>   son Aengus,
> mixes little in the affairs of Érin.[67]

Oidheadh Cloinne Lir   That is, the Fate of the Children of Lir, one of the 'three sorrowful tales of Ireland', the others being the Exile of the Sons of Uisneach (Longes mac nUsnig)* and the Fate of the Children of Tuireann (Iuchair and Iucharba).*

A story wherein the narration binds the poems, it was collected in manuscript form before AD 1500 and belongs to the tradition of medieval Gaelic romances.

Lir, whose first wife had died, married the daughter of Bodb Derg, king of Connacht. Her name was Aebh, and she bore him twins Fionula and Aodh, and later Fiachra and Conn. This was followed by her death, and, seeking the comfort of his father-in-law, Lir was persuaded to marry yet again, this time to Aebh's sister Aoife.

Aoife became jealous of Lir's children and the attention paid by Lir to them. Ill with jealousy she took to bed, summoning a druid to her side for advice. She took the children to Loch Derravarragh in Co. Westmeath where her charioteer was to kill them. This he would not do, so Aoife and her retinue pushed the children into the lake and, with the druid's wand, she turned them into swans. Lir found out about this and turned Aoife herself into a grey vulture, doomed to live in the cold and windy air until the end of time.

The Children of Lir lived on Loch Derravarragh for three hundred years. They then flew to the sea of Moyle, the North Channel, Fionula chanting this lay:

> Arise, my brothers, from Darvra's wave,
> on the wings of the southern wind;
> we leave our father and friends today
> in measureless grief behind.
> Ah! Sad the parting, and sad our flight.
>
> To Moyle's tempestuous main;
> for the day of woe

shall come and go,
before we meet again!

They spent another three hundred years on the North Channel between Ireland and Scotland. Fionula chanted:

> Our life is a life of woe;
> no shelter or rest we find;
> how bitterly drives the snow;
> how cold is this wintry wind!
>
> From the icy spray of the sea,
> from the wind of the bleak north east,
> I shelter my brothers three,
> under my wings and breast.
>
> Our stepmother sent us here,
> and misery well we know;
> in cold and hunger and fear;
> our life is a life of woe![68]

Fergus and Aed, the sons of Bodb Derg, set out to find the children with a host of the Tuatha Dé Danann,* eventually finding them on the Moyle. They reported back to Lir and Bodb Derg that the swans were alive but enduring 'unspeakable suffering'. Later, the last three hundred years of their exile was spent on Irrus Domnann off Erris Head, Co. Mayo.

> The hour has come; the hour has come;
> three hundred years have passed;
> we leave this bleak and gloomy home,
> and we fly to the west at last!
>
> We leave forever the stream of Moyle;
> on the clear, cold wind we go;
> three hundred years around Glora's isle,
> where wintry tempests blow!
>
> No sheltered home, no place of rest,
> from the tempest's angry blast:
> Fly, brothers, fly, to the distant west,
> for the hour has come at last![68]

137

In the west they met Ebric who, legend has it, wrote down their tale. They then went to Inis Glóire, off north-west Mayo, where they died as humans with the grave of Fionula in the centre and her three brothers surrounding her. This grave can be seen today as four standing stones about a well. It is situated in Inis Glóire.

Oilill Olum His original name was Aongus Olum; he was called Oilill Olum (*oilill* meaning great blemish, *olum* meaning 'bare ear') after he ravished Áine, daugher of Eógabal. Áine bit his ear off in retribution for his rape of her and for his part in the death of her father. He had three deforming blemishes: he was 'ear cropped', his teeth had become black and his breath had become foul. He killed Áine with his spear: 'he drove his spear through her body into the earth'.[5]

Oilill Olum had nineteen sons, nine by Sadb, daughter of Conn Cét Chathach:

> Nineteen pleasant sons had the chief —
> The beauteous Oilill Olum;
> Of one sole trio the race did not decay,
> From whom have sprung the property of the free-born.

Oisín The great poet of the Fenian Cycle of Irish tales. Son of Finn mac Cumaill,* his mother Blaí is said to have borne him whilst she was in the shape of a doe. He is said to have returned to the *síd* of Blaí when he died. His name is said to mean 'little deer' or 'little seal'.

> Oisín mac Fhinn fear go n-goil
> ro geanoir a gCluain Iochtair
> ingein dheirg a mháthair mhaith,
> torrthach naoi míos ón mór fhlaith.

> Oisín, son of Fionn, a man of prowess,
> was born at Cluain Iochtair;
> the daughter of Dearg was his worthy mother,
> she bore him nine months in her womb.

It was the function of the *fili* or poet to record pagan or pre-Christian Ireland. Oisín is our perennial laureate and, indeed, the Fenian Cycle is sometimes referred to as the Ossianic Cycle and vice versa. However, the Fenian Cycle begins with the battle of Cnucha or Castleknock in

AD 174 and ends with the battle of Gabhra* or Garristown in AD 283, whilst the Ossianic Cycle goes beyond this historical period, firstly because Oisín survives the battle of Gabhra and secondly as he enters the Otherworld,* returning to Ireland after three hundred years.

Oisín takes part in many of the Fenian tales. Together with Finn, Caoilte,* Innsna, Oscar and Conán Maol, Oisín constitutes the *fian*,° the body of six warriors whose many adventures are recorded widely, notably in the works of Eoin MacNeill[36] and P.W. Joyce.[68] The Pursuit of Diarmuid and Gráinne* (Tóraigheacht Diarmada agus Gráinne) is perhaps the greatest saga from the Fenian Cycle. At the beginning of this story Gráinne is equal in her desire for both Oisín and Diarmuid but, as she is to be wedded to Finn, Oisín's father, she decides to elope with Diarmuid. Oisín supports Diarmuid in the elopement but warns him of the wiles of Finn. Thus begins the true adventure of the Fiana — flight and pursuit. It is these treks across countryside on horseback that Oisín memorably recalls:

> Erect your hunting spears, wherewith we once wounded the
>   white does:
> when we were in arms we made no fasting journey.
> Steer ye your rounded hulls to the brave knolls of Lochlainn;
> with your stout lances we slew slow-glancing Raighne.
> I am Oisín, though ancient: I have trysted with gentle women:
> grayness is nearest to brownness, bentness is nearest to
>   erectness. Erect.[36]

The Ossianic poem, the Lay of Oisín in Tír na nÓg, is, according to the nineteenth century scholar B.O. Looney, a poem which exhibits characteristics of a later date, as poems written between the fourteenth and eighteenth centuries. (He actually states that Tír na nÓg was written by Michael Comyn about the year 1749.) The poem gives an account of Tír na ndaoine maite (land of the good people), the Elysium of the pagan Irish. This account is told by Oisín to St Patrick, on his return to Ireland after a long time in the Otherworld.* (According to O'Looney Tír na nÓg is a small and beautiful city marked by white breaking waves between Lahinch and Liscannor, Co. Clare.)

Oisín tells how Niamh, a princess, arrived on a white horse by Loch Léin where the fian were hunting. She told Oisín to accompany her to the Otherworld:

> It is the most delightful country to be found,
>   of greatest repute under the sun

trees drooping with fruit and blossom
and foliage growing on the tops of boughs.[71]

Oisín leaves his father Finn and travels with Niamh due-west until
they come to the land of the 'King of Youth'. En route, he slays a giant.
In Tír na nÓg, he is given to Niamh of the Golden Hair as consort
forever by the king. He has two sons and a daughter by her.

After three hundred years Oisín returns to Ireland on a white steed,
with the warning from Niamh not to dismount, 'for if thou alightest
thouself, thou wilt be an old man, withered and blind'. On his return
Oisín found the famous fortress of the Fiana at Almu (Hill of Allen,
Co. Kildare) overgrown and unguarded. Then, at Glenasmole (glen of
the thrushes) in Co. Wicklow, a crowd of men asked his help in raising
a huge stone onto a wagon. He stooped to do so, but the reins snapped
and Oisín fell to earth. The white steed returned to the Otherworld, and
Oisín became an old man.

In his old age Oisín met St Patrick, the discussions between them
giving rise to Agallamh Oisín agus Phátraic (Dialogues of Oisin and
Patrick). It is said that, Oisín being feeble and unable to care for
himself, St Patrick took him in so that he might convert him.[69] Patrick
is angered by Oisín:

> Each silliness thou recountest
> O Oisín of the spoils, we would permit,
> save only the speaking reproachfully of God,
> by whom fell the fianna of Finn.

Oisín's answer to Patrick is related in the concluding verses of the
Lay of Sliab Guilleann.

> I abhor thee and thy God,
> I abhor thy clerics bawling;
> I would not need leave from thee or them
> to be forever displeasing Him . . .
>
> O Patrick of the croziers bright,
> by thy hand, I tell no lie,
> we would prefer to heaven itself,
> to have Finn in his health and appearance.

A more definitive reply from Oisín to Patrick is contained in the
Duanaire Finn, a poem that has an older ring to it.

Woe for them that wait on churchmen, that are not heard on the hardy fray.
Woe for them that are checked by decay, unsightly end of shelter.
Woe for a king's son that is faint hearted, that imposes not his fear on man.

Woe for him who forsakes his pointed lance for a horned yellow staff.
Oisin am I, the prince's son: I was wont not to put off battle:
To many a hero on the steed of strife I have given cause of woe.
Woe for them.

Another unambiguous reply to Patrick is given in 'The Hunger of Críonlach's Church', also from *Duanaire Finn*.

The hunger of Críonloch's church, I cannot bear it;
last of the royal prince's sons,
we have suffered a scanty fare.
Oscar, my heroic son, for whom songs of praise were made,
were he alive at present.
he would not leave me to hunger.
My curse upon thy churchmen, Patrick, and mayest thou rot!
If I had Oscar, he would not leave me to hunger.
I am Oisín ruddy-cheeked, son of Fionn, of honourable spirit:
I have had in my pay twenty hundred that knew no hunger.

The hunger.[36]

Finn, Oisín's father, had prophesied to him that he would be forced to carry stones for the Tailgeann (adze-head), a name applied to St Patrick. It is said that he did have to carry stones for St Patrick at Elphin, Co. Roscommon. A poem from a Belfast MS called 'Cold Elphin' describes the isolation and loneliness of Oisín.

I make no music, I find no feast,
I slay no beast from a bounding steed,
I give no gold, I am poor and old,
I am cursed and cold without wine or mead.[70]

It is chiefly as a poet revitalising sagas through verse that Oisín is remembered. The poem, 'The Battle of Gabhra'* (or Garristown) is attributed to him.

I myself was in the fight,
on the south side of the green Gabhair;
I killed twice fifty warriors,
it was I who killed them with my hand.
Music, boating rewarding,
the prey most difficult I chose;
I would kill a boar in the hard wood,
I would rob a vengeful bird of its egg.

That Ogam which is in the stone,
around which fell the slain,
were Finn the fighter of battles living,
long would he remember the Ogam.[85]

It is said that Oisín left St Patrick and was taken to a *gallán* or pillar stone on the plain of Kildare. He had his companion dig up the earth beside the *gallán* and there he found Finn's spear and war-horn.

A number of stories exist which tell of Oisín fighting a black bull for St Patrick. Oisín kills the bull and eats its flesh and, when St Patrick goes to find how the fight went, he sees Oisín asleep in the bull's hide. Oisín's request, in return for killing the bull, is that he be buried facing east on Slieve Gullion, Co. Armagh. It is said that Oisín is buried in the hide of the bull on Curran Mountain, near Manorhamilton, Co. Leitrim. A standing stone is said to mark this spot.[47] It is also said that he is buried at Síd Airceltrai, Downpatrick, Co. Down.

I throw down the chain of small stones!
When life in my body has ceased
I will go to Caoilte, and Conan, and Bran, Sgeolan, Lomair,
and dwell in the house of the Fenians,
be they in flames or at feast.[72]

Ollamh An *ollamh* was a poet and distinguished teacher who, according to the Brehon laws, should know and practise the *teinm laeda*,° the *imbas forosnai** and the *díchetal do chennaib*.°

It appears that the first of these was a druidical verse or incantation which bestowed the power of understanding. (It has been translated as 'gnawing the marrow'.) The second involves the receiving and imparting of knowledge in an inspirational way, and the third is the capacity to improvise in verse. The *ollamh* was also responsible for maintaining the genealogies and etymologies of names in Ireland.

There were four divisions of knowledge involved: (i) genealogies, synchronisms and the reciting of historical tales; (ii) knowledge of the seven kinds of verse, and how to measure them by letters and syllables; (iii) the ability to judge the seven kinds of verse; (iv) the contemplation and recitation of verses 'without even thinking of them before'.[34]

The *ollamh* was part of the king's court and he often combined the roles of poet, historian and storyteller, his function being to preserve historic stories in the 'original state' and recite them at feasts and assemblies. He was charged with knowing at least one seventh of the historical narratives. The institution of the *ollamh* lasted up to the sixteenth century. During the latter century William Camden, the Oxford antiquarian, recorded: 'These lords [i.e. the Irish kings and chiefs] have their historians about them, who write their acts and deeds; they have their physicians, their rhymers whom they call bards, and their harpers; all of whom have their several livelihoods, and have lands set out for them.'

Although the word *ollamh* is generally applied to the professions of poetry or history, it also meant a certain level of attainment in other areas. *Ollamh* was the highest rank one could attain in profession or art, thus we read 'Ollamh Builder' and so forth.

Quite often the *ollamh* would have students under him, working their way towards the position of *ollamh*, corresponding to 'master' builder or poet or whatever. Sometimes the number of students was large enough to constitute a school. Fees were paid for tuition, 'instruction without reservation, and correction without harshness, are due from the master to the pupil, and to feed and clothe him during the time that he is learning'.[53]

According to Brehon law also, the pupil was bound to help the *ollamh* in old age, supporting him if necessary. At certain times the *ollamh*, with his students, went on a *cuairt* (circuit), presenting his poetical compositions to kings and chiefs and receiving their hospitality and the gifts which were expected.

The Ollamh Finntan is quoted in the *Book of Lecan* as the authority on the colonies of Partholón* and on Nemed* of the Firbolg.* The Ollamh Eochaid Ua Floinn is quoted as an authority on the Tuatha Dé Danann* and the first battle of Mag Tuired.*

An example of the best in the *ollamh* tradition was Giolla Brighde mac Con Midhe, a thirteenth-century poet from Tyrone. He was of the bardic family Mac Con Midhe who settled around Ardstraw in Co. Tyrone. He was patronised by the O'Donnells and the O'Neills; a number of poems extant are to the O'Donnell family. His poems remained in use up as far as the sixteenth century. The following is an

143

extract from one of mac Con Midhe's poems in praise of the O'Donnells:

> Ó Domhnaill is dó budh cuibhdhe
> Ceannas Éireann as gach fháth,
> don rígh is fhearr san dá obair:
> teann sídh, teann cogaidh ar cách.

> Is é is fhearr d'fhulang an chonáigh
> nach cuirfeadh fa lár a locht;
> Is aga budh fhearr a gcumhang,
> treall fada d'fhulang a n-olc.

Ó Domhnall, it is to him that the leadership of Ireland would
be due for every reason, to the king who is best at the two
occupations: firmness in peace, firmness in battle against all
comers.

He is the best to sustain prosperity, a man who would not lay
his own people low; it is best that their straits should be borne
by him, so that he might tolerate their misfortune for a long
time.[73]

Otherworld   The world of the spirits and gods, also known in the
tales as *Mag Mell* (plain of honey), *Tír Tairngire* (land of promise), *Tír
na nÓg* (land of perpetual youth), Tír Beo (land of life), Tír n-aill (land
of the cliff) and Mag Már (the great plain).
  Mag Mell was the way to the Otherworld in the imrama*; it
consisted of the golden path the sun makes over the ocean between the
horizon and the observer. Thus Mag Mell was the route to eternity. The
Celtic doctrine is that the first ancestor of the human race is the god of
the dead. This God inhabits a distant region beyond the ocean. In Greek
mythology, the heroes that perished at Thebes and Troy found a second
existence 'at the ends of the earth'. Tetra the Fomorian and Kronos the
Greek god reside over 'the isles of the all mighty and the blest, near
the deep eddying ocean'.
  An underlying theme in many of the stories portrays the Otherworld
as a land which lies over the water; it produces inexhaustible food and
its inhabitants are invisible when they choose.[39] This Happy Otherworld or Celtic Elysium, as in the stories of Bran (Imram Brain*),
Connla and Oisín,* consists of a never-ending round of simple and
sensuous delights. Frequently in the stories the hero is summoned by

144

an Otherworld woman who is filled with love for him.

Michael Comyn, eighteenth-century poet, describes Niamh, who carried Oisín* to Tír na nÓg:

> Redder was her cheek than the rose,
> fairer the face than swan upon the wave,
> more sweet the taste of her balsam lips
> than honey mingled with red wine.

He also described the land:

> Abundant there are honey and wine,
> and aught else the eye has beheld,
> fleeting time shall not bend thee,
> death nor decay shalt thou see.

Overseas voyages to the Otherworld are known as the *imrama*,* these voyages bringing their crew to the Otherworld which is often situated off the west coast of Ireland in the Atlantic. The Otherworld has similarities with the Scandinavian Valhalla, wherein battles are fought and enemies conquered. Alfred Nutt has seen a connection between old ideas concerning the Otherworld's location and their resemblance to the land of Falga. This seems to have been an old name for the Isle of Man, home of Mannanán,* lord of the Otherworld. Nutt states that the notion of the Otherworld as a Western isle harks back to the time when the Gaels inhabited Britain and the Isle of Man was to their west.[39]

Equal in antiquity to the overseas Elysium is the identification of the *síde* or mounds as the dwelling place of the Otherworld gods. In the present day these gods have all but vanished, though there still exists a residual belief in fairies. Two main elements enter the *síd* belief. Firstly the veneration paid to great natural features, mountains and rivers being originally conceived as animated by a life of their own (for example, the Mórrígan* tells the trees and rivers of the outcome of the Táin*). Secondly, the *síd* are regarded as being the dwelling places of beings that are wiser and more powerful than man.

Regardless of location some would say there was in Irish pagan belief but one Otherworld, a joyous place of sensuous pleasure. With the spread of Christianity the Otherworld began to shed some of its more erotic components and thus, in the story of Connla, we find him living with his faery women in perpetual contemplation of each other, without any 'fleshly sin whatever'. A folk rhyme from the highlands of Scotland illustrates the survival of belief in Otherworld spirits and deities up to the turn of the nineteenth century.

> Bho gach gruagach is ban-síth
> Bho gach mí run agus brón. . . .

> From every witch-demon and ban-shee,
> from every evil wish and sorrow,
> from every nymph and water sprite,
> from every fairy mouse and grass mouse,
> from every spectre among the hills,
> from every demon hard pressing me,
> from every half man half goat within the glens,
> Shield me till the end of my day.[9]

Connla in the Otherworld

Connla, son of Conn Cét Chathach* is approached by a damsel on top of the hillside of Uisneach* who invites him to Mag Mell, the Plain of Delights. She departs, but leaves him an apple upon which he feeds for a month without any diminution of its size. When she returns she tells Connla of another land 'in which there is no one save only women and maidens'. Connla bounds into her gleaming currach, 'her ship of glass'. They sail away and are never heard of again. Mag Mell, where Connla went, is a land whose inhabitants live in a continuous present. Inhabitants of this plain choose certain mortals to whom they offer freedom from death and decay. People here seem to live on a magic food and return to earth is impossible.

Cormac mac Airt in the Otherworld

Cormac mac Airt* meets a grey-haired warrior on the Hill of Tara,* bearing a silver branch with three golden apples.

> Very sweet music did that branch make, wounded men and women in labour, and folk enfeebled by sickness, would be lulled to sleep by it.[74]

The stranger told Cormac that he came from 'the land of truth'. Cormac asked him for the branch, and this was granted him in return for three wishes. These wishes were for his daughter Ailbe, his son Cairbre and his wife Eithne, who were taken from him over the following three years. In pursuit of them with his men, Cormac was overcome by a thick mist. When this cleared, he was on a large plain in the Land of Promise, Tír Tairngire. Here, reunited with his family, he was given a golden goblet and the silver branch 'to soothe and solace you'. He was told that on the day he died they would be taken from him. His host in Tír Tairngire revealed himself to be Mannanán mac Lir. Next morning when Cormac awoke he found himself back at Tara.

Tír Tairngire is said to contain beneath its sea the Well of Segais, the source of all wisdom and occult knowledge. (A similarity with Norse mythology is that the Well of Mimir is the source of all the rivers of the earth.) The Tír Tairngire well was surrounded by hazel trees, from which fruit dropped, causing bubbles of mystic inspiration to form on the streams issuing from it. Every seven years these hazel nuts passed into the river Boyne. Those who ate these became seers. According to some, Finn* obtained his wisdom by eating a salmon which had in its turn eaten a hazel nut from the Well of Segais.

Tadg mac Cian in the Otherworld

Tadg mac Cian sailed from Munster against Cathman mac Tabarn, who had carried off many of his people into captivity.[7] As in other stories of voyages there are visits to many strange islands. On the Isle of Birds those who eat the eggs have feathers sprout out all over them. On Inis Locha, ruled by the two sons of Bodb,* Tadg is met by a woman who tells him that here live all the kings of Ireland from Conn Cét Chathach. Here Tadg meets Connla and the faery woman who took him away. On this island is the apple tree whose fruit lured Connla away from Ireland. Tadg sails away, having spent a year in the Otherworld.

The Adventures of Nera in the Otherworld

Echtra Nerai is an early tale from possibly the ninth or tenth century. Beginning during Samain* in Connacht during the reign of Medb* and Ailill, it tells of a prize being offered to anyone who can put a piece of twig around the foot of the two captives hanged by them. 'Demon women appear on that night always', and Nera is the only one who accepts the challenge. Finding difficulty in carrying out the task, he is eventually told by the hanged man that he must persist until he succeeds. When he eventually does so, the hanged man tells him that he is thirsty. Nera carries him away on his shoulders in search of a drink.

Arriving at the *síd* of Cruachain,* Nera stays and is offered a wife. This fairy wife tells him that the *aes síde* or people of the *síd* are planning to attack Ailill's court the following Samain. (Tradition has it that during the Samain the *síde* or mounds are opened and their spirits are free to roam.) Nera asks his wife to give him some proof of his stay in the *síd*, and she gives him fairy fruits. Nera tells his earthly wife that he has been in the *síd* and, as a result, Medb and Ailill destroy the *síd* at Cruachain.

Stories relate that it was Nera who brought from the Síd ar Cruachain one of the cows which was a contributory cause of the Táin Bó Cualgne.* Another story whose beginning has a related theme to Nera's tells of a dead body flung on a spit to roast. A man is set to watch the body to ensure the flesh does not burn: his mind wanders and he is taken to task by the corpse itself.[39]

Partholón   Said to have led the first colony to Ireland two hundred and seventy-eight years after the flood, the date given for his arrival being AM 2520 (2678 BC). Arriving from Greece with his wife, three sons and a thousand followers, he landed in Donegal Bay and settled close to Assaroe at Ballyshannon. According to John O'Donovan,[5] the *Annals of Clonmacnoise* synchronised the arrival of Partholón with the twenty-first year of the Patriarch Abraham, and the twelfth year of the reign of Semiramis, empress of Assyria. The *Book of Leinster*, referring to Partholón, says:

> Ro gabh dóibh ar an maigh
> Partholón is Fomaraich.[41]

> He engaged them on the plain,
> Partholón and his Fomorians.

From this it would appear that he and his people were Fomorians,* though they are quite often called the Partholonians: these 'were a branch of the tribes that originally held possession of the promised land, and who spread themselves from the African coasts to the islands of the Chersonesus Cimbrica'[75] (present-day Denmark). Also called Lochlannaigs, a name whose origins may lie in the fact that they were pirates or else because their country of origin was indented with 'lochs' and inlets. It has been suggested[75] that they were a division of the Canaanites who had been expelled from their country by the Israelites under Joshua. Partholón must have had the same eastern origin as Nemed,* ancestor of the Firbolg,* of whom it was said that he was nephew of Partholón.

Partholón and his people later settled on Moynalty, the plain in Dublin between Tallaght, Clontarf and Howth. It was here, Sean-Mhag Ealta-Étair (the old plain of the flocks of Etar) that they were destroyed by a plague, six hundred years after their first arrival. Nine thousand of them are said to have died in one week.

The first recorded battle in Irish history is that fought between Partholón's people and eight hundred Fomorians under Cical and his mother Lot Luaimneach. The battle of Mag Ith took place near Lough Swilly in Co. Donegal near the river Finn in the year AM 2530 (2668 BC). It was likely that this was a battle between two branches of the Fomorians. Four years after this Partholón died at Moynalty in Leinster.

Samain

Badair oslaicte sídha Érenn im Samhain do gres, air ni feta diamair dia Samna for sidaib.

All the *síde* of Ireland were open at the Samain to the warrior guests, for on the day of the Samain nothing could be concealed upon the *síde*.

Oidche Samhna, All Hallows Night, or Hallowe'en, the night before 1 November. The word means 'the end of summer', from *samh* (summer), and *fuin* (end). On this night legend has it that the *síde* or mounds are open and the spirits or *lennán síde*° issue forth. From the síd ar Cruachain in Connacht comes the Ellén Trechenn,* the Mórrígan and the spectre of hosts led by a flock of copper-red birds, led in turn by a three-headed vulture.

It was during this time that the great idol Crom Cruach* was worshipped at Mag Slecht* in Co. Cavan. During Samain the people sought through worship and sacrifice to appease Crom, god of corn and agriculture.

Tributes were paid at this time. One was paid to the king of Ulster from the Western Isles of Scotland, though this probably came to an end after the battle of Mag Rath in AD 637. Others were paid generally to kings.

> He himself, the king of noble Cashel, is entitled
> to three hundred suits of clothes at Samain,
> to fifty steeds of a dark grey colour
> in readiness for every battle . . .[34]

A *feis*° was held at Tara* during Samain every third year. This was the most celebrated of all the ancient meetings. (By the fifth century, however, it was only held at the beginning of a king's reign.)

> Three days before Samain, at all times,
> and three days by ancient custom,
> did the hosts of high aspirations
> continue to feast for the whole week.[34]

This feis or convention, with the king of Tara and the minor kings and chiefs together with the *ollamhs*,* was commenced three days before Samain and lasted until three days later. The remnants of this feast are still preserved in the festivities of Hallowe'en, as indeed are other aspects of Samain. Athough the spirits from the mounds might be felt to have been quelled by Christian influence, the belief that fairies are abroad on Samain night still exists in parts of Ireland and pockets of Scotland. On this night fires are still lit everywhere in cities and countryside, the spirits are captured through masks and there is general feasting with fruits and nuts. The masks may be ancient mythological representations of animals, etc. For many ancient names include 'horse-head', ram-head', 'red-stripped' etc. It has been suggested that when genealogies were being read out, people may have worn these masks as images representing their ancestors

Eoin mac Néill records some verse which he heard at the Samain:

> Here comes I, old Beelzebub
> And over my shoulder I carries a club,
> And in my hand a dripping-pan,
> And I think myself a jolly old man.

And another:

> Here comes I the devil himself,
> If you don't give me money I'll break all your delf,
> Money I want and money I crave,
> If you don't give me money I'll sweep you all to the grave.

According to mac Néill, writing nearly 80 years ago, in some localities the devils were accompanied by Oliver Cromwell.[99]

It was during Samain that the Dagda* went to the Fomorians'* camp. His massive cauldron was filled with milk, flour and fat together with pigs, sheep and goats and the whole mixture was boiled. This was poured into a hole and the Dagda ordered to eat it all by the Fomorians. He did eat it all but would not have done so voluntarily, the food being offered to the earth spirit at this time of year.

After this he had intercourse with Indech's daughter, and he is also recorded as having had intercourse with Boand* and also the Mórrígan. This ritual mating of the god and goddess, i.e. the Dagda and the Mórrígan, would seem to be an integral part of Samain, it being a time when fertility rites were carried out. (Samain is a favourable time for a woman to conceive for purely practical reasons.)

The underlying theme of stories or myths associated with Samain show an attack by the Otherworld on mortals followed by the occasional counter-attack. It was at Samain that Aillén mac Midna, one of the Tuatha Dé Danann,* burnt Tara every year until he was killed by Finn.* As well as fire, water plays a part in the stories. Dwellings are set afire, people are drowned in vats. The Roman historian Lucan states that the Gaulish god Teutates was propitiated at Samain by the drowning of victims in a vat, and another Gaullish god Taranis by burning in a wooden vessel.[49]

Samain is a time of fertility and sacrifice. Stories concerning it remind us that in ancient times the supernatural could assume a menacing character and propitiation was equally terrible.

Scáthach Scáthach (the shadowy one) was a female warrior or Amazon who lived along the Western Isles of Scotland and is associated particularly with the Isle of Skye. A teacher of warrior-craft, Cúchulainn* went to her to complete his warrior training. In order to force her to teach him everything, Cúchulainn 'leaps on to her breast and threatens her with his sword'.[49] As her student he helped her against her enemies in return. Scáthach granted Cúchulainn three wishes — to instruct him carefully, to give him her daughter without a bride-price, and to foretell his future career. Among the feats Cúchulainn learned from Scátach was the Gaé Bolga* and the Torannchles or 'Thunder Feat'.

Scáthach is regarded as an Otherworld* figure. Comparison has been made between her presenting the Gaé Bolga to Cúchulainn and the presentation of King Arthur's sword by the Lady of the Lake.[2]

In the battle between Scáthach and the warrior-princess Aífe, Cúchulainn overcame Aífe and made her promise to give hostages and never oppose Scáthach again. He also made her spend that night with him, bearing him a son who should go to Ireland after seven years.

Cúchulainn also consorted with Scáthach's daughter Uathach, and with Scáthach herself, wresting from her 'the friendship of her thighs'.[78] This union with the Amazonian woman of the Otherworld whilst learning warrior-skills has connotations of the sexual undertones in craft initiations. It is mentioned[8] that the relation of a craftsman to his craft and materials is similar to that of husband and wife; an example cited from the Chisinga of Zimbabwe says that a smith would be guilty of adultery if he slept with a human wife while his forge was 'pregnant with iron'. The union of Cúchulainn with the female warriors is seen as a union of an apprentice with his vocation.

Scota   According to Keating Scota was the mother of the sons of Míl.*[4] The same source has it that of the fourteen names by which Ireland was known, the ninth was Scotia. The sons of Míl, thus, called the island after their mother. She, according to legend, was daughter of the reigning pharaoh of Egypt, Nectonibus. Other accounts have it that the Island was called Scotia because of some invaders' connections with Scythia. '*Cineadh Scuit ó'n Scotia*'; the Scots came from Scythia.[4]

Legend has it that the first Irishman was a Scythian called Fénius Farsaid. He settled in Egypt where his son Niul married a daughter of the pharaoh. Their daughter was Scota. She in her turn had a son called Goídel (hence Gael), and his great-grandson was Éber* Scot. 'The whole genealogy being probably invented to explain the origins of the three names by which the Gaels called themselves Finn, Scot and Goidel'.[67]

Scota left Egypt when Fénius was expelled for refusing to join in the persecution of the children of Israel. After living in Africa for forty-two years, passing through the present-day Algeria and Morocco, Scota went into Spain.

Scota has associations in folklore with Sliab Mis and Caherconree, both in Co. Kerry.

Síle na Gig   Sheila na Gigs are a group of female sculptures found not only in Ireland but distributed also in Britain and France. The sculpture is a nude figure, generally represented face on, with legs splayed and the hands placed behind the thighs with fingers opening the vulva.

The original Irish form of the word is said to be Síghle na gCíoch (Síle of the breasts). Dineen's dictionary defines Síghle na gCíoch as a 'stone fetish representing a woman, supposed to give fertility, generally thought to have been introduced by the Normans'.

These sculptures are generally found in castles such as the one on the south-facing wall of Ballaghmore Castle (an 15th century keep at Borris-in-Ossory, Co. Laois) and churches such as the one at Holy Cross Abbey, Co. Tipperary, and date from the 12th to 16th century. They are also found in round towers and to a lesser extent on standing stones, wells, walls and bridges.

Sheila na Gig at doorway to old church
at White Island, Lough Erne, Co. Fermanagh

Within the British Isles there are approximately 75 in Ireland, 21 in England, 7 in Wales and 3 in Scotland. In Ireland they are to be found in greatest concentration in counties Tipperary, Cork, Offaly, Clare and Meath.

Anne Ross has stated that the origins of the Sheilas have eluded scholars and that they are of 'indeterminate date'.[32] Their presence in mediaeval castles, it has been suggested, was to ward off evil. Also, it has been said that they are fertility figures connected with pagan cults.

Although the majority of Sheilas fit into the Romanesque style, some older carvings may be said to resemble Sheilas. An example of the latter is the stone image from Boa Island, Co. Fermanagh, and the stone figure from Tara,* known as St Adamnán's Cross. Likewise another stone figure from White Island, Lough Erne, precedes the mediaeval Sheilas and 'shows the descent of the motif from pagan to Christian settings'.[76] It would thus appear that there are stone images of pagan origin which fit into the Sheila prototype and which were forerunners of the mediaeval Sheilas. So, in trying to understand the Sheilas as a phenomenon one may ask to what extent did the later carvers draw on the pagan past?

The Sheila na Gig found in the parapet of the bridge at Clonlara, Co. Clare is said to have come from the nearby Newtown Castle. Locally this is known as 'The Witches' Stone'.[77] It is dated as early sixteenth century.

The Seir Kieran Sheila now in the crypt of the National Museum, Dublin, is regarded by Andersen[76] as 'rooted in the Celtic Past'. He states that despite its age scholars have never dealt with it in detail. In terms of these possible pagan origins, the idea of the *cailleach** comes to mind. The sovereignty motif of mythology had it that the king-to-be must first mate with an old hag or *cailleach* before becoming the sovereign. This Seir Kieran figure, in common with some others, has holes drilled into the stone. These holes may or may not have been part of the original.

Certain carved circular discs are associated with Sheila na Gigs. An example is the figure from Lavey Church, Co. Cavan, now in the National Museum, a carving which may be compared with the disc or ball on a quoin of Copgrove Church in Yorkshire, England. Another example of this association may be that between the Sheila na Gig in Ballyvourney, Co. Cork and a black ball which is touched during the pattern of St Gobnat in Ballyvourney.

Sior Gallomhai A sun deity and son-in-law of the Lord of the Otherworld.* His love is the Otherworld queen, the queen of the Isle of Women. Sior Gallomhai is part of the Highland tradition in Scotland, in Tiree and South Uist. One story tells how he rescues a lady from a giant-lord, this giant only being killed by his own weapon. Sior Gallomhai is regarded as being synonymous with Sir Gawain of the Arthurian Tales.

Sláinge   The Firbolgs took possession of Ireland $c.350$ BC.[5] Sláinge, who landed at Inber Sláinge, which is the mouth of the river Slaney, is also called Sláine. He and his four brothers, sons of Dela, the son of Lóch, divided Ireland into five parts. He was given Leinster, his territory extending from Inber Colptha (the mouth of the river Boyne) to Cumar dTrí nUisce° (Waterford harbour).

Sláinge's section of the Firbolg* people were the Gálioin.* At the end of his year's kingship he died at Dinn Ríg, also called Duma Sláinge (mound of Sláinge). This is on the River Barrow at modern day Leighlinbridge, Co. Carlow. The source of this story is the *Book of Leinster*[41] but the *Dindshenchas* has it that he died at Slane and was buried there 'with a mighty mound erected over him, and that the hill was named after him'.

> A year had Sláinge, this is true,
> till he died in his fine mound;
> the first man of the Fir Bolgs of the peaks
> who died in the island of Ireland.[15]

Sovereignty Myth   This myth is at the core of our mythology. It tells of the ancient power of the goddess or *cailleach** in conferring kingship. Unless the goddess conferred sovereignty, the king was not a proper king. The goddess herself was sovereignty and only through her could the king claim legitimacy.

> Atbér-sa fritt, a mac mín:
> limsa fóit na hair-ríg:
> is mé ind ingen seta seng,
> flaithius Alban is hÉrend.

> I will tell you, gentle boy,
> with me the high-kings sleep;
> I am the graceful, slender girl,
> the Sovereignty of Scotland and Ireland.[42]

The myth of sovereignty is simple enough to tell: a young man meets an old woman in a wood and mates with her; she turns into a young woman and confers sovereignty on him. He becomes king and is accepted as such. As an old man he is in a wood where he meets a young woman, he mates with her; she turns into an old woman and kills him.

She is represented as a lady wearing a golden crown and seated on a crystal throne, having before her a vat of red liquor, from which she pours a draught into a golden cup which she gives to each successive king of Ireland.

As an old woman she often appears quite hideous; she appeared to Lugaid Laigde and his brothers as a loathsome hag, with black bony knees and a paunchy belly and a head of hair like 'a furzy hillside'. Such was the horror of the brothers that they preferred to be buried alive rather than look at her. Then the hag addressed them all and said: 'One of you must sleep with me tonight, or I will devour you all, unaided, hound and strong man alike.'

Lugaid said that in order to save the lives of his brothers he would sleep with the hag or *Cailleach*. But as the firelight fell she changed into a young woman, 'three shafts of sunlight in each of her eyes: where her glance fell all was bright'.

> Roscuch in cúach corcra cain
> dia cíchib sís cen sentaid
> co mbenfaide frigde friss
> 'sin tig ar shoillsi a cóem-chriss.

> Down slid the crimson mantle fair
> from her breasts, untouched with age,
> till the flesh worm might be crushed in the room
> by the light of her lovely body.[42]

The goddess said that the son's name would be Lugaid mac Con*, that he would be seer, prophet and poet and would be king of Tara*.

The ceremony of inauguration with sovereignty was known as the *banais rigi* (*banfheiss* = woman feast or sleeping feast).

All the goddesses were sovereignty, but the chief one was Ériu*, the mother goddess. O'Rahilly[2] says that these goddesses represented the solar goddess; he states that the sun goddess 'was also the goddess of earth and of its springs and rivers . . .'. In other words the earth goddess was the consort of the son god. This ceremony may well have its origin in the fertility rite from the Bronze Age where the earth goddess wore a golden lunula to represent the moon and the son god wore beaten discs of gold on his back and chest. However, this Bronze Age ritual was not to confer sovereignty but rather to seek continued harmony between the earth, moon and sun.

Finally, if Mór Muman*, who conferred sovereignty, did die as the annals say in AD 632, then the *banais rigi* or sovereignty ritual lasted into a comparatively late period of Irish history.[102] The 17th-century poet Daibhí Ó Bruadair, from Barrymore, Co. Cork, referred to a king as the 'spouse of Cashel' and the 18th-century poets referred to Ireland as the spouse of her lawful kings. Dr D.A. Binchy in discussing secular institutions writes: 'At the top of the pyramid in each tuath stood the king, originally beyond all doubt a sacred personage, tracing his descent to one or other of the ancestral dieties and mystically invested with sovereignty by means of immemorial inauguration rites, which survived — though doubtless in attenuated form — down to the destruction of the Gaelic order.'[103]

Sualdam mac Roich   Reputed to have been the foster-father of Cúchulainn,* legend has it that Cúchulainn was conceived when his mother swallowed a may-fly during her wedding feast, Lug* the sun god revealing later to her in a dream that it was he she had swallowed.

Another version has it that Cúchulainn's mother Dechtire, who was half sister of King Conchobar mac Nessa* was already pregnant when betrothed to Sualdam. Ashamed of this, she induced a miscarriage and conceived again by Sualdam.

Sualdam is mentioned as Cúchulainn's father in the Lay of the Heads.

> Cumhadh Mhic Sualtam shéimh
> ni bhfeil aige féin air for

> Mourning the son of Sualtam the worthy
> — thereof no knowledge has he.[79]

Sualdam is mentioned in the description of the 'armed chariot' of Cúchulainn: 'It was then the champion and warrior, and perfection of martial heroes above all the men of the earth, namely Cúchulainn the son of Saoltann'.[34]

Sualdam's kingdom was Cuailgne (Cooley), Co. Louth, and he would have lived at the same time as Fergus mac Roich,* king of Ulster. He had the right to the produce of all cattle in Cooley which included Muirthemne, in present-day Louth. Evidence that this kingdom was separate from Ulster may be seem in the fact that neither Sualdam nor Cúchulainn was affected by the Cess Noínden Ulad* (debility of the Ulaid) during the Táin* Bó Cualgne.

Sualdam is said to have tested Cúchulainn's valour in the 'Champion's Covenant' at Dún Rudruige, where Cúchulainn preserved the honour of the Ulster heroes. It is stated[9] that this test may preserve 'a really archaic feature where the relation of the magician to the hero was that of father to son'.

During the Táin, Sualdam was sent by Cúchulainn to rouse the 'sleeping' warriors at Emain Macha.* Sualdam rode there on Cúchulann's horse, the Liath Macha. On his arrival he shouted, 'Men are wounded, women are captives, cows are driven away'. He received no reply as the Ulaid were bound not to speak before their king and the king was bound not to speak before his druids. Sualdam then addressed Cathbad* the druid with the same appeal to action but was told, 'It is better to allow the man who offers such combats to a king to come on to death and destruction'. Leaving in a fury, Sualdam was decapitated by the edge of his own shield as the horse Liath Macha reared up. The horse then galloped through Emain Macha with the severed head of Sualdam, crying out, 'Men are wounded, women are captives, cows are driven away'. This eventually aroused the Ulaid to arms.

Suibne Geilt   Son of Colmán Cuar, a seventh century chief of the Dál nAraide.* Often regarded as a mythological figure, he appears nonetheless in the story of the historical battle of Mag Rath which took place in AD 637. The battle was between Congal Caech, king of the Ulaid, and his foster-father Domnall, king of Ireland. (Domnall had his fort at Dún na nGedh on the Boyne and later at Ard Fothaid, near Donegal town.)

Congal had the support of Suibne, based in Co. Down and part of Antrim, and also of the Scots. Both Congal and Suibne were 'cursed by the bells and croziers of the clerics', all of whom supported King Domnall. Suibne's entry to the battle is described:

> The standard of Suibne, a yellow banner,
> the renowned king of the Dál Araidhe,
> yellow satin over that mild man of hosts,
> the white fingered stripling himself in the middle of them.[80]

However, the sight of the battle horrors drove him mad, and he fled, 'filled with intoxicated tremor, horror, panic and . . . flightiness . . . so that his body was converted into a confused shaking mass, from the effect of fear'.[80] It is said that 'the vigour of his brain in the cavities of his head was destroyed by the clamour of the conflict'.

It has also been said that Suibne was driven mad by a curse of St Ronán, with whom he had a conflict about the building of a church at

Drumiskin, Co. Louth, but J.G. O'Keefe[81] feels that this may be a later interpolation. (Suibne had entered naked into the church and thrown the psalter into the lake. He was doing likewise with the priest when summoned to the battle. The curse was that he would be forever wandering naked, eventually to be killed by a spear.)

When Suibne went mad at the battle he leapt onto the shield of a warrior and then onto a tree, in which there were many old and debilitated people watching the battle. They screamed at him to return to the fray. Rushing hither and thither and recognised by the armies, his frenzy became greater. He continued in this state (*míthapaid*) until a shower of hailstones fell. He then disappeared, turning his back on mankind and living in the wilderness.

> This was my first run, —
> rapid was the flight, —
> the shot of the javelin expired
> for me with the shower.[80]

In an unbalanced state of mind (*gealtacht*) from then on, his adventures are described in the romance entitled Buile Suibhne.[81] This romance displays that strong love of place, a feature of early Irish writing, and we thus find Suibne extolling his love of the country whilst bemoaning his own state.

Suibne spent the rest of his days in the bushy branches of tall trees, living on water and watercress, 'my trees hard and bare or close sheltering are my friends'. He occasionally went home to Glenn mBolcáin, near Rasharkin in Co. Antrim. Legend has it that Glenn mBolcáin was where the madman of Ireland used to go.

> Alas that I have been parted here
> from my mighty armed host,
> a bitter madman in the glen,
> bereft of sense and reason . . .
> sad forever is my cry
> on the summit of Cruachan Aighle
> from Glen Bolcain to Islay
> from Cenn Tire to Boirche.[81]

A pagan hermit wedded to nature — 'Sweeter indeed were it to me to hear the voices of the cuckoos on the banks of the Bann . . . than the grig-graig of the church bell' — Suibne imagined himself as a bird flying about Ireland for seven years.

Eidir corraibh Cúailghne Saimh
eitir chúnaibh o thig gaimh,
fo chéibh chaille gach re seal . . .

In summer amid the herons of Cuailgne,
among the packs of wolves when winter comes,
at other times under the crown of a wood . . .[81]

Many old poems are attributed to Suibne, including the following
from an Irish MS in the monastery of St Paul in Carinthia:

Suibne the Lunatic

My little oratory in Tuaim Inbir, it is
not a full house that is . . .
with its stars last night, with its sun,
with its moon.
Gobban hath built it — that its story may
be told to you —
my heartlet, God from heaven, he is the
thatcher who hath thatched it.
A house wherein wet rain pours not, a place
wherein as though in a garden, and it
without a fence around it
wherein thou fearest not spearpoints,
bright as though in a garden, and it without
a fence around it.[33]

Seamus Heaney has translated Buile Suibhne as *Sweeney Astray*.
  Suibne had three dwellings, all apparently in the Dál nAraide
territory — Tech Mic Rinneda, Cluain Crema and Ros Earcain. However, he was generally wandering, his journey bringing him to many
remote places — from Sliab Aughty in Co. Galway to Sliabh Mis in
Co. Kerry to Sliab Bloom in Co. Offaly to Inis Murray off Sligo. He
spent six weeks at a monastery of the Island of Eigg, off the west coast
of Scotland. He spent another six weeks at Carrick Alastair (Ailsa
Craig, in the Firth of Clyde, Scotland). When he left Carrick Alastair
he said aloud:

Duairc an bhetha-sa
bheith gan maeithleaptha,

160

adhbha úairsheaca,
garbha gáoithshnechta . . .

Gloomy this life,
to be without a soft bed,
abode of cold frost
roughness of wind driven snow.

Cold, icy wind,
faint shadow of a feeble sun,
shelter of a single tree,
on the summit of a table land.

Enduring the rain-storm,
stepping over deerpaths,
faring through greensward
on a morn of grey frost.

The bellowing of the stags
throughout the wood,
the climb to the deer-pass,
the voice of white seas . . .

Ulaidh in harvest time
about quivering Loch Cuan
a summer visit
to the race of enduring Eoghan.

A journey at Lammastide
to Taillten of fountains,
fishing in springtime
the meandering Shannon.

For my sustenance at night
I have all that hands glean
in dark oak woods
of herbs and plenteous fruit.

Suibne settled down for awhile at Tech Moling in Co. Carlow and Moling began to write down his story. Taking pity on Suibne, Moling told his cook to give him some of each day's milk. She used to 'thrust her heel up to her ankle in the cowdung . . . and leave the full of it of

161

new milk there for Suibne'. Suibne would come cautiously into the yard to drink the milk.

The cook's name was Muirgil, wife of Moling's swineherd Mongán. Mongán's sister set him jealous and this resulted in him throwing a spear at Suibne as he was drinking the milk. The spear passed through 'the nipple of Suibne's left breast and broke his back in two'. At this Suibne, Moling and Mongán uttered a lay between them, Suibne speaking the following:

> There was a time when I deemed more melodious
> than the quiet converse of people,
> the cooing of the turtle dove
> flitting about a pool.

> There was a time when I deemed more melodious
> than the sound of a little bell beside me
> the warbling of the blackbird to the mountain
> and the belling of a stag in a storm.

> There was a time when I deemed more melodious
> than the voice of a beautiful woman beside me,
> to hear at dawn,
> the cry of the mountain grouse.

Suibne died and was buried, each man placing a stone on his tomb. He was buried at Tobar na nGealt (the madman's well). Though not identified, it may be assumed to be near St Mullins in Co. Carlow.

> Robadh rígh, robadh geilt glan,
> rop fher oirnighe úasal,
> ag sin a lighe, líth ngle,
> dobhris mo chroidhe a thrúaighe.

> He was a king, he was a madman,
> a man illustrious, noble, was he;
> there is his grave — bright festival —
> pity for him has rent my heart.

Tailtiu   Sometimes referred to as the daughter of *Mag Mór* (large plain)[15] and elsewhere as daughter of Umor Mór (arable ridge).[7] The wife of Eochu mac Eirc, king of Ireland, she is often regarded as being from Spain, from where she was taken by Eochu who was the last of the Firbolg* kings.

Cian, also known as Scál Balb, son of Dian Cécht, gave his son to Tailtiu in fosterage. This son was Lug,* hero of the Tuatha Dé Danann.*

Tailtiu lived in Tailtiu, the present-day Telltown, Co. Meath. It was she and her people who cleared the forest of Coill Cuan that was here, the task taking them a year to complete. She gave the region her name; this is consistent with the earth goddesses' desire to be associated with place, e.g., Macha with Armagh, Tea with Tara, and Ériu* with Ireland. Tailtiu was buried on the plain that she cleared in accordance with her request.

In response to Tailtiu's request at her death-bed that funeral games be held every year on the plain to lament her, her foster-son Lug held games for a fortnight before and after Lugnasa* (1 August). Lug sang a song of lamentation at these games. Activities including games, feats of battle and horse racing from Cnoc Aidi, just north of Kells, to Telltown. The ancient assembly here was known as Oenach Tailten.

It is said that Tailtiu's participation in cutting down the woods and clearing the roots of the trees was the cause of her death, and that the clearing of the forest resulted in the fertile plain which is now Co. Meath.

Tailtiu was in later years the site of a local festival which continued to be held until 1770. According to P.W. Joyce,[53] the Fair at Tailten, 'on the the north bank of the Blackwater in Telltown, Co. Meath, was attended by people from all over Ireland as well as from Scotland'. Marriages formed a special part of the fair, these marriages being held in a place called the 'marriage hollow'. Tailtiu is mentioned by the thirteenth century poet Giolla Brighde mac Con Midhe.

> Taillte is Nás Laighean na learg,
> Oileach is Eamhain Fhíndearg
> — gan teacht tuirseach uatha d'fhior —
> Uisneach is Cruacha is Caisiol.

> Taillte and Nás Laighean of the slopes,
> Aileach and Eamhain, red with wine
> — no man leaves them sorrowful —
> Uisneach and Cruachain and Caiseal.[73]

Táin Meaning 'cattle-raid', this driving of cattle from other people's property was a very old and significant occurrence which, although greatly diminished, has existed almost up to the present day. What some regard as the most famous tale of ancient Ireland is the Táin Bó Cualgne and, though other raids are recorded, these are generally preludes or *remscéla* to the major story.

The Táin Bó Froích includes an account of an expedition by Fraech to the Alps to recover stolen cattle as well as his wife. He travelled from Ulster to Scotland and then through 'north-Saxon land' to the English Channel, then to the Alps and the land of the Lombards or Long-Beards. As the Lombards did not appear in Italy before the sixth century, this would appear to be a later story reworked in order to act as a preliminary to the Táin Bó Cualgne. (All these epics are supposed to have taken place between 500 BC and AD 100.) The oldest manuscript authority for the Táin Bó Froích is the twelfth century *Book of Leinster*.

The Táin Bó Dartada is related in the eleventh century *Lebor na hUidre*.* Eocho Bec, king of Clíu on the south bank of the Shannon, was feasting at Cruachain Connacht* with Ailill and Medb.* Ailill requested 'one cow from each farmer who is under thy lordship'. Eochu agreed but, on the way home, his party was attacked by one hundred and forty warriors from Mayo under the sons of Glaschú. Eochu's sons were killed in this skirmish. Following on this, Ailill sent his son Orlam to seize the cattle of Dartaid, Eochu Bec's daughter. She and Corp Liath fought and killed many of the Connacht raiders; but, in the end, she was carried off with her cattle, forty milch cows and fifteen heifers. She died as a result, hence the name Imlech Dartada, the lake shore of Darta, on the south bank of the Shannon. Each passage in this story commences with a woman appearing to the protagonists whilst they are asleep and foretelling the next stage in the story.[82]

The Táin Bó Flidais concerns a raid on Ailill Finn from present-day Castlerea in Co. Roscommon. Fergus mac Roich* goes to Ailill Finn's castle and, after much battle, carries off Ailill's wife Flidais and a hundred milch cows, a hundred and forty oxen and three thousand calves. Queen Medb then decrees that Flidais live with Fergus and, feeling that the proceeds of this raid will sustain her army whilst on the Táin Bó Cualgne, requests Flidais to provide food for them every seventh day during the expedition.

The Táin Bó Cualgne is set during the reign of Medb and Ailill, rulers of Connacht about the first century BC Generally referred to as the Táin, it is preserved in fifteen MSS ranging in date from the eleventh to the nineteenth century. The earliest version is that in the *Book of Leinster*; later transcriptions include that of 1750 at Clonmacnoise and that of 1870 by Professor O'Looney of the Royal Irish Academy.

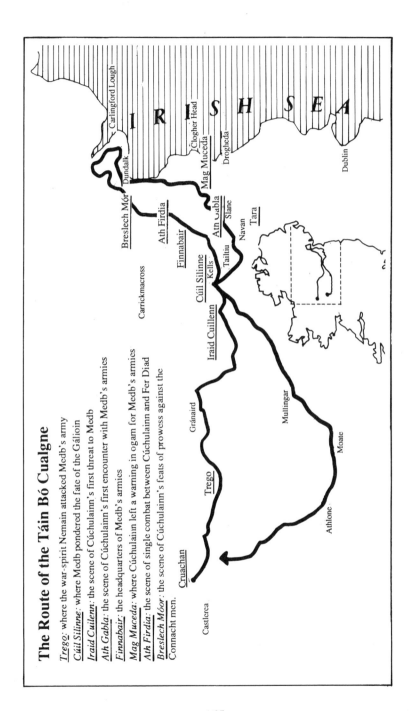

The Route of the Táin Bó Cualgne

Trego: where the war-spirit Nemain attacked Medb's army
Cúil Silinne: where Medb pondered the fate of the Gáiloin
Iraid Cuilenn: the scene of Cúchulainn's first threat to Medb
Ath Gabla: the scene of Cúchulainn's first encounter with Medb's armies
Finnabair: the headquarters of Medb's armies
Mag Muceda: where Cúchulainn left a warning in ogam for Medb's armies
Ath Firdia: the scene of single combat between Cúchulainn and Fer Diad
Breslech Móor: the scene of Cúchulainn's feats of prowess against the Connacht men.

165

In the story certain aspects of pre-Christian Ireland are portrayed such as 'totem and tabu, headhunting and fighting from chariots', according to David Greene.[56] The society depicted in the story is essentially pastoral, though descriptions in the *Book of Leinster* suggest that elaborate personal adornment was a feature of dress.

The story concerns war between Connacht and Ulster, centered round the desire of Medb for the Black Bull of Cooley. This great supernatural bull, known as the Donn of Cualgne, was attributed with large powers of fecundity (a quality obviously desirable in a stock-raising pastoral community).

O'Rahilly[2] has it that the struggle for the bull was between Meath and Ulster, that is between Tara* and Emain Macha,* rather than between Cruachain and Emain Macha. Whatever about that, the story is told as of east-west conflict, with the cattle thieves coming from the west. Joseph Raftery states[83] that the Táin gives some account of political events during the Iron Age in Ireland 'under which Ulster and the rest of the country were striving for hegemony'.

The Táin Bú Cualgne falls into the following sequences and sections in the *Book of Leinster:* Prologue; The gathering of the hosts of Erin and preliminary movements of the forces of Medb; Episode of Cúchulainn's* boyhood deeds; Combats and progress of the host, ending in the Brislech Már Maige Muirtheimne (the rout of Mag Muirtheimne); Final conflicts; The awakening of Ulster; The gathering on the Hill of Slane; The final battles of Gairech and Ilgairech and the deaths of the two bulls, the *finnbennach* (white-horned) bull of Medb and the *donn* (dark, black) bull of Cualgne.

Tara   A hill, five hundred feet above sea level, situated about six miles south-east from the town of Navan, Co. Meath. It is regarded as having been the centre of ancient Ireland and was the seat of kings from earliest times to the sixth century. It appears also to have been a centre of ritual significance, tribal gatherings being held in commemoration of divine ancestors buried in the local mounds, and also a place for kings and chiefs to gather in time of war and significant events.

The *fes Tara* was held here every three years at Samain; during this time a convocation of kings met and a great festival was held for three days before the Samain and for three days after. On certain occasions when a high king had to be chosen, the ancient rite of the *tarbfes** was carried out.

The kings of Tara have been referred to as priest-kings. Injunctions placed on them to observe the sun rising and setting may be connected to solar worship ritual. The 'burning' of Tara every Samain* by Aillén mac Midgna of the *síd* of Finnachad may suggest ritual fires during this pagan festival. A further connection is the prohibition against lighting fires in the district until the sacred fire of the druids* had first been kindled at Tara.

One of the oldest descriptions of Tara is to be found in the fourteenth or fifteenth century version of the *Dindshenchas*,° attributed to the poet Amorgein mac Amhalghada. Part of this is also found in the twelfth century *Book of Leinster*.

Nemnach, a well which is at the elf-mound in the north-eastern part of Tara. Out of Nemnach comes a stream named Nith. 'Tis on this that the first mill was built in Ireland for the benefit of Ciarnait, Cormac's bondmaid.

The Kings Fort beside the fort of Loegaire on the north. In this are three strange things; to wit, the site of Cormac's house in the south-eastern part of the fort on the side to the south of Raith Loegairi; the site of the high seat beside the site of Cormac's house on the east; and between them Tea's Rampart, from which was named Temair, i.e., Tea-múr, that is, the hillock between the two ramparts on the southern side.

[Legend has it that Tea was the wife of Éremón,* one of the sons of Míl.* Tea is an earth goddess and another place named after her is Temair Luachra about ten miles west of Kanturk on the mountainous Cork-Kerry border].

The Mound of the Cow, to the west of the Mound of Hostages. The Mound of the Hostages, to the north- east of the site of the high-seat (called after the hostages or foster children who would sit at the mound in order to get a better view of the festivities). Fál beside the Mound of the Hostages on the north, to wit, the stone that used to roar under the feet of every king that would take possession of Ireland. Of that stone the name was Fál, i.e. Fo-ail (understone), i.e. a stone under a king.

The stone of the Fians is to the east of a road in front of the Fort of the Synod.

The House of the Women, that is Tech Midchuarta, is north-east from the eastern mound. Thus was the site of that home settled, the lower part of the north and its high part to the south, and the erection of a wall about it to the east and west. The northern side of it is a little bent north and south it ought to be. It has the form of a long house with fourteen doors, seven to the west and seven to the east. And men say that there the feast of Tara was consumed. That was reasonable, for the choice of the men of Erin would fit therein, and this is the Great House with a Thousand Soldiers.[84]

These early descriptions also include that of a place called the site of Cúchulainn's* Shield, situated to the north-east of Tara. As well as the shield, his right hand is also reputedly buried there. The body of Loegaire, son of Niall, is said to be buried with his 'shield of valour' in the external rampart of Rath Laoghaire, 'with his face to the south, fighting the Leinster-men'.

Golden torques were found in a bank or mound near the Tara churchyard in AD 1810. Of a spiral or screw pattern, these are of great beauty and consistent with ancient descriptions of dress and ornamentation at Tara. Cormac mac Airt,* a high king of Tara, is described as wearing 'a fine purple garment, a golden brooch in his breast; a mun-torc, or gold collar, around his neck; a belt ornamented with precious stones about him'. It was generally considered that the wearing of torques was peculiar to the Celts; they were found among Gallic tribes throughout Europe, and Livy mentions that Publius Cornelius, in his victory over the Gauls, collected a spoil of fourteen hundred.[48]

As stated in the quotation from the *Book of Leinster* mentioned previously, it would appear that there was a mill at Tara, although it is commonly held that mills were unknown in Ireland until the eighteenth century. The poet Cua Lotcháin mentions the mill in his eleventh-century poem:

> Cormaic, I hear, the grandson of Con,
> brought a millwright over the great sea,
> (who erected) the first mill of Cormac mac Airt,
> which was of assistance to Ciarnaid.[48]

Both the *Yellow Book of Lecan* and the *Book of Leinster* describe the social composition of the Teach Midchuarta (Banqueting Hall) at Tara. In this hall, said to have been built by Nuadu,* all the social groupings had their own specific places.

Each person by his trade or craft or profession was assigned a particular place within the Hall. Thus horsemen, harpers, brehons and men of literature etc. had a place in the external division to the left. Huntsmen, charioteers, historians and rath-builders had their place in the external divisions to the right. The Banqueting Hall thus contained a microcosm of the wider society showing its hierarchical organisation and positions of relative status.

However, it must be said that it is not agreed that there really was any such Banqueting Hall or arrangements like this on this site. It is said that the depicted arrangements at various tables in the Banqueting Hall were simply attempts by scribes to show social organisation both from bardic tradition and from their own knowledge of social differentiation present in their own time. Scholars today feel that the Banqueting Hall was simply a grand entrance to the Royal Enclosure along which heroes would gallop before dismounting. It is also accepted now that it was a circus for the public holding of events such as races.

Tara has similarities with Ailech in Donegal and Emain Macha in Armagh. Royal residences existing at the same time, all present earthen remains of a similar nature. All present commanding panoramas of the countryside. They present 'striking vestiges of their ancient importance'.

Tarb fes The Bullfeast. 'Is amlaid dognithe in tarbfes sin' (it is thus that the bull feast was carried out then): 'firstly a white bull was killed and one took his fill of the meat and of the broth, and, satisfied with that, slept, and four druids chanted an incantation for finding truth over him, and it was seen from the dreams he had the kind of man who would be king, and from the spectre in the dream a description was made; thus the work was done. The man awoke from the dream and told the vision to the king: A strong noble youthful warrior with two red circles over him, standing above the pillow of a man in decline in Emain Macha.'[35]

The bullfeast was how the early Irish chose their kings. This rite was carried out at Tara;* it lasted for at least 400 years. Among those chosen were Conaire Mór and Lugaid Reóderg. The latter is referred to above in a translation by the author from *Lebor na hUidre**.

The *tarb fes* shows the significance of dreams in early Irish society. The result of the dream determined who would be king, regardless of the prevailing politics; thus Lugaid Reóderg was chosen king of Tara* despite the consensus of all the provinces to exclude the Ulaid or men of Ulster.

This rite came to an end with the spread of Christianity; it had originally been outlawed by St Patrick.

Tigernmas King of Ireland in the year c.150 BC, one hundred years after the Milesian invasion. He is said to have reigned for seventy-seven

169

years.[5] Tigernmas is firmly rooted in the mythological cycle of Irish legend. It has been pointed out that he bears a similar relationship to Ireland as that of Theseus to Athens or Minos to Crete.

Legend regards Tigernmas as the first of the Irish kings to work gold. Keating says that Tigernmas was also the first Irish king to establish the custom of distinguishing the ranks and classes of the people by the different colours of their dress.[4] A quote from the *Annals of Clonmacnoise* mentions this:

Ancient mind, *worn over forehead and covering ears*

He was the first who caused standing cuppes to be made, the refining of gold and silver, and procured his goldsmith (named Ugden), that dwelt near the Liffie, to make gold and silver pins to put in men's and women's garments about their necks and also he was the first that ever found the dyeing of coloured clothes in Ireland.[5]

Tigernmas is said to have fought victoriously in many battles. The battle of Carn-Fearadaig in the barony of Coshlea in south Co. Limerick; the battle of Cnám-Choill (wood of the bones) in the barony of Tireragh in Co. Sligo; the battle of Congnach at the fort of Benbulben in Co. Sligo; the battle of Beare in West Cork and seven battles at Loch Luigech (Corrane Lough) in the barony of Iveragh in Co. Kerry. He is also credited with fighting against the Firbolg* and, at Cúl Fobhair east of Lough Corrib, against the Érainn.

During Tigernmas' reign, according to the *Annals of the Four Masters*, nine lakes erupted — Loch Uair in Co. Meath; Loch n-Iairn; Loch Cé in Co. Roscommon; Loch Siglenn in Co. Cavan; Lough Foyle; Loch Gabair; the Black Lough in Co. Louth; and Loch Dabaill near Armagh. Three 'black rivers' are also said to have burst forth during

170

his reign — the Úna river in Co. Tyrone, and the rivers Torann and Callan in Co. Armagh.

Tigernmas died with 'three-quarters of the men of Ireland about him' at Mag Slecht* whilst worshipping Crom Cruach,* the chief idol of adoration in Ireland. This occurred on the night of Samain* or Hallowe'en, he and his people being sald to have died of plague. After his death Ireland is said to have been without a king for seven years, during which time the plague spread, decimating the people.

> Ba maith Tigernmas tamda,
> ba flaith fineamnas fiannda;
> fear ro chlái, ba rath rigda,
> trí nái cath ria cind mbliadna. . . .

> Good was Tigernmas who suffered plague,
> he was a prince, wood-hard, warlike;
> a man who won, it was a royal grace,
> thrice nine battles before the end of a year'.[15]

Togail Bruidne Da Derga The Destruction of Da Derga's Hostel is the principal tale in a cycle of tales beginning with Tochmarc Étaíne, the Wooing of Étaín. It is one of the longest of the sagas, and among the few complete narratives preserved. It existed in written form as early as the eighth or ninth century.

It is a story from Leinster. The hostel in question is situated[14] in Wicklow, west of Lough Bray and just south of the present-day Glencree Reconciliation Centre. It is reputedly built over the Dodder river.

Conaire Mór was king of the Érainn;° he is included in the lists of kings of Ireland,[41] dated at times between 105 BC and 27 BC, and he is the central character in the story. However, the story begins with the coming together of Eochaid Airem, king of Ireland, and Étaín, a woman of the mounds; Eochaid Airem is here synonymous with Eochaid Feidlech, father of Medb* of Connacht. Hunting, he came upon this fairy woman by a well (this is the familiar watersprite theme of folklore). Loosening her hair for washing and combing it with a golden comb, she invited him to wed her forthwith or die.

Eochaid and Étaín married, having one daughter also named Étaín, whom Cormac king of Ulster married. When his wife only produced one daughter, Cormac ordered that she be taken to a pit and killed. Those responsible for this task let her go free, and she was taken to the

171

calfshed of the cowherds of Eterscél, king of Tara.* There, her name became Mes Buachalla° (the cowherds' fosterling). Whilst living there a bird alighted on the skylight and, 'leaving its birdskin on the floor', said to her, 'You will be big-bellied by me and you will bear a son, and this son must not kill birds, and Conaire will be his name'.

Conaire thus, as son of a birdman, has as one of his *geasa* (*see*: geis*) not to hunt or kill birds. This association between birds and gods and heroes is not unusual. The Children of Lir, Aengus* and the war goddesses all change into birds.

The story then has it that Eterscél took Mes Buachalla as a wife, paying her the bride price of seven bondsmaids. It was thus that Conaire was seen as the child of the king. He was fostered out and security given by his foster-parents for his protection.

After King Eterscél's death, a 'bull-feast' (*tarbfes*) was held to determine who should now be king. This feast involved the killing of a bull, of which one man would eat his fill and drink its broth. He would then fall asleep, an incantation chanted over him. In his sleep the person he should see would be king, and were the sleeper to tell a lie about this he would be killed. This rite, known as *imbas forosnai** was forbidden by St Patrick because it was accompanied by sacrifice to demons. In this particular dream, the sleeper saw 'a naked man carrying a stone in a sling coming after nightfall along the road to Tara.'[56]

Conaire, at this time, was in his chariot with his foster-brothers on a plain south of the Liffey. They went to the bull-feast but Conaire took off on his own towards Dublin. There he saw great white speckled birds (*conu findbreca móra*) and pursued them to Merrion Strand, Dublin, casting his sling at them. He caught up with them at the sea and the birds, quitting their bird skins, attacked him with swords and spears. However, one of these birds- turned-warrior, Nemglan, told him it was against his taboos to be attacking birds. Nemglan told him to go naked to Tara.

Conaire went to Tara by the roadways; arriving naked, he was accepted as king. He took sureties, received his king's *geasa*, and was told that his reign would be honoured. However, the breaking of his *geasa* eventually led to his downfall.

After intervening in Thomond (Tuadmumain) in order to establish peace between the two Cairpres, his fosterbrothers, Conaire broke one *geis* after another. He went for refuge to the hostel of Da Derga, the Red God, being preceded there by three men on horseback. 'Red were they all . . . both steeds and men'.[91] In allowing these red warriors to ride to the house of Da Derga before him, Conaire broke yet another taboo. The red warriors said that they rode the steeds of Donn Desscorrach from the fairy mounds; 'though we are alive we are dead'. When Conaire heard this he said, 'All my taboos are broken tonight'. The three phantoms from the mounds went into the palace, leaving their horses at the door.

During this period of Conaire's reign, 'a third of the men of Ireland were marauders'. These included the sons of Donn Désa, the sons of Medb and Ailill, as well the Red Hounds of Cuala, three Leinster warriors named Cethach, Clothach and Conall.

Conaire had expelled these marauders to Britain, but they returned with Ingcél, a British pirate, who later became king of Ireland. So, as Conaire was on his way to the hostel in north Wicklow, going along the Bray Road (Slige Cualann), Ingcél was sailing off the coast of north Dublin to Howth. Ingcél and the sons of Donn Désa, on board the ships, then heard of Conaire's movements and so sailed from Howth across Dublin Bay, landing at Merrion Strand (Trácht Fuirbthenn).

In the meantime, Conaire on his arrival at the Bruiden Da Derga was addressed by a woman, a *banscál*. She told him that 'neither fell nor flesh of thine shall escape from the place into which thou hast come, save what birds will bear away in their claws'. Asked her name, and told it was Cailb, Conaire said that that was not much of a name. Calib responded that she was also known as Sinand ... Samain ... Caill ... Coll ... Dáirine ... Nemain ... Noenden ... Badb, and so forth, all names of earth and war goddesses.

Conaire asked her what she wanted and was told that she wished to stay in the hostel. He replied that it was a taboo of his not to allow a woman in after sunset. However, the *banscál* was eventually admitted, spending the night with Conaire.

Ingcél and the sons of Donn Désa took to their ships again, travelled down the coastline and disembarked at Leamore Strand, Co. Wicklow. They crossed the marshland between the sea and present-day Kilcoole, and on to Lecca Cind Shlébe (Lough Bray). When each man left his boat he carried a stone so that a cairn could be made to cover the bodies of those killed by the 'destruction'. Ingcél went to reconnoitre the hostel, observing the gathering 'through the spokes of the chariots wheels', reporting back to his men the details of Conaire's retinue. His descriptions are vivid examples of the storyteller's art.

In the hostel, he said, he had seen Cormac Conn Loinges, the son of Conchobar mac Nessa,* and three Picts wearing short, black cowls with long hoods. In the room of Conaire's champion, Mac Cécht, he saw a shield with a boss 'the depth of a cauldron'.

The two bald men thou sawest by the man with hair (Mac

173

Cécht) these are his two knees by his head. The two lakes by the mountain which thou sawest, these are his two eyes by his nose. The slender stream of water which thou sawest whereon the sun shines and its trickle down from it, this is the flickering of his sword.[91]

Ingcél's description of the rest of Conaire's retinue includes Manx giants, Da Derga the host, the room of 'three chief champions 'in their first greyness', Sencha, Dubhtach and Goibniu.* He describes the room of the Fomorians,* of Muinremur mac Gerrcind* and Birderg mac Ruain and Mál mac Telbaind, and finally the room of Conall Cernach* and that of the three champions of the mounds.

Just before the attack the howl of Ossar, Conaire's *messán* or lapdog, portends the coming of the battle.[91] Lomna the Buffoon was first to enter, his head being struck off by the doorkeepers and then flung in and out the door three times. The hostel was set on fire three times, three times the fire was put out. Eventually the attackers were driven back.

Conaire then needed water, a great thirst having been placed on him by the attackers' druids. Mac Cécht went away in search of water, of which there was none left in the hostel. The attackers returned and, on Mac Cécht's coming back, he saw them cutting off Conaire's head. He uplifted a pillar stone and drove it through a marauder's spine and then poured the water he had brought back into Conaire's severed head. The severed head spoke to him: 'Excellent is Mac Cécht, good is Mac Cécht who brings a drink to a king and performs a deed of valour'.

The story then ends, after Mac Cécht had buried Conaire Mór at Tara, with his return to his father's Amorgein's house at Tailtiu. Amorgein condemns him for coming back alive when his king is dead, but when he sees his wounds he commends him for his valour. Mac Cécht replies, 'Many are they to whom a drink of death was given before the hostel'.

Conaire died, it may be seen, for breaking his *geasa* and becoming the victim of 'relentless fate', or maybe because of the vengeance of Midir.* Conaire was the grandson of Étaín, whom Midir had lost to Eochaid Airem in order to save his síd.

However, the battle between Conaire Mór and the sons of Donn Désa is seen by O'Rahilly[2] as simply another version of the defeat of the Érainn, of whom Conaire was king, by the Lagin. Donn Désa was a legendary king of the Lagin. Another name for him was Labraid Loingsech,* king and ancestor deity of the Lagin who, in the story of the destruction of Dind Ríg, appear as heroes. This latter story may be the same tale of conflict, told from the point of view of the invaders. Thus both stories tell simply how a king of the Érainn was killed in Leinster by a force of Laginian invaders from overseas. The Laginian conquest of Connacht is instanced in the battle of Mag Tuired.*

Of the Togail Bruidne Da Derga, O'Rahilly says, 'when this great tale is divested of its mythological accretions we are left with a story which has all the appearance of having been based on historical fact'.[2]

Tuatha Dé Danann   The people of the goddess Anu or Danu, a mother goddess and mother of the gods, connected with fertility and nurture. Her name is preserved in twin hills in Co. Kerry known as the Paps of Anu (Dá Chích Anann.)

The Tuatha Dé Danann are said to have been the fourth of the six legendary or prehistoric colonies which invaded Ireland, arriving in c.350 BC. They are said to have come from Greece, though this is disputed (some saying that they are synonymous with the Cimbri from Denmark), and to have been celebrated for their magical skills.

The pantheon of Celtic gods in Ireland has been associated with the Tuatha Dé Danann; the remnants of a genealogy of the gods are complied in the *Lebor Gabála*. This is described as 'the most complete documentary account of any European non-classical pantheon'.[15]

Legend has it that the Tuatha Dé Danann came from four cities in northern islands of Greece, and that it was there they learned their druidry, knowledge, prophecy and magic. These cities are named as Failias, Goirias, Findias and Muirias. (It was from Failias that they brought the Lia Fáil;* from Goirias the spear of Lug;* from Findias the sword of Nuadu;* and from Muirias the cauldron of the Dagda.*)

> Their origin is uncertain, whether
> they were of demons or of men;
> but it is said that they were of the
> progeny of Beothach son of Iarbonel the Giant.

Two differing accounts describe the arrival of the Tuatha Dé Danann in Ireland. One has it that they came without vessels or barks, in dark clouds, by the might of druidry (*tre nert draidechta*), landing in the mountains of Conmaicne Réin in Connacht. The second version tells that they came by sea, burning their ships on arrival. The two stories are joined together by another, stating that they came in a fog of smoke emanating from their burning boats.

It is said that the reason they burned their boats was to avoid

175

discovery by the Fomorians* and so remain in Ireland. They defeated the Firbolg* and soon came into conflict with the Fomorians, opposing them in the second battle of Mag Tuired.* This battle is open to interpretation as a conflict between chaos (Fomorians) and light (Tuatha Dé Danann) and also a struggle for dominance by two tribes connected by a series of intermarriages.

Five chieftains of the Tuatha Dé Danann took part in this battle. Nuadu, Dagda, Ogma,* Goibniu* and Dian Cécht. Nuadu was beheaded, and Ogma was killed also. Lug then took over the kingship. The Tuatha Dé Danann ruled until defeated by the Milesians. Their last kings were Mac Cuill, Mac Cécht and Mac Gréne, whose wives were Ériu,* Fódla* and Banba,* three queens representing three different aspects of Ireland. (The hazel, associated with wisdom, was Mac Cuill's god, the ploughshare Mac Cécht's, and the sun Mac Gréne's.)

In addition to Lug, mentioned above, who was the Irish Apollo, the pantheon of Tuatha Dé Danann gods includes Brigit,* goddess of fertility and patron of poets, and Mannannán mac Lir,* the Irish Neptune. It also includes those gods associated with the Boyne Valley (Bruig na Bóinne)° such as the Dagda, the Irish Zeus, his wife Boand* (white cow goddess) and their son Aengus,* harper to the gods and symbol of the irrespressible mythological spirit. Belonging also to the Tuatha Dé Danann is the famous triad of fearsome sexual war goddesses, Badb,* Macha* and the Mórrígan.*

Certain of the Tuatha Dé Danann gods reappear in later stories. Lug appeared as protector to Cúchulainn* in the Ulster Cycle and Aengus to Diarmuid ua Duibhne in the Fenian Cycle. The war goddesses make constant reappearances, with the Mórrígan appearing as late as the battle of Clontarf in AD 1014.

Following their defeat by the Milesians, the Tuatha gods entered the underground beneath the hills and vales of Ireland, each taking possession of his or her domain. From particular centres there, generally places where tumuli (síde) existed, they ruled and marshalled their invisible hosts. Caoilte mac Ronáin,* the Ossianic hero, says of one of them, 'I am mortal, for I am of the race of man, but she is immortal for she is of the race of the Tuatha Dé Danann'.

Particular mounds or burial spots are still associated with various gods of the Tuatha Dé Danann. Manannán's father Lir is associated with Síd Fionnachaidh, on top of Sliab Fuait near Newtown Hamilton in Co. Armagh. Bodb Derg's* mound is Síd Boidb, south of Portumna in Co. Galway. Midir's mound or síd is Brí Léith, near Ardagh in Co. Longford. Ogma's* síd is called Síd Airceltrai (since despoiled), near Downpatrick, Co. Down. Manannán's son Ilbreach has the mound of

Mullachshee (Síd Essa Aeda Ruaid) near Bally-shannon in Co. Donegal. Finnbarr, to whom the Dagda gave Síd Meda (Knockma) about five miles west of Tuam in Co. Galway, figures in the Fenian stories. Finnbarr is said to be king of the *aes síde°* (the people of the mounds), ruling with his wife Onagh.

Cinerary urn found in Co. Carlow tomb, approximately five inches wide

It is thus the Tuatha Dé Danann who are the *aes síde*. It is they who have become the fairies of today and as such survive in popular folklore.

The Irish poet Mac Ria wrote in the *Book of Ballymote*,[89]

> Behold the *Sídh* before your eyes,
> it is manifest to you that it is a king's mansion,
> which was built by the firm Dagda,
> it was a wonder, a court, an admirable hill.[34]

Tuathal Techtmar Tuathal the Legitimate, recorded as king of Ireland in the second century AD. One account states that 'he has all the characteristics of reality about him'. His earliest name, *Teuto-valos*, means 'ruler of the people'. His accession was about AD 130. Tuathal is attributed with subduing the Aithechthuatha or vassal tribes of Ireland. The story has it that, after three tribes under Éllim mac Conrach of the Dál nAraidi* rose up killing his father Fiacha, his mother went to Scotland, pregnant with Tuathal. When grown up he returned, avenged his father and became king.

Tuathal arrived at Inber Domnann, Malahide Bay, with a fleet of foreigners and won to his side warrior-bands belonging to the king of Tara* and the king of the Lagin. He defeated the Firbolg,* the Dom-nainn and the Gálioin.* O'Rahilly[2] says that Tuathal was himself a foreigner, seeing him as an historical character who led the Gaels* across the sea, gradually conquering Ireland. Some say he was a Roman

177

legionary who, supported by the Gaels, successfully invaded Ireland and imposed taxes on the defeated tribes. Thus he reduced the small kingdoms to the position of tributary states.

Tuathal created the kingdom of Meath by adding the *meidhe* or neck from Ulster, Leinster and Connacht. He included here the four great meeting places of Tailtiu,* Tlachtga, Tara and, finally, Uisneach* where he is reputed to have lived. However, although Macalister[57] shows a sketch of what he calls the Uisneach House, which he states is Tuathal's actual residence, later excavations in the 1930s and 1940s resulted in the statement that 'little was found to support the identification of the site as a royal residence'.[86]

Uisneach   A hill between Mullingar and Athlone which is said to mark the centre of Ireland. The point where the provinces were said to have met was marked here by a great stone called Ail na Uírenn, the Stone of the Divisions.

> About the stone in cold Uisneach
> in the plains of Mide of the horseman-bands,
> on its top — it is a fair co-division —
> is the co-division of every province.[15]

The most ancient divisions of Ireland included two 'Munsters' in the number of provinces. Later there were five provinces, which number included Meath. The five provinces, each with their own king, constituted a pentarchy.

> The points of those provinces
> to Uisneach did they lead,
> each of them out of its . . .
> . . . till it was five.[15]

It was at Uisneach, a major assembly point, that fires were lit in honour of Bel* on the first day of May. Beltaine, meaning Bel's fire, is the Irish word for this festival and also the whole month of May. Two fires were kindled in Bel's name, cattle being driven between them to protect against disease, the ceremony organised under solemn incantations by the druids.* P.W. Joyce[53] maintains that during these ceremonies young cattle were offered to the idol. Legend has it that it was Mide, druid of the people of Nemed* who lit the first fire at Uisneach. The assemblies here were held under a sacred ash tree.

According to O'Rahilly the may-day assembly was known as *Mórdáil Uisnig*.[2] He draws a parallel between this and meetings amongst the Gauls in the druidic assemblies in the territory of the Carnutes.

Uisneach seems to have been a place of religious significance associated with both druids and with a fire-cult. Although not a very tall hill, it commands a wide view and the first fires lit here could be conveyed to many distant hills and from them to the coast. The first may day fire would have been lit here, all the others of Beltaine lit in imitation. Excavation during this century[86] on the Hill of Uisneach found an enormous bed of ashes which had burnt the earth red to a depth of some inches.

Macalister[57] asserts that Uisneach contained living quarters and that it was here that Tuathal Techtmar* had his house. However, excavations mentioned above showed no evidence of this in that there were no findings of pottery, the only significant find being a bronze pin with a silver inlay in its head.

Finally, Uisneach has associations with Lug*, who was killed here by the three gods Mac Cuill, Mac Cécht and Mac Gréine.

Special Notes

aes síde (modern sp. *aos*): the people of the mounds. Popularly, the fairy-folk.

aire échta: a clan-officer whose duty it was to avenge fellow-kinsmen.

Alba: from Latin *albus*, white; referring to the chalk cliffs of Dover. Alba in early texts referred to Gaelic Britain or Gaelic Scotland.

Alt na Síon, also *Ailt na Síon*: *lit.* high glen or ravine of stormy weather; a wild glen.

Ardachad: *lit.* high field (*achadh* is a field, plain or hill); it is located in Sliab Fuaid, near Newtown Hamilton, Co. Armagh. The body of Conchobar mac Nessa was taken as far as here by his servant Ceann Bearroide.

Argatros: Silverwood (*airgeat,* silver; *ros,* wood) situated in the parish of Rathbeagh on the river Nore in Kilkenny. Said to derive its name from the silver shields which were made there.

Ath Fhirdia: present-day Ardee in Co. Louth, meaning Ferdia's ford.

bachlach: a churl, a large rough person, a giant, a rustic, a boor.

bó airech: member of the nobility, who was entitled to payment in cows (*bó*, cow) for any wrong done to him. Also a man rich in cattle.

bocánach: a goblin; also *bocán*.

bruidne: plural of *bruiden*, a hostel, a fairy palace.

Bruig na Bóinne: *bruig* (modern Irish *brugh*) means a palace or distinguished residence, also land or a farm. Bruig na Bóinne is a place on the river Boyne near Stackallen Bridge, Co. Meath. It is one of the chief burial places of kings of pagan Ireland. The Dagda and his son Aengus are buried there.

Cailleach Gearagáin: *cailleach*, *lit.* a veiled woman; popularly, a hag; older meaning, a witch; *gearagáin = garb óg*, a rough ogress. *Cailleach Gearagáin* was a sorceress connected with Kilinkere parish, Co. Cavan.

Caladbolg: *lit.* hard (crushing) lightning; more correctly, a lightning sword. This is connected to the *cloidheamh solais* or sword of light. This sword (Caladbolg) was possessed by Fergus mac Roich. It is said that when it was in the act of striking that it was as 'big as a rainbow in the heavens'.

Casdubh: *cas*, curly; *dubh*, black, referring to Cairenn's hair.

Cianacht: a tribe from north Leinster. Or more particularly from the river Liffey to Dromiskin, Co. Louth.

Ciarraige: Kerry; earlier it referred to North West Kerry, that is from the harbour of Tralee to the Shannon.

cnoc: hill.

Cnoc Ailinne: a hill near Old Kilcullen, Co. Kildare.

Cnoc Áine: Knockainey hill in the barony of Small County, Co. Limerick.

Conmaicne-Cuile-Toladh: district which extends from south Mayo, from the river Robe to the Black river at Shrule. It includes the barony of Kilmaine.

Corca-Baoiscne: the people or race of Bhaiscinn; an area in south-west Clare.

Corca Duibhne: the present barony of Corcaguiny, in Co. Kerry.The old district corresponded to the baronies of Corcaguiny, Ivreagh and Magunihy in Kerry.

Cormac Connlonges: lit. Cormac head of the exiles; said to have been an incestuous son of Conchobar mac Nessa, he was exiled when he sided with Fergus mac Róich against his father.

Craeb Ruad: one of the three houses of Emain Macha, the Red Branch Knights, also the Hostel of Kings, centered at present-day Navan Fort, Co. Armagh, as opposed to Craeb Derg, the hostel where the skulls of enemies slain, and other trophies of war, were stored. The townland near Navan Fort (Emania) is known as Creeveroe; it is situated near the river Callan.

cruit: harp or lyre; *cruitire*: a harper.

cú: a hound, a champion.

Cúl Ceasra: lit. the heap (of stones) of Ceasair; the carn or mound of Ceasair, said to be situated near the river Boyle in Connacht.

culdee: from the Irish *Céile Dé*, meaning society of God; a monastic movement which began towards the end of the eighth century and is largely associated with St Maelruain of Tallaght, Co. Dublin, who died in AD 792.

Cumar na dTrí nUisce: the confluence of the rivers Suir, Nore and Barrow near Waterford. The limit of the province of Leinster as possessed by Sláinge, king of the Firbolgs.

Dáire dá Baeth: a place in Connacht, where the brain-ball was lodged in the head of Conchobar mac Nessa.

Dál Fiatach: the historical Ulaid or Ulster tribe. Kings of the Dál Fiatach are noted in the regnal lists of Ulster. Their power began to subside during the fourth and fifth centuries AD.

Dál nAraidi, also *nAriade;* a tribe from south Down whose ancestor is said to have been Conaire Mór.

Dál Riata (modern Irish *Dál Riada*): *lit.* the division or tribe of Riata. Their ancestor deity was Eochaid Riata, whose epithet O'Rahilly interprets as 'travelling on horseback or in a chariot'. This tribe is associated by legend with the northern part of Antrim in Ireland and with northern side of the Clyde estuary in Scotland.

Danu: of Ana, Anu, the mother-goddess.

deas soil: right, with the sun. People at ceremonies walked clockwise with the sun. To walk opposite to the sun's apparent motion was said to bring misfortune.

Déise: a tribe originally from the North (Boyne basin), which settled in Waterford and whose territory extended from there to Tipperary. Said to have fed one of their members (Eithne Uathach) on human flesh in order to fulfil a prophecy. Later their king, Domhnall O Faolain of Tipperary, made war on Brian Boru. The name Déise is represented in the modern baronies of Decies within Drum and Decies without Drum, Co. Waterford.

delc n-óir: a pin of gold.

dét fis: wisdom from the tooth, that is from the rite which involved chewing the marrow from a bone.

díchetal do chennaib: *lit.* an incantation for prophesying, permitted by St Patrick as it involved no offerings to the gods.

Dindshenchas: book of legends and stories written by Amergin, poet of Diarmuid mac Cearbhaill. Tracts both in prose and poetry are to be found in the *Book of Leinster*, the *Yellow Book of Lecan* as well as in a MS in Rennes Library. Stephen Gwynn edited much of the poetry for his Todd Lectures to the Royal Irish Academy.

Dub Commair: black confluence; the confluence of the Boyne and the Blackwater. As well as Eochaid Múgmedón, Fiachaidh Sraibhthine is also said to have been slain here by the three Collas.

Dun na mBarc: *lit.* fort of the ships; cf. Dunnamark fort and castle on Bantry Bay. According to Keating's *History of Ireland*, Dun na mBarc is on Ballinskellig Bay. The sound between Valentia Island and the mainland is known locally as Loch mBairc.

éiric: fine, or ransom or retribution, also a blood fine.

Eiscir Riada: the continuous line of low gravel hills stretching from Dublin to Clarinbridge, Co. Galway. In ancient times they divided Ireland into two parts, one part being Conn's or Leath Chuinn and the southern part being Leath Mogha or Mogh Nuada's half. Names associated with the Eiscir Riada are Esker, near Lucan, Co. Dublin and Eskerboy near Loughrea, Co. Galway.

Eochaid Ollathair: Eochaid the father of all.

Eochaid Sálbuide: Eochaid Yellowheel, father of Nes, the mother of Conchobar mac Nessa.

Enna Airgtheach: Enna the Plunderer.

Érainn: a pre-Gaelic race said to be descended from the god Dáire (i.e. Cúroí mac Dáire) through his son Lugaid mac Dáire. They came to Ireland from Britain. They are found throughout Ireland, particularly in Ulster and Munster. Regarded by O'Rahilly as synonymos with the Fir Bolg.

Ess Ruaid: the waterfall of Aed Ruad, also known as Assaroe Falls on the river Erne at Ballyshannon, Co. Donegal.

fénechas: ancient jurisprudence of Ireland. This was the law of the *féne*, or free land-tillers.

fes (early modern Irish *feis*): a feast, an assembly, a parliament. *Fes Temrach*, the assembly of Tara (the triennial representative parliament of ancient Ireland).

fian (plural fiana and *fianna)*: a troop of professional soldiers and also a band of roving men whose principal occupations were hunting and war. There were usually six warriors in a *fian*.

fidchell: often translated erroneously as the game of chess; though it may have been a board game with wooden pegs.

Findloch: *lit.* white lake, the white lake known as Carrowmore lake in the barony of Erris, Co. Mayo, is one of the three lakes found by Partolón.

finnbennach: white-horned or white-antlered.

Fir Domnann: a tribe included under the general name of Fir Bolg. They are associated with Iorrus Domnann in the barony of Erris, Co. Mayo.

giolla (plural *giollaí*): gillie, servant, attendant.

Glen Etive (Scotland): flows into the Firth of Lorn. It is south of Glencoe.

Glen Masan (Scotland): on the north side of the Clyde estuary near Lennox.

Glen Urchain (Scotland): Argyll.

Grianan Ailig: *lit.* the sunny spot of Aileach from where the Dagda, the Irish Zeus, is said to have come. Grianan is often translated by Irish-Latin writers as *solarium*, and *terra solaris*; also as a palace on a hill, the most celebrated of these being Grianan Ailig, in Co. Donegal, six miles north-west of Derry.

Im Bolc (also *Oimelc*): sheep's milk; the ancient fertility festival associated with Brigit. This feast fell on 1 February.

in tEllén Trechend: ancient and original form of Ellén Trechenn, three-headed Ellén.

leanán síde or *lennán síde*: a fairy lover, a familiar sprite, or local spirit familiar to the *síde*.

Leath Chuinn: *lit.* Conn's half. This half was the northern half of Ireland, (north of the Eiscir). This was the half led by the descendants of Conn (the Dál Cuinn).

líos: the enclosed ground of an ancient dwelling place or ring-fort.

Loch Ló: in Co. Roscommon between the Shannon and the Suck.

Mag Bolg: the plain of the gap (?) at Moybolgue near Kells in Co. Meath and partly in Co. Cavan, near Bailieborough.

Mag Da Chó: in Connacht between Cruachain, Co. Roscommon and Athlone, Co. Westmeath. Also, according to Hogan, it is in Hy Maine.

Mag hAgha: a plain including Telltown, in the barony of Upper Kells, Co. Meath.

Mag Muccrama: the plain extending westwards from Athenry, Co. Galway.

Mes Buachalla: originally known as Étaín, she married Cormac, king of Ulster. Having only one daughter, Cormac ordered that she be taken to a pit and killed. She was subsequently set free however and went to tend to the cowherds of Eterscél, king of Tara. Here she mated with a birdman and bore Conaire, who was later to become king of Tara.

Mes Gegra: his brain was soaked in lime and hardened as was usually done with the heads of those who were decapitated in battle. It was put in a sling and landed in the head of Conchobar mac Nessa during a battle. Conchobar is reputed to have survived this ignominy for a number of years.

Mesca Ulad: The Intoxication of the Ulstermen, a tale from the Ulster Cycle included in the *Book of Leinster*.

muirisc: a sea-side marsh. As a placename to be found near the river Easkey in north Sligo, and in a narrow plain between Croagh Patrick and the sea in Co. Mayo.

Múscraige: a tribe descended from Cairbre músc. Their territories included the baronies of East and West Muskerry, Co Cork, Upper and Lower Ormond and Clanwilliam, Co. Tipperary.

nes (gen. *nessa*; old Irish, *nis*): wet, damp, river. Connections have been made with Loch Ness in Scotland.

Osraige: the ancient territory comprising the barony of Upper Ossory in Offaly and almost the whole of Co. Kilkenny, the rough limits of the territory being from the river Suir to the Barrow and from the Slieve Bloom mountains to the sea at Waterford Harbour. Presently known as Ossory.

péist (old Irish, *béist*; Welsh, *bwyst*): dragon, serpent or monster.

ráth: a ring fort, a low circular bank surrounding early Irish residences, a barrow or artificial mound.

Rath Achaill: The rath of discourse; the place where druids would divine the future for kings, queens and princes, near Screen, Co. Sligo.

Rath Árda Súird: the hill of Rath tSiúird, half a mile north-west of the old church of Donaghmore, near Limerick.

Reilg na Rí: burial place of the kings of Connacht at Cruachain.

rí: king, monarch, ruler or (early) abbot.

rofheassa: lit. great knowledge.

rosc: rhetorical composition, chant; *rosc catha*: battle-chant, war cry.

síd (plural *síde*): mound, fairy hill.

síd an broga: lit. the mound in the field. The mound in Bruig na Bóinne wherein Aengus is said to lie.

Síd Fionnachaid: at the top of Sliab Fuaid, Co. Armagh, the abode of Lir, father of Manannán and his people.

Súil Bhalair: lit. the eye of Balor; the evil eye, the sun, a bewitching eye.

Sliab na dé dana: also known as Sliab nGuaire in Co. Cavan.

Teamhrach: genitive of *teamhair*, meaning 'an eminence of wide prospect standing by itself', this Irish word has been popularly anglicized as Tara; seat of the kings in Co. Meath.

teinm laeda: lit. to gnaw the marrow. A pagan rite, banned by St Patrick on account of the fact that it involved 'offerings to demons'. Finn mac Cumaill is said to have acquired his knowledge through *teinm laeda*.

Tír Tairngire: lit. the Land of Promise. One of the many ancient Irish Otherworlds.

tobar: well, fountain, spring, source.

Tobar Áine: the well of the goddess Áine, in the parish of Lissan, Co. Derry.

Traigh-Eochaile: Beltra Strand, at Ballisodare, Co. Sligo.

Trí Dee Dánann: The three gods of artistic skill: *na trí dee dan* (from *dán*, genitive plural *dána*, art, poetry etc.) Sometimes written as the *trí dee Danann*, which O'Rahilly saw as being due to the influence of Tuatha Dé Danann. The phrase *na trí dee dána* 'began at an early date to be corrupted to (*na*) *trí dee Danann*'.

uaisne: proudly.

Source Material

Each book in this list is given a number; the typescript numbers which appear in the text of the Guide refer to books as numbered on this list.

1   Meyer, Kuno, *Death Tales of the Ulster Heroes* (Dublin, 1906).

2   O'Rahilly, Thomas F., *Early Irish History and Mythology* (Dublin, 1946).

3   Gregory, Lady Augusta, *Collected Works*, vol iii (London, 1970).

4   Keating, Geoffrey, *Foras Feasa ar Éirinn (History of Ireland)*, trs. David Comyn and Patrick Dineen (London, 1902-14).

5   O'Donovan, John, (ed.), *Annals of the Four Masters* (Dublin, 1851).

6   Meyer, Kuno, (ed.), *Sanas Cormaic* (Dublin, 1912).

7   O'Grady, S. Hayes, *Silva Gadelica* (London, 1892).

8   Rees, Alwyn, and Brinley, *Celtic Heritage* (London, 1961).

9   Henderson, George, *Fled Bricrend* (ITS, London, 1899).

10   Barron, Thomas J., *Guth agus Tuairm*, vol. IV.

11   Chibnall, M., (ed.), John of Salisbury, *Historia Pontificalis* (Edinburgh, 1956).

12   Mason, T.H.. 'St Brigid's Crosses', *JRSAI*, lxxxv, pt iii, 160-167.

13   D'Aliella, Count, *The Migration of Symbols* (London, 1894).

14   Morris, Henry, 'Where was Bruidhean Dé Derga?', *JRSAI*, lxv, pt ii, 297-313.

15   Macalister, R.A.S., (ed.), *Lebor Gabála* (Dublin, 1938).

16   Macalister, R.A.S., *The Archaeology of Ireland* (London, 1928).

17   Hull, Eleanor, *The Cuchullin Saga* (London, 1898).

18   O'Beirne, Crowe, *Kilkenny Archaeological Society*, 1870.

19   Colum, Padraig, *Anthology of Irish Verse* (New York, 1922).

20   O'Flaherty, Roger, *Ogygia* (London, 1685).

21   Chadwick, Nora, *The Celts* (London, 1970).

22   Kinsella, Thomas, *The Táin* (Dublin, 1969).

23   Kennedy, Patrick, *Legendary Fictions of the Irish Celts* (London, 1866).

24   Mac Neill, Eoin, *Celtic Religion* (London, 1912).

25   Mac Culloch, John Arnott, *Religion of the Ancient Celts* (Edinburgh, 1911).

26   Rhys, John, *Hibbert Lectures for 1866* (London, 1898).

27   Joyce, P.W., *A Concise History of Ireland* (Dublin, 1900).

28   Dinneen, Patrick, *Irish-English Dictionary* (Dublin, 1927).

29   Stokes, Whitley, 'Glossarial Index', *Ériu*, iv, 56.

30   Hull, Eleanor, 'Old Irish Tabus and Geasa, *Folk-Lore* xii, no. 1, 1901.

31   Brislech Mór Muirthemne, MS 1712. Brit. Mus. Egerton, 123 fol. 1.

32   Ross, Anne, *Pagan Celtic Britain* (London, 1974).

33   Stokes, Whitley, and Strachan, John, *Thesaurus Paleo Hibernicus*, vol. 11, 1903.

34   O'Curry, Eugene, *Lectures on the MS Materials of Ancient Irish History* (Dublin, 1861).

35   Best, R., and Bergin O. (ed.), *Lebor na hUidre* (Dublin, 1929).

36   MacNeill, Eoin, (ed.), *Duanaire Finn* (ITS, London, 1908).

37   Clarke, Austin, *The Vengeance of Fionn* (Dublin, 1917).

38   Dillon, Myles, and Chadwick, Nora, *The Celtic Realms* (London, 1967).

39   Meyer, Kuno, and Nutt, Alfred, *The Voyage of Bran*, 2 vols. (London, 1895-7).

40   Stokes, Whitley, 'The Voyage of Mael Duin', *Revue Celtique* ix, 247-295 and x, 50-96.

41   Best, R., and Bergin, O., (eds.), *The Book of Leinster*, 5 vols. (Dublin, 1954-67).

42   Gwynn, Edward, (ed.), *The Metrical Dindshenchas*, 5 parts (Dublin, 1903-35).

43   Meyer, Kuno, (ed.), *Rawlinson B503 facsimile edition* (Oxford, 1909).

44   Freud, Sigmund, *The Interpretation of Dreams* (London, 1974).

45   Butler, Hubert, *Ten Thousand Saints* (Kilkenny, 1972).

46   Meyer, Kuno, 'Baile in Scáil', *Zeitschrift Für Celtische Philogie* 3. 457-66.

47   Mac Neill, Máire, *The Festival of Lughnasa* (Oxford, 1962).

48   Petrie, George, *History and Antiquities of Tara Hill* (Dublin, 1839).

49   Sjoestedt, Maire Louise, *Gods and Heroes of the Celts* trs. Myles Dillon (London, 1949).

50   Wilde, Sir William, *The Beauties of the Boyne and Blackwater* (Dublin, 1849).

51   Stokes, Whitley, 'The Second Battle of Moytura', *Revue Celtique* xii, 52-130.

52   Long, Andrew, *Custom and Myth* (1893).

53   Joyce, P.W., *A Smaller Social History of Ancient Ireland* (Dublin, 1906).

54   Mac Airt, S., (ed.), *Annals of Innisfallen* (Dublin, 1951).

55   Mac Cana, Proinsias, *Celtic Mythology* (London, 1970).

56   Dillon, Myles, (ed.), *Irish Sagas* (Dublin, 1959).

57   Macalister, R.A.S., *Ancient Ireland* (London, 1935).

58   Wade Evans, W.W., (trs). Nennius, *Historia Brittonum* (London, 1938).

59   Cross and Slover, *Ancient Irish Tales* (London, 1937).

60   Knott, Eleanor, 'Why Mongán was deprived of noble issue', *Ériu*, viii, 155-160.

61   Meyer, Kuno, *Bruchstüche der älteren Lyirk Irland* (Berlin, 1919).

62   Walsh, Paul, 'Irish Ocha, Ochann', *Ériu*, viii, 75-78.

63   Macalister, R.A.S., *Corpus Inscriptionum Insularum Celticarum*, 2 vols (Dublin, 1946-49).

64   Plummer, Charles, 'On the meaning of Ogam stones', *Revue Celtique*, xl, 387-391.

65   O'Curry E., and O'Donovan, J., *Transcripts of the Brehon Law Commission*, 15 vols (Dublin 1850-60).

66   Raftery, Barry, 'A late Ogham inscription from Co. Tipperary', *JRSAI*, lxxxxviii.

67   Squire, Charles, *Celtic Myth and Legend* (London, 1901).

68   Joyce, P.W., *Old Celtic Romances* (London, 1914).

69   Meyer, Kuno, *Anecdota from Irish Manuscripts* (Dublin, 1913).

70   Hyde, Douglas, *Legends of Saints and Sinners* (Dublin, 1915).

71   *Transactions of the Ossianic Society*, iv (Dublin, 1854-61).

72   Yeats, W.B., *The Wanderings of Usheen*, 1912.

73   Williams, Nicholas (ed.), *The Poems of Giolla Brighde Mac Con Midhe* (ITS, Dublin, 1980).

74   Stokes, Whitley, *Irische Texte* iii.

75   *Transactions of the Ossianic Society*, ii (Dublin 1854-61).

76   Andersen, Jorgen, *The Witch on the Wall* (London, 1977).

77   Rynne, E., 'A Sheela-na-Gig at Clonlara, Co. Clare' *North Munster Antiquarian Journal*, 1962-67.

78   Stokes, Whitley, 'The training of Cúchulainn', *Revue Celtique*, xxix, 109-152.

79   Cameron, A., *Reliquiae Celticae*, vol. i (Inverness, 1892).

80   O'Donovan, John, *The Banquet of Dun na n-Gedh and the Battle of Magh Rath* (Dublin, 1842).

81   O'Keeffe, J.G., *The Adventures of Suibhne Geilt* (ITS, London, 1913).

82   Leahy, Arthur, *Heroic Romances of Ireland* (London, 1905).

83   Raftery, Joseph, *Prehistoric Ireland* (London, 1951).

84   Stokes, Whitley, 'The Rennes Dind Shenchas', *Revue Celtique*, xv, 277-289.

85   *Transactions of the Ossianic Society*, i, Dublin (1854-61).

86   Report of the Archaeological Committee, R.I.A. (Dublin, 1900).

87   Julius Caesar, *De Bello Gallico*, vi.

88   Toland, John, *Critical History of the Celtic Religion* (London, 1815).

89   *Book of Ballymote* (Dublin, 1887).

90   *Inquiry into the History of Scotland* (1814).

91   Stokes, Whitley, *Togail Bruidne Dá Derga* (Paris, 1902).

92   Wood-Martin, W.G., *Traces of the Elder Faiths of Ireland* (London, 1902).

93   Binchy, D.A., (trs.) 'Bretha Crólige', *Ériu*, xii, 1-78.

94   Thurneysen, R., *Studies in Early Irish Law* (Dublin, 1936).

95   Windisch, E., *Irische Texte* (Leipzig, 1880).

96   Jackson, Kenneth, H., *A Celtic Miscellany* (London, 1957).

97   Thurneysen, R., *Die Irische Helden-und Königsage*, (Halle, 1921).

98   Kelly, Fergus, *A Guide to Early Irish Law* (Dublin, 1988).

99   MacNeill, Eoin, *Celtic Ireland* (Dublin, 1921).

100   Watson, W.J., *Celtic Placenames of Scotland* (Edinburgh, 1926; reprinted Dublin, 1986).

101   Campbell, Joseph, *Creative Mythology* (Dallas, Pennsylvania, 1968).

102   Mac Cana, Próinsias, 'Theme of king and goddess in Irish Literature', *Étude Celtique*, vii (1955).

103   Dillon, Myles, *Early Irish Society* (Cork, 1959).

104   Pedersen, Holger, *Scéalta Mháirtín Neile* (Dublin, 1994).

105   Meyer, Kuno, *Ancient Irish Poetry* (London, 1913).

Index

Compiled by Brad Morrow

196